THE BLUE RAJAH MURDER

THE BLUE RAJAH MURDER

Harold MacGrath

COACHWHIP PUBLICATIONS

Greenville, Ohio

The Blue Rajah Murder, by Harold MacGrath
© 2015 Coachwhip Publications

The Blue Rajah Murder was published 1930.
(Individual stories published 1929.)
No claims made on public domain material.

ISBN 1-61646-304-X
ISBN-13 978-1-61646-304-5

CoachwhipBooks.com

Dead, in front of his rifled safe, and
the great Blue Rajah missing . . .
the fabulous diamond that had behind
it seven known murders!

Part I

Impromptu

1

A BILLOW OF REDDISH DUST rolled over the roadster as it came to a sudden halt. It was not a smart machine. One had only two guesses about it. Either its owner had purchased it second-hand or he could not afford to buy a new one. The rumble seat in the rear had been thrown back. The foot space held a suitcase, a tin box, and an aluminum rod case. All over the great North Woods there would be cars similar to this in appearance, luggage, and ownership.

The young man at the wheel leaned back and contemplated the stream. It had everything—white water, pools smooth and rippled, deadfalls which reached halfway across the stream, big granite boulders and, above all, music. The run had been chanting lovely symphonies since the beginning of the new time, and countless trout had died of old age on the bottoms.

"Lord, what a trout run!" the young man cried out.

He had caught glimpses of the stream for the past half hour; but here was a vista. He saw the stream clearly through an arcade of lordly pines, and it drew him irresistibly. The floor of this natural arcade was richly carpeted with reddish-brown needles, with here and there a pattern in vivid green. An Ispahan worthy of Shah Abbas.

A blue jay flickered across the opening. From far above a crow called. A squirrel peeked from a hole in an oak. A chipmunk was busily engaged digging into the pine needles. A hedgehog waddled toward the stream.

"The Forty Thieves!"

The young man chuckled. Every living thing in this forest was a thief—a natural-born thief. What I want, I take. Eternal warfare. And back yonder, in the great cities of the earth, they were abolishing war on paper. The chuckle developed into laughter, not without a quality of irony. The predatory instinct, the dominant human instinct. Roll up the other way, said the visionist to the Niagara! A man must live; and so long as he must, to prey upon others was obligatory. Predatores—a kind of insect which devoured others and was itself devoured. It was lawful that one insect should devour another, because man hadn't written anything to the contrary.

The pioneer, when confronted by a colossal obstacle, does not laugh, but clamps his teeth grimly and proceeds to overcome the obstacle. The adventurer, confronted by an obstacle, laughs before he starts to overcome it. There is a sharp cleavage between the two, for their obstacles are not comparable. One dreams of cities where there are none and proceeds to create them. The other must find the poles, the highest peak, the virgin jungle, go where no other man has gone, do what no other man has done, just for the fun of it.

"Thieves on land and cannibals in the water! Life!"

"Caw, caw, caw!" answered the crows.

The young man glanced upward. "No doubt you are perfectly correct. But you must admit that people are more likely to accept me as a bird of paradise than as your brother."

His wrist watch informed the young man that it was five o'clock in the afternoon. The sky was cloudless, but that did not matter, since there was no sunlight on the stream or on the forest floor. Only the tops of the pines were in the waning sunshine, resembling points of flame. The air was delicious with the perfumes of the saps. Just the right time.

Plus-fours, golf stockings, and sport shoes. The young man laughed again. Why not! Who the devil cared if he did what probably no one had done before—wade this stream dressed as he was, sartorially correct for any golf course. A game he did not play because anybody could play it and nearly everybody did! Without opening the side door he vaulted to the road and made a grimace of pain. That shin of his! Very well.

He sat down at the side of the road and rolled down his stocking, revealing an ugly bruise along the shin. In the middle of the bruise was a ragged horizontal cut, fresh. A horse could not have landed a more effective kick, save that the iron shoe of a horse would have broken the shin bone. He liberally daubed the wound with an aromatic salve, then pulled up the stocking carefully. He was going fishing. He was a fool, he had always been one, but nevertheless it was a great business, so long as you were no man's fool.

He stood up and listened. Such sounds as he heard were native to the woods. He had perhaps twelve hours' leeway; that would be enough. He was going fishing. He had brought along rod and tackle for that very purpose. He would have been a fool if he hadn't. Good camouflage.

He strapped his wrist watch to the broad ribbon which ran around his pearl-gray fedora. From his hip pocket he brought forth a small automatic pistol. This he transferred to the left upper pocket of his Norfolk jacket. Keep your watch and your powder dry. Next, from the little pocket at the top of his trousers, he took out a small rubber pouch. Now, where the devil would he put this? For if water got to it he was done. Good. He would hang it around his neck. But first, a reassuring look. Presently upon his palm lay a crystal, perfectly transparent, yet vaguely blue as the sky. Lovely and mysterious fires leaped forth. It was the size of a pecan nut and of similar shape. A stone which, it was evident, had never known any metal setting.

"Clever," thought the young man grimly. "As clever a job, probably, as ever was conceived and executed."

He shook his head as if there were something in all this perplexing beyond measure. Knots came into his jaws, and his handsome blue eyes grew hard and bitter and relentless.

Things began to happen to the diamond. It disappeared magically and reappeared. Intelligence would know what was happening to the stone—remarkable legerdemain—but no human eye could fix upon the point where the stone disappeared or reappeared. Lean strong hands they were, well kept, with nails cut almost to the quick; a fighting hand or a musicianly hand, or both.

The music of the water began to call him away from his somber thoughts. He returned the diamond to its waterproof casing. Then he got out his fishing tackle. But first he snipped off enough line to make a loop around his neck. With this he secured the rubber casing and drew the loop over his head. It took him about ten minutes to rig a beautiful five-ounce rod, with backbone enough to handle a moderate salmon or muskellunge.

"Now, then, Mr. Salvelinus Fontinalis!"

"Caw, caw!" cried the crows.

They were always about—crows. He had seen them in Darjeeling, in the Sudan, all over Europe and Asia. In drawing rooms too—not so raucous but just as thievish.

"Hang it all!"—with a reckless laugh.

Carrying the rod carefully extended before him, he made his way to the water and stepped boldly into it. His shin stung for a moment, followed by cool relief. He began to whip the air to limber up. When he concluded that his wrist was acting properly he launched the flies upon that part of the stream which ran darkly under the bending alders on the far side. Three casts convinced him that there was nothing in that inviting spot. Above him was a large boulder. He cast upstream just beyond the boulder, skittering the flies. There was a splash. The line flew into the air behind him.

"Not so good," he murmured.

The next cast, however, rewarded him. He reeled the captive to his side, stooped and, with his hand under water, freed the trout, which was small.

He moved downstream, whipping this spot and that, wherever instinct told him there would be trout. Twice he got caught in the alders, but each time he laughed. He nearly went under, however, as he freed the flies the second time. Fun! Up to his vest pockets once. He had a good deal of difficulty with his feet—the rubber soles would not grip substantially the moss-covered stones. All in the game, though. This was fishing.

He was reminded of an episode in the Ardennes two years ago. On a wager he had waded a stream in his dinner clothes, ten o'clock at night, in the rain. Fool, yes; but it was fun being that kind of fool.

All he wanted was a three-pounder; a fight, chances in favor of the trout, and no moral problem to vindicate. Over three pounds, trout were generally logy. Only the salmon or the muskellunge knew the fighting worth of each pound he possessed.

He waded perhaps three quarters of a mile down the stream, hunting for the spot. Occasionally he sighed aloud as some lovely vista opened unexpectedly before him! Ha! There it was—the delectable spot. If there wasn't an old golliwhopper in that pool, there wouldn't be one in the stream anywhere else. A regular Bastille of a place!

The young man had by now forgotten time and place, the brilliant, the loaded pistol, the desperate project which had brought him into this paradisaical wilderness. By the color of the water he judged the pool to be anywhere from six to ten feet deep and fast. You could not cast a fly from the shore, for the height and thickness of the alders; you had to stand in water which tried to buckle your knees. Across the stream, touching both sides, lay a giant pine, storm-riven, bleakly gray—a natural bridge. But that wasn't all. Many gaunt limbs reached into the water, draped with dead grass and branches from other trees; in one place the stream was clogged by a fence post in a snarl of barbed wire. You might hook your trout, but to keep him in the clear—that would be a real fisherman's job.

The young man fiddled about for a substantial footing and, having found it, made a cast. Nothing happened. Fussing over flies would be useless; the trout in this stream would take anything, provided they were hungry. And it was evident that they weren't hungry, for he had had indifferent luck so far. He would give the pool ten minutes' time; then he would toddle back to the car.

Snugging the rod under his arm, he got out his pipe, primed and fired it. Then he made his second cast, lightly skittering the flies against the current. There followed a mighty upheaval of water, a living silver arch, and a plop which sounded like a stone striking the water. The line zoomed and the rod bent. The young man's teeth clicked against his pipestem. The gorgeous moment of which every fisherman dreams had arrived.

Of course there were exceptions to all rules. Once in a while you hooked a monster who was still pulling down a million in gate money. The young man understood perfectly that he was in the ring with the Gene Tunney of this neck of the woods. Lord!

As one prize fighter outthinks the other, so the absorbed fisherman outthought the trout, who straightway made for the entanglements. No go. He crossed to the middle of the stream and shot at the fence post. No. He whirled, leaped, returned to the bottom of the pool, rose and darted toward the fisherman's legs. No go.

Now then on the right bank of the stream there appeared a girl. Perhaps it would be more exact to say a young woman. She wore laced boots to her knees, which were partly hidden under a cream-colored linen skirt. She wore a coat of the same material, a white silk shirt, and a flowing green tie. She was hatless, and her wind-tossed hair was as ruddily brown as the pine needles under her boots. To get on, it is necessary for some women to be beautiful. This young woman had no need of beauty—beauty of the Bouguereau type. Some women are born queens who never come to thrones. Her hands stuffed in her pockets, she stood imperially. She would think and act imperially, naturally. Her lips were vividly red. Her eyes were deep blue and calm. But both lips and eyes gave testimony of interest and amusement. Beautiful women and imperial women are not generally humorous, but when they are, watch out.

She had been on the point of calling out to the fisherman, when she observed that he carried neither net nor creel. She decided to see the play through because she was normally curious. She knew this pool, the very best in a fifteen-mile run. And he had discovered it instinctively. Fishing in a golf suit, without net or creel! A real sportsman; he would be worth watching. There wasn't the least doubt of it; he had hooked Old-Timer, whom she had lost ten times if once. True, she had never let him make the entanglements. But when he had turned and rushed at her!

No ordinary poacher, this; almost handsome, though a bit lantern-jawed. Nonchalant. Poacher though he was, she liked the way he kept his pipe going, with a battle of this caliber on his hands. He knew what had happened to him; he recognized the surrounding perils. Nonchalant outwardly, yes; but she knew very well that he was boiling with excitement inside. He wouldn't have been human else. Of course in the end he would lose; not even Saint Peter himself could have landed Old-Timer without a net. Already she had learned something—the way to hold the rod when Old-Timer lunged toward you: arm's length above the head. But could she maintain her balance at the same time? More than once her knees had buckled and she had had to turn and wade to save herself from a good ducking.

There was a swarm of black flies, but the fisherman seemed to be immune.

She sighed with envy. No use lying to herself. It took more than skill; it took muscles of iron; and no woman had any right to be as strong as this good-looking poacher. What queer streak of impatience had impelled him to wade the stream in a golf suit?

Every lunge and leap and twist of Old-Timer was adroitly met. By and by he turned on his side, beaten.

"He's done it," whispered the lone spectator.

Slowly the young man began to reel in. He knew these big game fish; they generally had second wind, and if you weren't exceedingly careful you lost out. He was in the act of reaching for the trout when she spoke:

"Beautifully done! But for all that, this is private property, and I must ask you to let the trout go." The fisherman all but lost his balance, so greatly was he surprised. His jaws opened and his pipe fell into the water. He made a desperate but futile effort to save it, but it bobbed under the pine and vanished.

"Hang it all," he said whimsically; "that was the best pipe I ever had!"

2

HER FACE REMAINED GRAVE, but laughter bubbled into her throat perilously. For a poacher, the young man had marked peculiarities. He had been surprised, but there was no evidence of abashment. He coolly reached down to the trout and freed it from the hook with a flip of the wrist.

A barbless hook! He had caught and beaten Old-Timer with a barbless hook. Insult to injury! She had been witness to the unbelievable!

She felt compelled to ask, "Was that a barbless hook?"

"Yes. What's the use of killing things if you don't want them to eat? I did not mean to poach," he declared. "I saw no posted signs."

She pointed to the pine near which she stood.

He laughed. "Never saw it. Big as all outdoors, and I never saw it! I saw only the pool. There he goes!" he added as the trout slowly righted himself majestically, then sank. "He's tired; not particularly hurt."

"You came from the road?"

"Yes. I had my tackle and simply had to give the stream a try. I'm sorry."

Sorry, indeed! She knew that he wasn't the least bit sorry. In fact, he seemed to be very well pleased with himself.

"The trail to the highway is just beyond that posted sign on the other side."

He followed the direction of her finger and again burst into laughter. "Two of them!"

"I advise you to hurry," she said. "You will find it very cold presently."

"Thanks. How far is this stream posted?" he wanted to know.

"Five miles above this pine and ten miles below."

"The King of Belgium cannot boast of such a trout run."

"Do you know the King of Belgium?" she could not resist asking. His nonchalance was a trifle over the line of her patience. A dig or two wouldn't hurt him.

But he did not respond. He loosed the leader and wound it around his hat. He reeled in the line, disjointed the rod, waded to shore, stamped and shook himself and turned. The black flies still swarmed about his head indignantly.

"You've been very sporting about it," he said, lifting his hat. "But I would do the same thing over again, under like circumstances. Evidently you're a fisherman too. You know how it is. When you beat a big fellow like that you like witnesses. I can always tell the story now, knowing that there is, somewhere on earth, a reliable witness who can vouch for my truthfulness. But who never will."

"Oh, I shall tell the story"—icily.

"You will? Well, that will be sporting of you."

"And I shall add that I never in all my life met a more coolly impudent poacher."

"Impudent? Why, I thought I was very polite. I might have lost that fish, and then you would have heard something."

What a stunning young woman! She looked like the Winged Victory restored. Who had been the sculptor? He had forgotten. But if the shade of Praxiteles— None of that! No woman in this picture. He plunged inland in search of the trail, which he found readily enough, being versed in all lores of the open.

Fool. But this bit of tomfoolery had turned out beautifully. He had beaten the biggest trout in the stream under the very eyes of Diana herself. But what would they think of him when they saw that he was wet to his vest pockets? He chuckled. He took off his hat and looked at the dial of the watch. Quarter after six. An hour and three quarters to reach his destination and change for dinner.

Well, there wouldn't be any women about, only men; so his condition was nothing to worry about.

The girl was right, though—he would be infernally cold and uncomfortable by the time he reached the Hood camp. He strode over the padded trail, no longer mindful of atmospheric effects but of the purpose which had brought him into this wilderness. He had waded the stream primarily because it had called to him irresistibly; secondarily, to cool his blood. There must be no sudden impulses to-night; he must follow his schedule absolutely. He would be among men who would be watching one another after the manner of strange but well-bred dogs. He himself would be a fox in dog's clothing; and if they scented him out— Well, there would always be that thunderbolt up his sleeve. But he was determined never to use this except in dire necessity.

None of them knew him personally, only by reputation. There was always the possibility of nothing being done to-night. It was on the knees of the gods. Step by step he had built up to this day; yet he knew that, because he was no superman, he had erred somewhere along the line. Where the weak link in the chain lay he could not guess. This hidden menace bothered him. If the gods denied him luck the game was up.

Why the devil must he meet such a girl at such a time? The picture of her would stick because the frame had been so unusual. Yet he was frank enough to admit that her face would have stood out in a crowd of feminine faces. It was beautiful, but its beauty was the antithesis of the accepted type. Verbally he could not have explained what he meant. She was beautiful; but he, a man never at loss for phrases, found himself inarticulate and beggared in words. A kind of beauty he couldn't find terms for.

He found his car where he had left it. There was gas enough to carry him two hundred miles. He climbed in lumbersomely, growling. He was cold and presently the wind would make him a good deal colder. The girl might laugh over the thought of his sartorial predicament, but she would always remember that he could have thrust his finger through the trout's gill.

All aboard! He started the car and went humming up the road in a cloud of dust. Presently the road veered north, then east.

There would be Van Cleve from Amsterdam, MacFarlane from London, Descamps from Paris, Morgan and himself from New York. Middle-aged men, who knew the history of every known gem. Great adventurers whose integrity was as impregnable as the Gibraltar— with the exception of Berks (himself) whose reputation was some- what speckled by rumor; who would sell out a client if there would be profit and security in the act. Unscrupulous, but. all the same, a great adventurer. And he would have to lay these rumors in the dust by his impeccable manners, his knowledge of the lore, his clear conception of what man was made of. The wheel turned upon the fact that they had never met him and had no proof that, from time to time, he had played a hand unethically.

There was a droll side to it. Like going to some lodge meeting; you had to have a passport, a secret sign. Proper credentials, or you wouldn't get into the Hood camp. Bidding for the Blue Rajah would take place in the morning. Perhaps.

But somewhere along the line he had made a mistake, being human and fallible. But there was this in his favor—the men he was soon to meet were, like himself, human and fallible. The mis- take might never be discovered.

Why hadn't she laughed when his pipe had dropped into the water? The picture must have been funny—shoutingly funny. Did he know the King of Belgium? She knew how to set a barb sting- ing, suavely. He sighed. He would have liked to know her, and under other circumstances he would have gone toward this desire boldly. The high road and the low road. She on the bank and he in the stream.

He wondered if Hood owned any of the stream. Hood. An eye for an eye, a tooth for a tooth. The oldest law. On and on he rode with reckless sped.

"Ha!" he cried aloud; for suddenly he observed twinkling lights in the distance. That would be the camp. And yonder was a by- road.

They called them camps, he mused. Hot and cold water, porcelain tubs. Persian rugs, all the comforts of a Park Avenue residence. When all a man needed was a war blanket, a pup tent, a gun, a rod and a hatchet.

He turned into the byroad and shortly rolled under the wooden porte-cochère and struck his horn. At once the door opened and the butler came down the steps. A gaunt man with a stony face.

"The name, please."

"I'm Berks—Roger Berks."

"Your letter of introduction?"

Eeny, meeny, miny, mo! Berks piped inwardly. Hood was a fool. Had he conducted this affair in New York, he would have been as safe as in a church. Miles from anybody. What would they do here if anybody had the toothache? He produced his credentials—a letter signed by Hood, with a blot of ink in one corner. All very childish. The blot, anyhow. Still, Hood had to know who was who.

"Very good, sir. Your luggage?"

"In the rear. Just the bag."

"Yes, sir. Why, you are all wet!"—astonishedly.

"That's true. Had to go fishing. I am unfamiliar with the habits of the house, but I shouldn't mind a stiff peg of whisky. Medicinal, of course."

"I'll bring up the peg, sir. Be so good as to follow me."

As they entered the house, Berks observed that all the rooms were empty of human beings.

"Have the others arrived?"

"Yes, sir. Came in shortly after luncheon."

"What time is dinner?"

"Eight o'clock, sir. This is your room. You will find hot water for bath and shaving."

"How about telegrams?"

"We relay them by telephone. Any urgent message, sir?"

"No. I might want to get in touch with my client."

"The telegraph office closes at nine and does not send or receive again till eight in the morning. But we can get long-distance to New York. The railways are thirty miles east and west of us."

"Seems to me you're pretty far off."

"We have our own gas station and three cars. Either way, we can make the railroad in less than an hour, unless there's been a cloud-burst. I'll have the whisky up in a jiffy, sir."

Jiffy. Come, come! thought Berks. The old gargoyle had something human in him despite his looks. Jiffy. He hadn't heard the word since boyhood. Evidently up here "Whoop" was still the word; "Whoopee" hadn't yet arrived. Heaven forfend that it should! Of the two kinds of American Indians, Berks preferred the red.

The door closed and Berks stared at the panels moodily. Long-distance to New York. Would the unknown mistake lie in that direction? Puddles on the birch floor. Off with these togs, and also good-bye to them forever.

Berks stood in his shorts before the shaving mirror, when a tap came on the room door. He hurried to it, half his face in lather. The saturnine butler passed in a small decanter and a tall glass.

"Thanks. That will do nicely."

"If you will leave your wet clothes in the hallway, sir, I'll see to it that they go to the drying room. Mr. Hood will receive you just before dinner."

"I'll be down as soon as I bathe and dress."

This time Berks locked the door, completed his shaving, finished with the tub, then attacked the whisky. A hot sling, which threw comfort and well-being over him at once, but which warned him that one would be enough. In his condition he responded too quickly. There were no tailor's labels in any of his clothes. That would not be the mistake. The bag, which he had purchased in a second-hand shop, was unidentifiable.

So then, at five minutes to eight he stood before the mirror and inspected a presentable young man, ready for Piccadilly or the Champs Élysées or Park Avenue after dark. In the lapel of his dinner coat was a bit of red ribbon. In regard to this his conscience was in good order; he could lawfully wear the Order of Leopold. It was absolutely necessary to impress his host and the other guests, to mitigate such dubiousness as they might hold for him.

"Do you know the King of Belgium?"

Hang the girl! There was no room in his thoughts for a woman; he must not wander mentally for a second this night.

He thrust the automatic pistol in the inside pocket of the dinner coat and the stone loosely in the left outside pocket. Ironically he glanced into a coat sleeve—the thunderbolt was there, ready to be launched. He kneaded his sinewy hands for a minute, then unlocked the door and proceeded downstairs.

Immediately he was gone, the butler came stealthily out of another room and silently entered Berks'. He deftly went through everything belonging to Berks, examining even the inside of the collars. Ready-made, everything. A scowl rippled over the butler's saturnine face. Quietly he stole out of the room and down the servants' stairs. A gentleman, with ready-made clothes, even to his collars, his military brushes unmarked, and no labels on the worn suitcase.

Berks saw a group of men by the fireside, and he approached with the air of a man who knew his way about. He recognized Hood instantly, and his body felt as if the stream was flowing over it. Introductions were made, perhaps somewhat stiffly. The other guests had met before.

"Make yourself at home, Mr. Berks," said the host, a handsome man about sixty, beautifully gray. "Magazines in the library. Dinner will be twenty minutes late. To-night you are simply my guest. No business till to-morrow morning."

The young man smiled, but inwardly grew cold. No business till to-morrow, when he had staked everything on to-night!

There was some desultory talk about the condition of the highways, the stock market, the German debt. Berks readily understood that they had drawn into their shells, gravely polite.

"Are you gentlemen armed?" he asked quietly.

The others fell back a step, dumfounded. Van Cleve was first to recover, and he did so good-humoredly.

"Yes, I am armed. The man who bids in the Blue Rajah may have to defend it on the way back to New York."

"My opinion, too," Morgan admitted, while MacFarlane and Descamps looked distressed.

"We are all armed, then?" Berks laughed. "The bootlegger, the dopester, and the bandit ride abroad. But it strikes me as droll—dining with guns in our pockets."

Leaving this bomb smoldering, he sauntered into the library, where he discovered a fine piano. Good. He had shocked them, now he would enchant them. He must win the respect of these hard-headed beggars. He was in the mood for Chopin; and he began the Fantasie Impromptu, C sharp minor. He played it exquisitely and with fire. When he had done he dropped his hands and bent his head, searching for something else to fit his mood.

"Beautifully done! But for all that, this is private property, and I must ask you—"

He leaped to his feet. Across the piano, smiling into his face, was the young woman of the stream.

"You?"—a whisper.

"So you do know the King of Belgium?"

3

EVIDENTLY SHOCKS WERE RUNNING deuces wild. He was speechless for a moment. He had an instantaneous picture of his project from a new angle. Detour. He was like a man driving furiously in the night and coming, with a shriek of brakes, upon an unlighted detour sign. He would have to rearrange his plans. But how? He recovered his mental balance.

"It isn't fair," he said.

"What isn't?"

"To surprise me two times in one day."

"You are Mr. Berks. I am Miss Hetherstone, Mr. Hood's niece. Why didn't you tell me you were coming here?"

"Word of honor, I didn't know where I was."

"I knew that there was someone playing. The mechanical touch is never quite the same as the human. And, oddly enough, that very piece is in the piano this minute. It is a player. What else do you do—beautifully?"

There was no irony in her voice now, but there was mischief. Very well; he would pick up the foil. Mischief for mischief.

"How many times have you lost that trout?"

"Too many times."

"I suppose my skill filled you with envy."

"I was glad to see you lose your pipe."

He laughed, attached the roll, and started the player. The difference between the human hand and the automaton was easily distinguishable. Even to the man peering into the window—a man with bleak gray eyes.

"Don't!" the girl cried. "It isn't the same at all."

"Nevertheless, it's Paderewski."

"I had the notion that you would be an older man."

So they had been discussing him? "I am very old," he gravely replied.

"You like Chopin. So do I. Are you on the concert stage?"

"No. I do not sell the gift; I give it away. For the fun of it."

He had need of some clear thinking, and he could not accomplish this while engaged conversationally with a young woman who, if he once let go, would set a spell upon him. Perhaps he had not committed any mistake; perhaps he had planned perfectly. But fate was always stronger than human perfections. He began one of Bach's lovely chorals.

With folded arms she leaned against the piano. Poise, he thought. She would have gone to Buckingham Palace with the same unstudied grace. Devil take it, she was in the way, and he would have to maneuver around her!

For the fun of it, she thought. Waded streams in golfing clothes. Threw away a gift which would have made him rich and famous, for the fun of it. Yet that wasn't the jaw of an idler. She was quite sure that there were serious actions in this young man's life. Gems. To be sure. He carried them across oceans and continents, at the risk of his life. Caution, alertness, doggedness, quick thinking—he would apply these attributes to his work. But when he played, it would be with whimsical recklessness. And to have a man like this enter the house when she was at the peak of her boredom! What intensely blue eyes he had!

He played a mazurka and a nocturne, but during the performance he did not look at her directly, which most musicians would have done—male musicians. Suddenly he saw light. She would be an asset rather than a liability. A young woman wanting the society of a young man who was not without attractions, in a house where all the other men were middle-aged. She was not the type to select companionship carelessly. He would use her interest in him, but not to her hurt. As a fisherman and a musician he had caught her fancy. It would raise him considerably in the eyes of the others.

He would not deviate a hair from the line. He might be defeated. Aviator, mountain climber, hunter—aye, and gambler—he had known defeat. Yet he had never retreated in fear of defeat. But unless the Blue Rajah was brought out to-night, his defeat would be absolute.

"Have you ever climbed mountains?" she asked irrelevantly when he had done.

"Why, yes! What put that question into your mind?"

"Up here we are rather informal. We ask questions frankly. We do not observe the amenities of convention strictly. You strike me as a man who must always be extending himself physically, not caring anything about the cost."

"This time you astonish me," he replied. "I haven't thought much about it, but you are quite right. I am always slam-banging into excitements. I like impromptu adventures such as this afternoon's. I always like to leave something to chance."

"Where angels fear to tread?"

"There came an angel in the wilderness," he quoted.

"I neither look nor feel like an angel."

"Oh, I don't know how you feel."

"But to you I look like one?" She laughed for the first time.

"My idea of an angel would be a woman who would let a poor devil of a poaching fisherman have his meed of sport before she called him to a halt. Who would, in the event of a serious injury, have gone instantly to his aid."

"You are a very wise young man."

"You say that with the air of Methuselah's wife. You are younger than I am, and I am only thirty. In these thirty years I have met many women."

"Yes?"

"They are all different."

She broke into laughter again. "Serves me right!"

"Pardon?"

"I thought I was going to be given a compliment."

"To some women it is not necessary to pay compliments."

"I'll accept that statement as one. You play beautifully. Under whom did you study?"

"Busoni. At twelve I decided to become a second Paderewski. At fifteen I gave one concert. I learned that I hated audiences, hated applause. At eighteen I decided to take up aviation."

"And you went to war and the King of Belgium decorated you. Then you became interested in gems, because there was risk in handling them. But frankly I do not like this business." Her eyes became troubled.

"You mean our being here?"

"Uncle Mark could have transacted the sale in New York. Suppose one of you buys the Rajah and you are robbed between here and New York? Secret? How can you keep a thing like this secret?"

Aye, how indeed? Did she love this uncle of hers? Was it possible that Hood could inspire love in anything that lived?

She went on: "This cannot be wholly a secret in your offices. There will be some untrustworthy man in the secret. The Rajah represents a fortune. It is one of the most beautiful diamonds in existence. Whenever it is in the house—in any of the houses we live in—I feel an oppression. I don't like it."

"Your uncle is a very rich man. Why should he wish to sell it?" The young man's nostrils dilated slightly.

"He has become superstitious about it."

"Superstitious?"

"He is sixty and not well. The stone has a sinister history, as you know, and it has begun to work upon his imagination. He is quite mad about the collection."

"He has his collection up here?"—incredulously.

"He cannot be separated from it."

"How did the others arrive?"

"They all came in one car."

"Well, whoever buys it will be protected by the other three."

"But you are here to buy it, and you will be going alone."

"True. But I'm afraid that Van Cleve will be able to outbid me. My client does not care to tie up too much money."

"Is it just adventure, or do you really care for gems?"

"I am quite mad about them. To have that stone in my pocket and to carry it back to New York!" He shrugged.

"I understand. The bright face of danger. But you are young and adventurous, and shortly my uncle will be an old man. I love him! He has been the only father I have ever known."

Berks lowered his eyes, ill at ease. Devil take the way fate intruded! Perhaps the finest specimen of young womanhood he had ever met. Why couldn't she have been somewhere else? His purpose was to wring her uncle's heart; indirectly he must wring hers too. His jaws stiffened. No deviation from the line.

"Do you live in New York?"

"Oh, no," she answered. "We really live in Paris. But every summer we have a month here. There's nothing like it in the old country. My uncle used to be an ardent fisherman, but now he leaves the rod to me."

"How about the servants?"

"Except for the chauffeur, all are old in service. The butler has been with us for twenty-odd years. He is English, but he speaks French very well. The caretakers live here the year around, and they sometimes act as guides."

"And all of them know about the collection?"

"I suppose so. But we have a very odd wall safe. A man might break into it and still not find what he sought"—enigmatically. "And where do you live?"

"I have no real home. Hotels, mostly. Probably that is why I am driven into excitements. I have no home life to tame me."

"Would you want to be tamed?"

"That depends"—smiling.

"Dinner is served."

The saturnine butler stood in the doorway, eying Berks coldly.

4

THE BLUE RAJAH HAD BEHIND IT seven known murders. Its history began with the rajah himself. No one knew where he had got it. He had worn the stone sewed in his white turban at a durbar. He was knifed in his tent pavilion that night. The stone popped up in Constantinople. Two murders there. It was next heard of in St. Petersburg. One murder. Berlin, Paris, London, Liverpool; in each city someone had paid. Then for twenty years the world lost track of it. Berks wondered what the history was previous to its possession by the rajah. It had not been cut by any modern machinery, the facets being without conformity. A medieval or pre-Christian gem. No one had ever thought to cut the stone in halves, thereby enhancing its commercial value. As it was, no woman would care to wear it with one half of its beauty always hidden. It was, in truth, a collector's stone. Seven murders and one man who had died of a broken heart.

Berks knew that he would always remember this dinner. Tension. If he sensed it, surely the others must. Drawn up here, miles away from civilization and the protections which civilization offered, the sinister history of the stone must be in the process of review in each mind. Everybody calm outwardly but jumpy within. He himself had not been conscious of nerves till the girl's voice had come across the piano. Indeed, he had not known how deeply the vision of her had impressed his imagination till he saw her the second time.

He sat at her right; Morgan, Van Cleve, the host, Descamps and
MacFarlane. To Berks each face was worth a study. Hood and Van
Cleve alone seemed normal. Morgan, Descamps, and MacFarlane
looked dour and suspicious. Naturally; they were on a queer business. Berks switched his glance to the butler and received a shock.
The man's eyes seemed like coals in his head. More than that, his
hand shook as he set down the bouillon cups. The old fellow's
phlegm seemed to have gone out of him. Guns—all of them were
carrying guns!

"What caused you to smile then?" abruptly asked the girl.

Caught off his guard, Berks stared at her bewilderedly. "Beg
pardon?"

"You smiled oddly. What struck you as amusing? Remember,
we are not formal here."

"A joke," he said. "You know how irrelevant things flash through
one's head. You were talking to Mr. Morgan, and this joke popped
into my head. Too infantile to repeat."

A colossal joke! If Hood did not show the Rajah to-night, the
enterprise would represent zero. And it would be the last chance
he would ever have. Part of the joke was that he himself might not
ask to see the stone. He must commit no act which would focus
attention, no act which related to the stone.

Yes; she was in the way, because of the loving glances she sent
down the table to her uncle and because of the loving glances her
uncle returned. Detour, red lanterns; and he must go smashing on!

"Mr. Berks, you play extraordinarily well." Van Cleve was speaking. He spoke English with but little accent. "You should be on the
concert stage instead of selling gems."

"Crowds bother me."

"I see. Stage fright?"

"No. I do not believe I am afraid of anything. Just do not like
crowds."

"That's possible," replied the Hollander. "I see you wear the
Order of Leopold."

"Aviation during the war"—simply. The truth, so why shouldn't
he tell them?

"Ah! Now I understand your distaste for crowds. The eagle is a lonely bird. He flies over the city, but never through it." Van Cleve smiled amiably. "I'd give a good deal to know who your client is."

"There, there!" interrupted Hood. "No business to-night, if you please."

"But surely," said Descamps, the Frenchman, "you are going to let us see the Rajah? To keep us on—what you say?—hooks—" He gestured excitedly.

"Tenterhooks," assisted MacFarlane, warming a little.

"On tenterhooks all night is not fair. An unofficial inspection. Eh?"

"Come, Mr. Hood," said Morgan. "We will promise not to quote prices or use our micros. We all know the stone, but none of us has seen it."

"I have," said Van Cleve. "When I was a young fellow. It came to my father. One of the ends was slightly chipped. My father himself polished it down."

"What do you say, Elsie?" Hood called down the table.

So her name was Elsie. Berks rubbed his palms upon his napkin. They were beginning to sweat.

"Let them see it," said Elsie. "They are human."

"Very well. Go and get it."

To Berks it was as if he had been holding his breath under water and his head was now in the air again. And yet, there was a cold ripple over his spine. Too easy. The whole affair had cut like cheese; and that wasn't fate's way. There would be a trip somewhere; it was inevitable. But being suspicious of fate was as good as being forewarned.

Elsie. He would never see her again. You had always to pay an extra price for the Rajah. The imagined woman. The physical reproduction of a dream. You met the one woman in a drawing room and did not recognize her. You met her under the sky and by the side of a wild stream, and you recognized her at once. . . . Damn his palms! They were like watersheds!

Elsie departed upon her errand. Berks became conscious that the butler, who stood behind Hood's chair, was eying him covertly.

But there was something else in the old chap's attitude. He was listening. What did he expect to hear? Was there more than one impromptu on to-night's program?"

Elsie returned presently, holding her handkerchief in her hand. She stopped at her uncle's chair and gently unrolled the contents of the handkerchief on the tablecloth. The elliptical ball of prismatic fires was plainly visible to Berks, even though he sat seven feet away. The pulse under his jaws began to thump. Could he do it? Well, if he failed, there was the thunderbolt in his sleeve.

Hood passed the gem to Van Cleve. The butler immediately stepped over to the light buttons.

"Henry!"

"Yes, sir."

"You need not worry about the lights," said Hood reprovingly. "This is not the cinema or a detective story."

The butler embarrassedly returned to his position behind Hood's chair, while the gem experts eyed him amusedly.

Van Cleve rolled the stone about. "The same. I never have forgotten it. If I were rich I should have the mania, too." He passed the stone along to his neighbor.

The experts had no reason to conceal their ecstasies. The highest bidder would take the stone away with him. Eventually the stone came to Elsie, but she at once pushed it in front of Berks.

He did not touch it immediately but stared at it with half-closed eyes. The others were looking at him interestedly. "Let's see what you know about it!" they seemed to shout at him.

"Old," he said. "But what puzzles me is what has become of the other great stones. The sea and the earthquakes and the fires cannot have swallowed them all. This is one evidence. *Adamas*—adamant—*diamant*—diamond. Pliny speaks of them. The story goes that this comes from the ancient sandstones of India. Am I right, Mr. Van Cleve?"

"Yes."

"Have you any notion how it was worn? I mean in olden times?"

Van Cleve answered. "My father told me that it hung in a little gold-wire basket, around a woman's neck. Though priests were also known to wear them that way."

Berks reached out to take the stone. As his hand hid it for a second he drew back both hands suddenly and gripped his side. His face became lined. The Blue Rajah still lay upon the tablecloth.

"What is it?" asked Elsie anxiously.

He smiled. "Stitch. Had a fall and smashed some ribs. Rheumatism. It's what I get for wading that trout stream this afternoon. There, it's gone. Sorry." With the tip of his finger he rolled the Rajah toward Elsie.

"I caught him at it, Uncle Mark," Elsie called down the table. "He had Old-Timer on a barbless hook."

"Old-Timer?" cried her uncle. "And he lost him?"—hopefully.

"Alas! I had to make him let it go, thinking he was poaching."

"In spirit I was," said Berks, straightening up and vigorously rubbing his side.

The laughter was general.

"Your butler saw the state I was in when I arrived." Berks touched the stone again. "What a queer business! Sometimes it amuses me to think what men will do to each other for something like this—a mineral with colors in it."

Hood stared at his plate and made bread crumbs absently.

"There is another phase," put in Van Cleve. "The collector has no successor. His heirs are always sure to put the collection on the market. Hence, our reason for being. I remember—"

"Drink a little of your wine," advised Elsie.

"I had a peg before I came down," replied Berks. "I never drink except when I need it."

"And you don't need it now?"

"There are other and better kinds of intoxicants" —looking directly into her eyes.

What she saw in his eyes caused some warmth to flow into her cheeks. Well, she had opened the door. She had told him that one spoke frankly here, by lip or eye. "Anyone wish to see the Rajah again?"

All shook their heads. So Elsie wrapped the stone in her handkerchief, and with a bright nod went her way to return the Rajah to the safe.

Suddenly the butler turned his gaze toward the hall.

"Is that the telephone, Henry?" asked Hood, looking up from his plate.

"Yes, sir."

After a few moments the butler reentered the dining room.

"Long-distance from New York, Mr. Berks," he said.

Berks sat perfectly still for the space of several wild heartbeats.

5

New York? What had happened down there? He pushed back his chair and rose.

"Excuse me for a moment, gentlemen. Probably my client. Where is the telephone?"

"Under the hall stairs, sir. Follow me," said the butler.

The telephone stood on a small stand; there was no booth. Berks sat down in the chair and took the receiver. He was about to call when he observed the butler, close beside him.

"I'm afraid this is going to be private," said Berks, smiling.

"I beg your pardon, sir. I wasn't thinking."

The butler walked slowly back to the dining room, wiping his palms on the sides of his trousers.

Meantime.

"Who is it?" asked Berks, low but clearly.

"Gerry," came from New York. "When I went back he was gone."

"Gone?"

"Yes. Watch your step."

"Thanks."

Berks hung up the receiver. He did not rise at once. It was now after nine. Nine hours. Berks knew that he would not dare make a get-away till all had gone to bed. Nine hours. And why hadn't he telephoned? No doubt he had solved the riddle by this time. Berks frowned darkly at the green-covered telephone wire. No fault of his; purely accidental, like the presence of this girl in the house. And all of them carried guns! Berks shot a glance over his shoulder. He was alone and unobserved. Swiftly he drew out a knife and sawed the telephone wire, applying savage strength. Then he proceeded to the hall door and casually opened it.

Now? The way was clear. No. Always the fool, he must see the girl again. The cold sweet night air refreshed him. Speculating, he forgot that his prolonged absence might be noticed.

The beggar had had ample time to warn Hood. But he hadn't. Well, the dice were on the green! Only a few hours ahead!

"Anything wrong, sir?" asked the butler.

"The stitch in my side recurred," said Berks. Was this chap watching him? Hang him! "I needed a bit of air. Gone now."

"I thought perhaps the door had blown open, sir."

"You may close it."

The butler peered into the night, then shut and bolted the door. He followed Berks into the dining room, and Berks returned to his chair beside Elsie.

"Are the grounds guarded?" he asked.

"It isn't necessary. We have an absolutely impregnable safe."

"A hundred resolute men, armed, could blow up the Sub-Treasury and loot it in twenty minutes."

"This would be different. Blow up this house, and there wouldn't be any gems, nothing but crystal atoms. But I don't like it. Have you ever felt that someone was behind you? That's the way I feel."

"There's always the man who put in this safe."

"I understand. But my uncle himself built this safe. Mechanism is his profession, though he no longer practices it. His inventions are used all over the world. Only Uncle and myself know the combination. But I wish he had not brought the collection."

"But what do you think can happen, when all of us are armed?"

"Something in the air."

"Imagination."

"Whatever it is, I feel it."

"Is your car locked, Mr. Berks?" asked Hood.

"Yes."

"I'm sorry there wasn't room for it in the garage."

"If it rains it will not matter. It's an old bus, not worth stealing."

"If you should need any gas or oil in the morning—"

"Thank you."

"Henry, coffee and liqueurs. . . . I believe," the host added, "that it will be pleasanter to remain at the table."

"Do you want coffee and liqueur?" whispered Elsie.

"No"—emphatically, from Berks.

"Then come into the library and play for me. It will take me out of myself. Come."

Berks arose with alacrity. To have her alone by himself! To build pleasant but impossible dreams! Besides, he thought with smarting irony, if anyone went to the telephone and found the wire cut, he could make a tolerable exit through one of the French windows. And in the library, while making a pretense to view the night, he loosed the window latch. So far as it was humanly possible he was not going to overlook a point.

Meanwhile Van Cleve turned to Hood. "I had a notion that Berks was older and—well, not quite so polished. Strange how we build up the character and appearance of a person by hearsay. I am something of a musician myself. This young fellow has soul as well as superb technique." Van Cleve paused. "I have a confession to make. I told a reporter just before we docked that I had come to America principally to try to purchase a diamond called the Blue Rajah. We will talk carelessly at times. But I did not know where the bidding was to take place. I met my rivals at Albany, and there we agreed to make the trip up here together. How far are we from the next camp?"

"Twenty-two miles. We never have any night prowlers," Hood replied. "Your talking hasn't done any harm. I should indeed be pleased if the bidder-in will announce it to the newspapers."

"Not I!" said Van Cleve. "I have a long way to go."

"Well," said Morgan, "if I'm the lucky man my firm will advertise it. Are you going to sell all the collection?"

"No." Hood stirred his coffee thoughtfully. "I have suddenly taken a distaste for the Rajah. It is the pariah of the collection."

Van Cleve took up the Venetian glass and inhaled the bouquet of the green chartreuse. He was not unused to these odd switchabouts. A mania which lasted a third of a lifetime, which one day began to crack suddenly, for no known reason. A real gem collector was, he had found, generally a man with a vivid imagination.

"Has anyone attempted to rob you?" he asked.

"No," answered Hood, still idling with his coffee. "I haven't added to the collection in twenty years. So my former activities are somewhat forgotten." Hood raised his head. "The truth is, I have been thinking about my niece. When I die the collection will unavoidably come into the open. Although I live abroad, I am still an American citizen; and the state inheritance tax will reveal the existence of the collection. A small army of rascals will learn that my niece has a portable fortune. She does not care for gems, except jade and chrysoprase. I can sell the Rajah, but it is utterly impossible for me to part with my emeralds—while I live."

"I understand," said Van Cleve, sipping the green nectar.

Gem collectors. There were rich men who bought gems without being particularly inquisitive as to how the seller had come by them. Of course, thought Van Cleve, it was none of his affair, but he couldn't recall the sale of the Blue Rajah to Marcus Hood. Certainly it was not recorded in the historical data which he had in his bag upstairs. Probably Hood had purchased the stone privately. In 1898 it had been in Amsterdam. The final registered purchase had been made by Jonathan Willard, who had been dead for many years.

Elsie drew a chair beside the piano and waited. Berks sat slumped on the bench, his chin touching his chest, his eyes closed. He had the appearance of a man delving into memories. As a matter of fact, his body was trembling, and he was waiting for this tremor to subside. He was sure of himself, of every future act till he was safe in New York. Yet here he was, attacked by vertigo which was not a reaction to his recent activities.

"Perhaps you are too tired?" she said interrogatively.

He sat up with a start. "I was trying to recall the Scherzo from Mendelssohn's Midsummer Night's Dream, but it escapes me."

"Play anything."

He did not observe that her fingers were tightly locked.

"Chopin," he said; and plunged into the fiery Fourth Étude in C sharp minor, as difficult as it is brilliant. Debussy followed, Grieg,

Mozart, the Tarantelle by Fauré, Liszt's transcription of Wagner's Spinning Song—now rarely played on the piano—Beethoven. It came to him like thunder in the night that he wanted this girl to remember him always, tell her by exquisite sounds that in other times she would have been the one woman in the world. And never could he tell her; for he was an implacable enemy to her house.

He concluded the program with the Fantasie Impromptu, knowing that he would never play it again without seeing the vision of her. You had to pay. As he played he ironically cogitated that, had she not entered upon the scene, he would have gone through the whole adventure sardonically amused. He had mocked the crows. By a queer twist of perspectives he saw that he had become one of them. He should have launched his thunderbolt boldly. Now it was too late.

As he ceased playing he turned. Her hands lay limp in her lap, her head rested against the back of the chair and her eyes were closed. He waited. Suddenly, yet dazedly, she opened her eyes.

"What a gift!" she whispered. "What a gift!"

"I did not tire you?"

"Never, never!"—quite vehemently. Then she happened to glance at the doorway. Five men stood there, dead cigars in their fingers. Elsie eyed them astonishedly.

Berks sprang up, smiling. "I forgot where I was!" So he had.

"We all forgot where we were," replied Hood gravely, his eyes vaguely puzzled. Had he ever seen this man Berks before? It was not the face, it was the quick smile that had in it something hauntingly familiar.

Van Cleve shook himself out of a dream. Never again would he judge a man by what he had heard about him. This young fellow was a thoroughbred; it was not possible that he had ever "sold out" or "gone partners" in a shady gem deal, as rumor strongly had it.

"I'm off for bed," he announced. "It has been a strenuous day."

To which the others agreed, and straggled back into the living room.

"Very strenuous," remarked Berks. "But I would go a-fishing!"

A moment alone with her, the last ever. He approached her and held forth his hand. She accepted it, struggling out of the hypnosis which had bound her. But when he bent and kissed her hand she withdrew it quickly, finding her mental balance.

"You go to the moving pictures?"—with light irony.

"Don't you ever surrender to impulses?"

"Rarely. I am afraid to. One throws a stone into the water, but one never knows how far the ripples will go."

"That is true." Aye, so it was! If anyone knew the price of impulses it was himself. "Will you be sorry to see the Blue Rajah go?"

"Sorry?" Her eyes flashed. "Sorry? I hate it!"

"But why?"—astonished.

"Men have killed other men for it. Whenever I am compelled to touch it I have the same feeling as when I see a snake. The other stones in the collection I don't mind, but the Rajah fills me with abhorrence."

"It is only a stone with pretty colors in it. You shouldn't revile it; revile mankind."

"Your voice sounds oddly."

"Perhaps I've caught cold"—lightly. "Good-bye."

"Good-night." She did not notice the finality of his salute.

He passed quickly from the room and she sat down again. A queer sensation laid hold of her. The room seemed empty and dead, like a theater when the audience was gone. She was becoming just a little afraid of this singular Mr. Berks. No man had ever before robbed her so completely of the initiative. She had been like an empty chalice into which some strange living wine had been poured, and drained. She was not musically emotional ordinarily, but to-night she had been swept off her feet. Perhaps it was because she had been so utterly unprepared for such a visitation.

Her uncle entered. "Remarkable young fellow, Elsie. All of them are remarkable men, particularly Van Cleve. None of them ever saw Berks before. He was not originally invited to bid. But in some manner he or his client heard of the deal, and he begged to be permitted to put in a bid. Rumor has it that Berks has been mixed up in several shady affairs."

"I don't believe it!"

"Well, after what we have seen and heard of him, it is mighty hard to believe."

"Don't you see, Nunky? It wasn't humanly possible to keep the affair secret. Why did you bring all the collection?"

Hood paced about for a moment. "Because I want them always with me now. I am sixty. Only a little time is left to me. Probably five years at the longest. Might as well face the fact." Hood sat down on the arm of her chair. "Have I been a good father to you, honey?"—tenderly.

"The idea!" She put her arm around him. "I love you better than all the world."

"There's no young man?"—teasingly.

"Indeed there isn't. Several times I believed I'd found the man, but subsequent events proved I hadn't. When I marry, Nunky, I'm going to be sure."

"How will you be able to tell?"

"When I meet the man, I'll know."

"But sometimes it's the right one and sometimes it's the wrong. Cupid is often a bad shot. What do you think of Berks?"

She did not answer at once. "Rather remarkable. I don't just know what to make of him. He isn't a bit like the others."

"He is young."

"That isn't it. He belongs to a different world. Ours—if you want the way I feel."

"Is our world always the best? Haven't we two seen mighty shady aristocrats?"

"Yes."

"Charming, intellectual, and all that?"

"Yes. Oh, I'm not in search of any Saint Michael or D'Artagnan. But he must belong to the world I belong to. Men and women should marry their kind, socially and religiously. I'm not a snob, but one is generally married a long, long time."

"Good girl!" Hood bent and kissed her ruddy hair.

And she looked down at the back of her hand. Men had kissed her hand before now, some perfunctorily, some with the air of worship. If he hadn't caught Old-Timer on a barbless hook, if he hadn't played the piano like a Paderewski— In the beginning he had been whimsically impudent, an impudence which had worn down her indignation perilously close to laughter. To-night he had been gravely courteous and companionable. A man might be a great fisherman and behave terribly at table, or he might be a prince in the house and a pest in the open. Berks seemed to belong wherever one put him.

"Come along to bed," broke in her uncle, pulling her to her feet and locking his arm in hers.

Henry, the butler, once in his room, his face grimmer than ever, knelt before his bureau and began to rummage the lower drawer. From a small leather box he extracted a letter the creases of which offered mute testimony of the many times it had been read. He did not read it to-night, but carefully stowed it in the inner pocket of his butler's jacket.

When Elsie got to her room she did not undress. She turned out the lights and sat in a wicker chair by the star-spangled window. The theme from the Fantasie Impromptu persisted in echoing and reechoing through her head. She was passionately fond of good music, but never before had music so deranged her emotionally.

The unusual episodes had had something to do with it. The wilderness which had reawakened the primitives. Her highly-strung nerves, tautened by the knowledge that there was more than half a million in gems in the house—enough to tempt a regiment of thieves. These had weakened the barriers. Her mood had been both receptive and unconventional to this sort of diversion; only, it had taken her beyond her depth.

Good heavens, yes! Had he kissed her lips instead of her hand she would not have been terribly indignant, at that moment. Somehow it came to her that he had set his will to the purpose of making himself unforgettable. Funny old world, wasn't it? Tomorrow he would or would not take the Blue Rajah away, and that would be the end of it.

She laughed softly. His pipe falling into the stream and vanishing, and his vigorous reproach. Fisherman, pianist, gem runner, aviator—and good looks. Why couldn't she have met him in the proper environment—say, Cap D'Antibes? But he was here in quest of a fat commission, and his honesty had been questioned—by rivals he had frequently beaten, no doubt. Envy was the mother of Rumor. These cogitations had taken perhaps the major portion of an hour.

Suddenly she gripped the arms of her chair and propelled herself to her feet. Music! He had stolen downstairs and was playing the Fantasie again. To draw her. Daring and whimsical impulses—that kind of man. Confident that no one but herself would be drawn. But she would be on guard this time. No sweeping her off her feet twice. She opened the door softly and walked to the landing. Very good. She would surprise him by permitting herself to be drawn. It was rather droll, and she wasn't the least bit afraid.

The pianissimo of the finale died away as she reached the foot of the stairs. The light was in the living room. She heard another sound. She ran into the dining room and peered into the night. An automobile was making for the highway! Who was stealing away, and for what reason? She tried in vain to make out the shape of the car.

She whirled from the window bewilderedly. There was the Fantasie again! The player, mechanically set to repeat! Here, where there were no walls between, she could readily discern that the human touch was absent. A car stealing swiftly away and the player set into action! She began to feel some difficulty in breathing and her thoughts revolved confusedly. She got hold of her emotions presently and ran into the living room.

Instinctively she focused the spot in the wall where the safe would be. The door was wide open. She smothered a cry with her palm. A thief in the house and the thief had got away! Her fears had not been imaginary. The freshness of the air warned her that one of the French windows in the library was open.

Between her and the fireplace stood a magnificent specimen of birch in the form of a center table. From where she stood this table obscured the hearth. Before she summoned help she decided to close and lock the window. As she passed the table she halted.

Huddled grotesquely on the rug before the fireplace lay her uncle in his dressing gown and Moroccan red slippers.

Silence for a space. Then Elsie screamed.

6

THERE FOLLOWED A SPACE OF TIME of which Elsie had no recollection. When she opened her eyes she was not sure of the visions presented to her. Faces out of some mummers' show, pale and almost featureless; slowly they took shape and distinction. The butler, Descamps, Morgan, MacFarlane, and Van Cleve; her gaze slowly traveled from face to face. Van Cleve dropped to his knees and offered her a glass of water mixed with aromatic spirits of ammonia. She drank and became fully conscious. She was in the library.

"Is he—" She could not complete the question.

"Yes, my child," said Van Cleve most distressedly. "A most terrible thing has happened. But you are a brave girl."

"Dead!"

"Yes."

"How?"

"The fire poker. Someone struck him with it. The music kept us from hearing the sound of his fall. Evidently he did not see the man who struck him. When I rushed down after your scream, the piano had started to play the Fantasie for the third time. Rather ghastly."

Elsie sat up, pushing back her hair, then holding her head between her hands. "Where is Mr. Berks?" she asked, quite certain what the answer would be.

"He is gone. His bag and most of his clothes are in his room. But his car is gone."

"Horrible!" she whispered. "Horrible!"

Van Cleve thought he knew what she meant. Double horror. The death of her uncle and the disappearance of the young man whom she had selected from them all as her companion for the evening. The double shock—the tragedy of death and the tragedy of disillusion.

"Henry!"

"Yes, Miss Elsie."

"The police!"

"He cut the wire after he had telephoned, Miss Elsie," said the butler, twisting his locked fingers.

"Splice it!"

"I fixed it," interposed Morgan. "The police will be here within two hours. They have Berks' description and the car's. All the highways and railroads will be covered. He will not go far."

"The safe door is open. Nothing but papers in it, Miss Elsie"— from the butler.

Van Cleve, who had, by his seniority in years, taken charge, stared at the butler curiously. There was a phase of agitation which did not seem to apply to the tragedy but to some outside fact. Terror as well as misery was evident in his eyes.

"The safe?" cried Elsie, struggling to her feet.

"You mean the jewels are gone? But no! Only Uncle and I knew the secret of the safe. Robbery was only attempted; it did not succeed."

"Nothing has been touched," said Van Cleve. "There should be plenty of fingerprints. My theory is that your uncle came down to look at the Rajah for the last time. He had opened the safe and was struck down then."

"Who turned on the lights?" asked Morgan.

"They were on when I came down the stairs," answered Elsie.

"Then he should have seen his assailant."

"But the gems, Miss Hetherstone—are you sure they are where you put them?"

"Oh, yes! But just now! . . . All I had in the world!" She rocked her body.

"I don't believe it would be wise for you to see him at this moment, Miss Hetherstone," Van Cleve advised. "Better wait till you are steadier. He did not suffer any. Bad business for us, gentleman. Have you your passports? I have mine. We shall need them."

Descamps and MacFarlane signified that they had theirs.

"That will help," said Van Cleve. "Police get queer notions in their heads. Fortunately you, Mr. Morgan, will not need a passport."

"On the contrary," replied Morgan, "I wish I had a passport. Aside from the letter establishing my identity, I have practically nothing."

"But we can all vouch for you," returned Van Cleve.

"Please, please!" cried Elsie, her palms going to her ears.

Van Cleve gestured helplessly. Still, he could not blame her for disregarding their personal safety. To him the affair was not only a horror but a disaster. It was as if the Blue Rajah had vanished. The will would have to be probated in law before the diamond would come into the girl's possession. He would have to return to Amsterdam empty-handed. Hood—even though he had come to his death so tragically—was not a friend, scarcely an acquaintance. He was terribly sorry for this lovely girl, and he would help her in whatever way he could, but, all the same, he had lost a fat commission.

Elsie dropped her hands from her ears. "I wish to see him. I am strong now. Please!"

Gravely they followed her into the living room. Strong she was; for she knelt at once before the silent body and reverently kissed the white forehead. There was a gray bruise on the temple, down which a threadlike trickle of blood was drying. As Van Cleve reached out to assist her to her feet she waved aside his hand and got up. Her face was like marble and her eyes were like sapphires in the sun.

"If he had come through the window, taking his chances, and surprised my uncle at the safe! But he accepted the hospitality of the house; he won our respect and admiration only to disarm us. I know of nothing more horrible. But he has done murder for nothing. I even told him that there was a trick compartment in the safe.

Oh, you will find the Blue Rajah in the case. If you gentlemen will step back into the library I will produce the diamond," she said. "You must go with them, Henry."

Three minutes later she called to them. She extended her palm. On it lay the Rajah, full of magic fires.

"You see?"—bitterly. "At present I have no lawful right to dispose of it. But if I had my will it would go into the bottom of the well. To me he was the dearest, kindest man I knew, for all his queer hobby."

Without knowing why he did so, Van Cleve swerved his glance from the stone to the butler's face. The man looked like a cadaver. His queer bald forehead was beaded with sweat. Why?

"May I look at the stone?" asked Van Cleve.

"Why?"

"I've a queer notion that it is not the Rajah."

"What?"—came from four throats simultaneously.

"It is just a notion. I may be wrong."

Elsie passed the stone to him, and he beckoned all that they should follow him into the library. There he drew down the lid of a small secretary, got out a piece of white writing paper, placed the gem on it, and sat down. Out of a pocket he drew an object which, to Henry, the butler, resembled a clip of cartridges for a rifle. The object was, in fact, a series of powerful microscopes. Van Cleve began to study the stone from all angles. The others were grouped about him, tense and almost breathless. Except Elsie, who stared at the piano somberly.

At length Van Cleve leaned back. "Perfect! As perfect a piece of work as I ever saw! Even to the chipped end my father polished. But it isn't the Blue Rajah."

"But it must be!" cried Elsie. "I took it out of the safe and I put it back. It was never out of my sight!"

"I am sorry. But wait till Mr. Morgan examines it."

Morgan promptly took the chair and the micros. When he was through he shook his head. "Mr. Van Cleve is right. Remarkable paste."

"It flashed through my head a moment ago," explained Van Cleve. "Do you remember when Berks had it, and the sudden pain that struck his side? Legerdemain—trick of the hand. Palmed the imitation for the genuine. Why should we distrust him? A great musician, the Order of Leopold in his buttonhole, steady eyes? I have heard rumors derogatory to his honesty, and I had begun to disbelieve them." Van Cleve shrugged. "There is nothing further to do. We must await the police. But, Miss Hetherstone, hadn't you better go to your room till they come?"

"No. I need no rest." Elsie stepped over to the French window and threw it wide open.

"The stone?"—hesitantly from Morgan.

"Since it isn't the Rajah, it is not necessary to replace it."

What a woman! thought Van Cleve. That red-brown head, the strength of the face and the courage of the heart! Berks might go far, but not far enough.

"Henry!"

"Yes, Miss Elsie."

"Get some sherry and crackers and ice water." She did not stir from the window.

The men sat down where they would, anxious and distressed. All knew that they would be questioned severely. They might even be detained, at a serious loss of time and money. When the butler returned he set down the tray with a clatter. He filled a glass with ice water and presented it to Elsie. She drew a small chair to the window, sat down with her face to the night and sipped the water.

"Anything more, Miss Elsie?"

"Yes. Sit down somewhere. You must not leave the room again till the state police arrive."

Henry found a chair in the obscurest corner and mopped his face.

Van Cleve could not keep his eyes off the man. Terror. But terror of what?

7

"HOW LONG HAVE YOU BEEN in the family, Henry?" Van Cleve asked kindly.

"More than twenty years, sir."

Van Cleve relapsed into silence. He could hear the clock ticking in the living room, the lights of which had now been turned out. From out the forest rim came the melancholy hoot of an owl. To Van Cleve, to come to a wilderness like this had been a tonic and an exhilarant. Through the afternoon and evening he had enjoyed himself thoroughly. Now it was become more God-forsaken than any other place he had ever known.

There was danger, too—real danger. Their alibis would be without corroboration. In the eyes of the police any one of them might have done the thing. They weren't house guests in the social sense. They were not Hood's friends. They had come up here to buy a diamond. The stone was gone and Hood lay dead in the next room.

The girl, there. She never stirred. No doubt her ear was straining to catch the first sound of the police automobile. A kind of military police, so Van Cleve had been given to understand, recruited largely from the vast army which had returned from France. Van Cleve had an almost intolerable craving to smoke, but the straight back of the girl persuaded him that the odor of tobacco would be distasteful to her. An hour passed and more. From time to time Van Cleve saw the flutter of the butler's handkerchief.

"I hear a car!" Elsie cried, standing.

Ten minutes later four troopers of the state police entered the house. Brisk, stalwart, personable young fellows they were. The sergeant in charge conducted the examination. Hood had died from a violent blow on the left temple. Death had evidently been instantaneous. The character of the blow precluded any free flow of blood. The fire poker weighed about ten pounds. Person or persons unknown.

"But he is known!" cried Elsie.

"A suspect, miss. He is guilty only after a jury has convicted him. I can tell better when you give me the story. You haven't touched anything—particularly the body?"

"No," replied Van Cleve. "We have been scrupulously careful."

The sergeant cast his glance about. During the war he had been in the Intelligence and had good background for a case like this. And it was a case; he could sense that without two tellings. He noted that the girl alone was fully dressed. The others had been in bed or were about to turn in. But you never could tell. The butler wore his coat, but neither vest nor collar. A gorgeous-looking girl, who had good hold of herself.

"Now, let's have the story," said the sergeant kindly. "In the line of duty I shall have to ask disagreeable questions."

Van Cleve turned to Elsie: "Shall I tell it?"

"If you will be so kind."

"Just a minute," broke in the sergeant. "George, get a sheet from somewhere. We can't move the body, miss, till the coroner views it."

"I understand."

"Then we'll have to take him into town for the autopsy."

The sheet was procured.

"Suppose we go into the next room and turn out these lights?" This was done. "Now, then, what happened? Don't leave anything out because you happen to think it unimportant. Everything you can remember about the evening."

Van Cleve told the story clearly, and frequently the sergeant nodded approvingly.

"Queer place for a business deal," was the sergeant's comment.

"We were agreeable. Three of us had never been in this kind of wilderness."

"And this man Berks and the diamond are gone. Opened the safe for more loot, and Hood caught him at it."

"But no one except my uncle and myself could open the safe!" Elsie protested. "Or the secret compartment."

"Miss, there are men in New York who can open any wall safe ever made. But this Berks is the lad, all right. Sleight o' hand. Who asked to see the diamond?"

"I did," said Descamps gloomily.

"I see. How were you going to pay for the diamond after you had bid it in?"

"Certified checks," answered MacFarlane, the Englishman.

"Have you all got certified checks?" The sergeant was astonished.

"We all have letters of credit large enough to cover the cost of the stone. Quite the same as certified checks," said Van Cleve.

"All new stuff to me. I must see these letters of credit and your passports. Understand, gentlemen, this is murder. Your letters of credit and your passports will be good alibis. You've all told me where you were when the thing happened. But none of your statements can be substantiated by your neighbors. . . . You're an American, Mr. Morgan. What have you got to show?"

"A blank check, signed by the treasurer of my company."

"Not so good."

"To-morrow you can call up my company and verify my statement. No one could get one of these special blanks except from the treasurer's office, from the treasurer himself."

"Bring them all to me, gentlemen."

They proceeded upstairs, followed by the troopers.

"What's your idea, miss?" the sergeant asked of Elsie.

"All I want you to do is to find him. He accepted the hospitality of the house. It was horrible!"

"Your uncle didn't seem to be very smart."

"What do you mean by that?"

"Coming up here in the middle of nowhere for a deal like this."

This silenced Elsie. This had been her thought, too.

"Well, we'll get the bozo; don't worry. The minute he tries to sell that stone—"

"No one will know anything about it. This man Berks will have some rich client who will not ask questions. Do you know anything about collecting gems?"

The sergeant uttered a short laugh. "Not likely."

"It's like a drug. It kind of makes you mad."

The four strange guests came down and gave the sergeant three passports, three letters of credit, and a signed blank check. The sergeant went over them, carefully. He gasped. Here were the representations of nearly three quarters of a million! Alibis, if ever he saw any before. He put the articles into a safe pocket.

"Merely a precautionary measure," he said. "They will be given back to you after the coroner has had a look at them. You won't have any trouble, gentlemen. It's this fellow Berks. Plain as the nose on your face. The description of Berks has been broadcasted. Telephone, telegraph, and radio; crooks don't get far these days. Now, you folks sit down while I prowl about. The player piano was going?"

"Yes."

The young officer returned to the living room and turned on the lights. He stared at the fireplace. The case was all cut and dried, motive a mile high. Only one hope for this chap Berks—the middle of the Amazonian jungle. Otherwise his goose was cooked. The fire rack and the medley of instruments had fallen against the fender. He did not touch the poker which lay about four feet from the hearth. He righted the rack, as if absently. With his eye he measured the distance from the long window in the library to the fireplace in the living room, the distance between the fireplace and the wall safe.

"Two of you scout around outside for footprints. George, you stay here with me. Now, George, run upstairs, get into a room and shut the door."

George obeyed without question. When his subordinate was gone, the sergeant pushed over the rack.

"Hi, George, did you hear it?"

The trooper called down: "Yes, but not loudly."

"All right. Go back into the room. Someone turn on the player."

"No, no!" cried Elsie, horrified.

"Sorry, miss, but I must know if it is possible to hear the over-turn of the rack while the music is going. We are obliged to do a lot of disagreeable things in search of the truth."

Elsie flew to the piano to guard it. "No! I could not stand it to hear the record! I couldn't!"

"Sorry, miss, but I must run it over to get the time."

"Put on some other record!" she begged.

"Duty, miss. Sorry can't oblige. It may mean a man's life."

This was the law, and she had to surrender. But when she heard the opening crescendo of the Fantasie Impromptu, she put her hands over her ears and closed her eyes, lest she see him at the piano. The agony was intolerable.

The sergeant again righted the rack and toppled it. The trooper upstairs came down. He had heard only the music.

"That's what I wanted to know. Seven minutes to play the thing. The average man can do a hundred yards in fifteen seconds. Seven minutes—plenty of time for a lot of things. Anything missing from the safe, miss?"

"Nothing"—dully.

"Telephone wire cut, window fixed for a getaway, a priceless diamond gone. Looks like rain for Mr. Berks. No one of you ever saw Berks till tonight? Humph."

"We all knew something of his reputation," said Van Cleve.

"Not so good?"

"Questionable methods, unethical."

"I see."

The sergeant was a new type of policeman. The accepted notion of a detective silent, mysterious, pussy-footed—was totally absent. And Elsie began to lean toward him mentally. He talked, explained his actions, thereby mitigating the nerve tension of the others. This apparent frankness was premeditated. If you scared folk they shut up like clams; if you could get them into ordinary conversation, sometimes they dropped a vital bit of information.

This business looked simple, all cut and dried; but experience warned him that it wasn't. No signs of any struggle. It was the player piano that created the fog. It did not fit into the right place somehow. If Berks had entered by the French window, he couldn't possibly have got to the poker without Hood seeing him. Hood had been killed without knowing what had struck him.

However, Berks might have been hidden in the library, where the piano stood. Hood had turned on only the living-room lights. The safe was on the far side of the fireplace. Hood might have been so intent on the safe that Berks— But the beggar had got what he had come after! He might have been sneaking out, seen his host at the safe, and the impulse had come to take all the gems. Confound the piano; it cross-trailed everything! Had it been going before or after death?

One of the troopers came in to report:

"Nothing, Sergeant—that is, no footprints. This kind of ground doesn't take footprints well. Nothing in the flower beds. Milo tires on the car, though— two new ones and two old. The dust took that. Balloons. I think he was headed for the dirt trail. He'll have to turn up somewhere near Lake George. One of the guides said the rear license plate was badly bent. He remembered the number."

"Good work. Go to the phone and shoot it out. That narrows things down a bit. . . . What's that—a car coming?"

Every head was turned toward the windows, and all stood in effect like a tableau. The sergeant did not move. He still had a man outside to take care of the stranger.

The blood pounded in Elsie's ears. If it were Berks returning!

But the man who entered with the trooper was not any man she had seen before. He was rather stocky, his face rubicund like that of a man who had lived well and carelessly. But nevertheless it was a strong face, with a large-bridged nose and thin straight lips. There were signs of recent physical activities. Across his forehead was a broad piece of adhesive, one of his eyes was discolored, and one of his hands was partly bandaged.

The sergeant observed that the adhesive and bandage were streaked with dust and sweat, several hours old.

"What's going on here?" the stranger demanded, somewhat truculently. "Where's Mr. Hood?"

"That'll keep," said the sergeant. "But first we'd like to know who you are." The sergeant stood between the newcomer and the quiet thing on the floor.

"Who I am? I'm Berks—Roger Berks."

8

BERKS! THE ANNOUNCEMENT had the effect—the stunning effect—of a thunderclap out of the blue. Even the troopers were silenced by their astonishment. Van Cleve was first to recover. Yonder person · was more like the man he had imaginatively built up out of hearsay. A bold fellow, not particularly hampered by ethics, and not quite a gentleman. Who, then, was the other, who looked and acted like a gentleman?

"That is not the man!" said Elsie, her voice stifled.

"You bet I'm not! I'm Berks. The other fellow was an impostor. Oh, it was neatly done. It isn't often they bamboozle me. Now, what's happened? What are the police doing here?"

"Hood was killed to-night. The weapon was the fire poker," the sergeant informed the questioner.

"Dead? Hood?" The stranger dropped into a chair as suddenly as if someone had cuffed him behind the knees. "Dead!"

"Yes. By violence."

"Did the chap get away with the Blue Rajah?" asked the original Roger Berks.

"Yes."

"I knew it! I knew that was his game. But he didn't look like a fellow who'd kill a man with a poker."

"Who is he?" Elsie wondered when this nightmare would end.

"I don't know, miss"—dejectedly. "Sounds foolish, but it's true."

"You don't know?" shouted the sergeant. "Come, now. You can't expect us to believe that. What did he do to you?"

"Plenty—plenty. Kidnapped me and took my papers."

"I see. Now we're getting somewhere," declared the sergeant. "And you put up a fight."

"I did, but I didn't get far. It was two to one. But I got loose about ten and here I am."

"And here you are! From where did you escape?"

"New York."

"Who was your client, the man you were working for?" interjected Van Cleve.

"He was! That's how he fooled me," Berks replied.

The sergeant shoved back his hat. "Seems to me you're telling the middle of the story. Begin at the jump-off. The fog is too thick."

"Which one of you is Van Cleve of Amsterdam, Holland?" asked Berks, looking about.

"I am."

"You've heard of me, haven't you?"

"Yes."

"But till now you never saw me?"

"That is correct."

Berks—for all understood now that he must be Berks—brought forth a wallet and handed it to the sergeant. "Please examine the contents. There's an old passport in there. Compare the original with the descriptions."

Which the sergeant proceeded briskly to do. "Gentlemen, this is the real Berks. You were entertaining an impostor. Now, then, Berks, get along with your side of the story."

Elsie noted that the trooper did not use the conventional title. On the other hand Berks apparently did not note its absence.

"Well, about two weeks ago this fellow came to my office. He had heard that the Blue Rajah was about to be put up for sale, which was more than I had heard. Said he wanted the stone. He had heard of me. That's my business—negotiating the sale and purchase of gems on commission. Said he wanted the stone, but that if he handled the job he might bid too deep. I'd heard of the stone, but had never seen it. Here was a fat commission, if the fellow was on the level. He looked and dressed like a swell. . . . I'd like a drink of water."

Elsie shivered.

The butler got Berks his water, and Berks emptied the glass.

"That's better. Been through a lot of dust. He was staying at one of the commercial hotels in the Forties. We had dinner a couple of times. Knew a lot about gems. Said he lived in Paris. Oh, he hooked me all right. Asked me casually if I knew any of you, and, like a fool, I said no.

"Why didn't you telephone when you got free?" demanded the sergeant.

"I'll come to that," answered Berks, apparently quite pleased with the interest he had aroused. "I was to do all the corresponding and all that. I finally got a letter from Hood giving me permission to come up and make a bid. When I reported to him that everything was ready but the financial side— Say, he took my breath away. He showed me fifteen ten-thousand-dollar bills!"

"Genuine?"

"Five of them were. I handled them; and I know real money."

"Cash," mused the sergeant. "We'll rake the banks and find out who drew fifteen bills as big as that."

Berks smiled. "He had me hypnotized. After a late breakfast he invited me to his apartment."

"In the hotel?"

"No. He was living at the hotel temporarily. He wouldn't be in town long enough to engage a cook, so he said. I went with him. Why not? He had a hundred and fifty thousand in his pocket."

"And he was going to turn it over to you?"

Berks smiled again. "That's what I thought. His apartment was in Seventy-eighth Street. Third flight up. Two lowers were vacant. I kept thinking of that roll and my commission if I got the Rajah."

Elsie hated him and the sound of his voice. She did not know why. It was one of those unreasoning sentiments. Probably this hate was aroused because he seemed to be enjoying himself.

"He opened the door of the apartment. And then the circus began. They took my letters and left me bound and gagged in a middle room."

"You got the number of the house?"

Berks gave it with a good deal of satisfaction.

"George, get headquarters in New York. Give a gist of the story. Find out who owns this apartment. Get Albany and Syracuse airports."

"Yes, sir."

"Now," said the sergeant to Berks, "what name did this fellow give you?"

"Bassett."

"Bassett?"

The others jerked their heads in the direction of the butler. He looked like a Venetian gargoyle—his forehead and cheeks marble white and his jaws—he had a heavy beard—black.

9

THE SERGEANT EYED THE BUTLER as though he had taken note of him for the first time.

"What name were you expecting?" the sergeant asked with sardonic amiability.

"I—it just came out," stammered the butler.

"Oh! Ah! Come across. You were expecting some name. What was it?"

"No, sir. But everything—the confusion, the terribleness of the night—I'm a bit hysterical."

"Did you hear the piano player?"

"Oh, yes, sir. But I thought nothing of it."

"Where were you at the time?"

"In my room, sir, preparing to go to bed."

The sergeant decided to hear the end of Berks' story before he resumed questioning the butler. "Go on, Berks."

"Well, I got free about noon. And my first thought was speed. So I got an airplane. It was just possible that I might beat out the crook. At any rate, arrive here before the bidding began, and expose him. I landed at Syracuse at about three. But it took me almost an hour to find anyone who'd risk renting a car going into the woods at night. Chap like me who didn't know the ropes."

"Syracuse. You should have been here by half-past ten."

"I know it now," Berks agreed. "You can find your way in the daytime, but it's a different thing at night. By ten I found myself miles up a dirt road. It was smooth and I took it for the state road, till it began to get humpy. That's my story. This part of the map is brand-new to me."

"Do you realize that if you had telephoned, Mr. Hood would not be dead?"

"I realize it now. Maybe I wasn't thinking clear."

"What time did this pseudo Berks get here?" The sergeant put the question generally.

Elsie spoke. "I saw him fishing in our stream between five and six."

"Fishing? Well, I'll be— I beg your pardon, miss! You say he was fishing?"

"Yes."

"Berks, how long did it take you to get to Syracuse from New York?"

"About four hours. It took me a long time to find a plane."

"Then this chap must have left New York by airplane. Landed at Albany. Otherwise he couldn't get here by auto and then fish before dark. Had his plane ready and lost no time. A good deal of fog. And he must have driven like the devil—yes, and known the way. Miss, did your uncle have a known enemy?"

"He couldn't have had. He was too kind and generous. May I retire? I'm dreadfully tired."

"Go to bed. I haven't any more questions to ask you. But you'll have to appear when the coroner arrives." When Elsie was gone, the sergeant approached the butler menacingly. "What name were you expecting?"

"I told you the truth, sir."

Van Cleve interposed mercifully. "We all have been badly shaken up, Mr. Officer."

"I know it, sir. But he didn't merely repeat the name—he shouted it. Exactly as if he had been expecting Jones or Smith instead of Bassett. Someone killed Hood. Everything points to the pseudo Berks. And yet, I don't know."

"You don't know?"

"Just what I mean. If he started the player it must have been before he struck Hood. And in the event of the player starting, Hood would have wanted to know why. See what I mean?"

"Sir," put in the butler, "Mr. Hood frequently came down and turned on the records when he couldn't sleep."

The sergeant struck his hands together. "Now we stand on something. The darned fog lifts. Thanks, Henry. I begin to see. Hood goes into the dark library and turns on that piece, returns, and opens the wall safe. The music going, he doesn't hear Bassett, who decides to get all the loot. Good boy, Henry. But you were thinking of another name, and when the coroner comes you'll be under oath."

Van Cleve smiled inwardly. No coroner would dig anything out of Henry, the butler. But Van Cleve felt saddened with life. He had this night been profoundly disillusioned. He had given, unasked, his friendship to an amazing scoundrel.

The trooper called George came in from the telephone.

"Shoot it!" ordered the sergeant.

"The owner of that apartment house in New York is Crabtree, the eccentric millionaire. He is seventy, and cussed the police when they woke him up. The man who called himself Berks evidently broke into the place. Berks arrived in Syracuse about the time he said. Man answering Bassett's description landed at Albany a little after one o'clock. Coroner on the way. No other news."

"A smooth customer, this Bassett. Do you notice that nothing has been left to chance? Mathematics. Cash. Got those bills outside of New York, or has half a dozen men working for him. And it will be deposited in several banks. Again, bootleggers in New York carry thousands. They may have helped him out with the cash. This bird, so it seems to me, has written a play for himself, and he won't be missing any cues. What name were you expecting, Henry?"

"No name, sir. But what will they do with the body?"

The sergeant eyed Henry thoughtfully; "The coroner will come with the village undertaker, and they will take the body back. And then the autopsy will be performed."

"Just what do they do, sir?"

"Open the head, open the body; examine the brain and the heart and the lungs. It is the coroner who will say that Mr. Hood was murdered. I only gather the facts. He examines both the facts and the body. Murder, by a man named Bassett. And you have to catch your rabbit in order to cook it. A man who can palm a diamond with all you experts about can easily fix his mug so that no one will recognize him. There'll be a lot of good dicks in Grand Central and the near-by flying fields. But they'll have a mental picture of an-other man than the one who will walk by them."

"What about us?" asked Morgan anxiously.

"Go to bed and snooze till the coroner arrives. I'll stay in the house, boys; you clear out and stay wide-awake on the hoof," the sergeant ordered.

"I'll sleep on the lounge here," declared Berks.

"Suit yourself."

Berks settled himself comfortably, with his back to the lights, and composed himself for sleep.

The sergeant eyed him moodily and dropped his own weary body into a comfortable chair.

The butler's room was above Elsie's; and she heard him tramp-ing, tramping, till at length she could no longer support it. There was a pole net in one corner of the room. With the butt of this she pounded the ceiling. The tramping ceased.

10

MEANTIME THE ACTIVITIES of the young man who did not know he was being hunted for murder.

The car rolled through the green tunnels of the forest toward his objectives. It would be nine or ten in the morning before the trick would be discovered. He had plenty of time, but he was going to pretend he hadn't.

He wasn't going ahead blindly; he had been over this road in another car to familiarize himself with it. Yet only once did he recognize a tree and a plank bridge over a trout stream. By compass he was going northeast; by the dash clock he was an hour and a half from the Hood camp. An hour later he would have to go on by foot—seven or eight miles, in time to catch the milk train south.

How green the tunnel was in the glare of his headlights! He had seen two deer and any number of hare; occasionally a clearing, with a darkened farmhouse or a sawmill. They could, of course, trace his tires to the spot where he was going to dump the car.

Elsie Hetherstone. That was the way it was with life. No matter how beautifully you wrote your copy, there was an Editor with ideas of His own, to cut, add, slash. The girl had changed the color of the adventure. It had been written in sardonic shades; it had become drab and grim.

The miles dropped behind; the hour hand of the dash clock turned. From afar came the shrill pipe of a whistle. The young man stopped the car and turned off the headlights. From the rumble he took out the tin box—which held something more than tackle—and an electric torch. He listened intently and heard the murmur of a stream near by. By the aid of the torch he found it. The tackle box was really a theatrical make-up box with a mirror in the lid. For twenty minutes he worked. Not so easy as might be. At last he held the light to his face and looked into the mirror. Heavy black eyebrows, a scrubby black mustache, the deep tan of the woodsman; it would pass. Next he searched for a balsam and smeared his fine hands with the sap, then he dug his hands into the leaves and muck. A hardened son of toil.

No one at the camp had seen the clothes he wore, so they could not be described. And no one had seen the cap. The clothes he had left behind could be found in a thousand shops of ready-made clothing. The milk train as far as Albany, then a day coach to New York. But he would drop off at Yonkers and take a taxi into town.

He buried the make-up box, the reel, and the barbless flies and went back to the car. Devil of a lonesome road, but it was miles out of the bootleg range; as safe for him as the middle of Colorado.

The gully on the other side of the road was thirty feet deep, rank with undergrowth and vines. He got into the car and fiddled till he had it headed for the gully. Then he shut off the power and the lights, put his shoulder to the rear and heaved several times. With elephantine clumsiness the car went over the lip of the road, gained momentum, and charged with a sounding crash to the bottom. Silence. The point was, it might be several days before the car was discovered, and perhaps several more days before it was reported. But some beggar would eventually find a mighty fine rod.

With his hands in his pockets he strode down the road, his stride the long swing of the hunter and the climber. He arrived in the little village just as the last milk cans were being put aboard the train. Biding his time, he climbed aboard a truck and squatted down in a corner, one shoulder propped by a can. He would be very stiff when he got to Albany.

At eleven o'clock that morning he was in Yonkers. He had no difficulty in finding a taxi to drive him into New York; and by noon he walked up the steps of a house in lower Park Avenue and let himself in.

It was an old house, with high-ceilinged rooms and plaster decorations around the chandelier pipes. Everything was under sheets, paintings as well as furniture. A melancholy house out of which even the human echoes had gone.

"Hi, Bud! Gerry Owen! Here's John—Chick—Murray Willard home again, and with the loot. The vendetta is over. Oh, Gerry!"

Living sounds kitchenward, and almost at once there entered into the drawing room a young man in the middle thirties, red-headed and freckled. He held a crumpled newspaper in one hand. His name was Robert Owen, but only his checks and legal documents were signed thus. Otherwise he was known to his intimates as Bud or Gerry.

"Chick, is it you?"

"As you see, but made up a bit. It was easy—too easy. But here I am, Blue Rajah and all. There was a fly in the amber, though." Willard paused. "Hood has a niece."

"Has?"

Willard did not catch either the vehemence or the inflection. He said: "I didn't know she existed. And when I saw that she adored Hood and that he worshiped her, y' know, the whole job went stale. But how was I to know? The mysterious note I received was unsigned. It stated simply that Hood was about to offer for sale the Rajah, at his camp in the woods. There wasn't any family history in the note."

Owen stared at him.

"Suppose," went on the oblivious Willard—"suppose you stepped out of a tunnel into the Garden of Eden? It was that kind of shock, seeing that girl. No clinging-vine stuff, no flapper—a young woman. On my word, I can't quite describe her. Funny, Gerry; what? A kind of sideswipe when I'm on the way to somewhere else. You'll laugh, but she's the one—the one each man of us searches for and seldom finds. There she was, and I had lost her even as I had found her. For how the devil am I ever going to explain to her? Any hot water? This make-up is pulling my face apart."

"There's hot water in the kitchen."

The adventurer did not observe Owen's face so pale that the freckles stood out like the spots on a snow leopard. "I say, how the deuce did Berks get loose? I gave him every sailor's knot I knew."

"He was gone when I returned."

"How about starting some bacon and eggs and coffee while I have my face lifted?"

"All right, Chick."

"I wonder," said Willard, looking about the room, "if I shall ever be content in any one place long enough to call it home?"

"I wonder, too, Chick." Owen's voice was unsteady.

Willard was lax this day; the hours of tension were gone. So he missed Owen's stark anxiety and that the latter's two hands were twisting the newspaper into dry pulp.

"Any kerosene?"

"I can get some."

"I'll need it for my hands. . . . What the devil are you doing to that newspaper?"—suddenly becoming observant.

"Chick, have you read any newspaper this morning?"

"No."

"Then you don't know?"

"Know what?"

"Thank God—thank God!" Owen wrapped his comrade in a fierce embrace.

Willard released himself roughly. "What's happened? Have they discovered the paste?"

"Hood was murdered last night at the camp. Some one struck him with the fire poker. By to-night your description will be in every newspaper and police office in the country. I warned you against the folly of this game!"

Willard stood perfectly still. He looked at his friend, eyes unbelieving. A momentary petrifaction, then he seized the newspaper and opened it. In a little while he let it fall to the floor. He sat down in the nearest chair, the sheet folding about him queerly. With terrifying clearness he saw his position. He hadn't one chance in a million—not one! The circumstantial evidence was impregnable. If he took the police with him, over step by step, explaining each step, it would only be handing his head on a platter to the district attorney. Done! Willard began to laugh.

The sound terrified Owen, who seized him by the shoulders and shook him. "Stop it, man; stop it, I say!"

The queer paroxysm died away.

"Looks kind of bad, Gerry"—now quietly. "But, gad, it was funny for a moment!"

"But you didn't do it!"

"No. Why should I? If he had caught me as I was making my get-away I'd have told him who I was—the truth. What edition was that paper?"

"Ten o'clock. I went out for it only a few minutes ago."

"Berks. He got there! And he knew nothing beyond the fact that I was after that stone. And he'll believe I did it! Not a loose knot in the rope around my damfool neck!"

"Chick!"—explosively.

"What?"

"The man who wrote that note to you! Luring you there, then killing Hood! Where is that note?"

"I tore it up. Gerry, we went to war together, I in the air and you in the underground. Neither of us ever reported and asked what should we do next. Well, I'm going to ask you. What shall I do, Gerry. What shall I do? I haven't a Chinaman's chance. I didn't kill Hood. But they'll send me to the chair all the same if they find me!"

11

THE CORONER'S OFFICE IS POLITICAL. In a small town it is a dull job, but sometimes the occupant can step from this office into legislature. The verdict of his jury is not conclusive, but it may be the foundation of criminal prosecution against the person or persons charged. The performance of the autopsy is not perfunctory; it is the one thing he has to do thoroughly. Upon the coroner's findings the district attorney must always depend. When he opens the case for the state he must know absolutely that there has been murder done; else the lawyer for the defendant may push him out on the end of a limb.

Magically, then, the coroner and the town in which he acted leaped into the spotlight from one end of the continent to the other. This was not an ordinary case of one bootlegger killing another, of a killing in a roadhouse brawl. A millionaire had been the victim in his beautiful camp. Some of the greatest gem experts in the world had been visiting the camp at the time of the crime. The coroner saw brightly into the future, himself at Albany, in the halls of legislature. There was even a dim vista of the national capitol.

The verdict of his jury—after the examination of all those who had been at the camp—was willful murder against the man who had stolen the diamond known as the Blue Rajah, who had given his name as Berks and as Bassett, in both cases assumed.

The autopsy revealed that the blow from the poker had crushed in the side of the head, death being instantaneous. It further revealed that Hood had a bad heart, due possibly to the reaction of an operation for appendicitis three years before. But with care he might have lived several years. The handle of the poker, octagonal in shape, but having no sharp edges, had crushed the skull without cutting the flesh to any noticeable degree. That there were no fingerprints on the end of the poker was of minor significance, since it was widely known these days that high-type criminals wore gloves. The playing of the record on the piano had given the criminal time to kill Hood, leave by the library window, make his car and get to the main highway before the alarm. Hood was dead, the man Bassett and the diamond known as the Blue Rajah had completely vanished. The evidence was clear.

The sharp wits of the metropolitan newspapers got to work. The foreign correspondents learned that the roster of the Order of Leopold offered no help, for the reason that it did not give a man's weight, height, or color or any of those identifiable marks indicated in passports. It was not possible to find the late Busoni's papers in relation to the names and nationality of his distinguished pupils. The reporters worried themselves into blind alleys. They had this much—a good-looking young man about thirty, brilliant blue eyes, a jaw verging on the so-called lantern, a great pianist, a skillful fisherman, and an airman of note. The pilot who had driven the man from New York to Albany swore that his passenger knew more about air busses than he did.

The reporters naturally gave a good deal of space to the niece— her unusual beauty, her dignity, the quality of her voice. They all agreed that she seemed cold. Not the warm vivacious type of the movie queens.

For a week the story occupied the front page; then a chorus girl shot her sugar papa in a night club and the Blue Rajah mystery was promptly relegated to the inside pages. There wasn't enough human interest in it.

Elsie decided not to close the camp till she had drafted a workable plan for the future. Another point: it seemed to her to be an admission of cowardice to run away and hide in a great city among strangers. She knew the trees here, the streams, the birds, the trails; and there was that in her that demanded isolation from the crowd.

One of the first things she did was to destroy the record of the Fantasie Impromptu. The deed had the appearance of childishness, but it was actuated by something far deeper than that—a dim, evasive clairvoyance that some night she might be drawn to the piano, irresistibly, and play the record; and see the man's face as it had been that night, mildly ecstatic as the melodies flowed out of his magical finger tips. A thought as fascinating as it was horrible.

She was lonely and bitter. She walked miles, broke new trails, but with no delight. She never went anywhere near the trout run, but wandered along the tributaries.

It was the treachery, the abysmal treachery, that kept her brooding ceaselessly. Never, never so long as she lived would she wear a jewel. She never looked at the back of one of her hands that she did not scrub it vigorously against her skirt.

The will had left her everything, aside from a few legacies. But her riches left her unstirred, indifferent. All his gifts had made Bassett's acts only the baser. Had he been from the underworld, had he come from anywhere else save from the circle in which she herself dwelt! Her sense of shame was at all times equal to her lust for vengeance. She had secretly given the man her friendship, not easily acquired, the moment she had seen him at the piano. Horrible—no other term seemed to have any strength. Had it been the real Berks she would have had neither shame nor desire for vengeance beyond that which the law would mete out.

Affairs at the camp went on about the same. The wardens kept the poaching fishermen away, and solemnly the gaunt Henry attended to his duties.

Her plans for the future did not mature quickly. She would never return to live in any place where she and her uncle had been happy together. This much she could, with definiteness, plan. In time she would put up the camp for sale and find some place where no one knew her.

Once a day Henry would ask: "Any news, Miss Elsie?"

And each time the answer would be: "No, Henry."

So deep was she in the sea of her own speculations and brooding that she did not observe that Henry was also brooding. Once in a while she would catch him tramping the floor at night.

"I can't sleep, Miss Elsie," he explained.

"But you keep me awake!"

"I am sorry."

Now Elsie's mind had not functioned keenly in relation to the happenings of that dreadful night—that is, she had not gone over the scenes and deduced from them any salient.

One night Henry was about to set the soup before her, when she happened to recall an odd incident.

"Henry, why were you so startled that night when that man Berks said the name was Bassett?"

The soup sloshed from the cup, which slid perilously near the rim of the plate. His queer face became ghastly.

"Why, what is the matter? . . . Henry, you are hiding something!" She got to her feet swiftly, her mind bell clear. "What are you hiding?"

Henry put down the soup. "Please, Miss Elsie!" he begged.

"You perjured yourself in the coroner's court! Did you see anything that night?"

"No. And that is God's truth!"

"What is it, then?" Henry began to back away. "Henry, if you do not tell me at once, I shall call in the state police!"—her eyes burning. "What have you been keeping secret from me?"

"Miss Elsie, I am half crazy! I have kept silent because I did not want to hurt you."

"Hurt me? How could you hurt me?" she demanded.

"Why not have patience? Soon or late, the police will find him."

"You know his name!" she cried. "You expected his name instead of Bassett! And that policeman understood it. But you lied in the coroner's office. I've been blind! What is his name, Henry? Oh, I will give ten thousand for his name!"

"Yes, I know it. But, Miss Elsie, if I tell it to you, your heart will break."

"It is already broken. You refuse to tell me?"—her fury rising. The reporters would not have called her cold had they seen her at this moment.

"If I tell you, you will be sorry all the rest of your life. The love which existed between you and your uncle was beautiful to all who beheld it."

"Be still! I want nothing from you but that man's name."

Henry bent his head, but he did not speak.

"Very well," she said, with passionate vehemence. And she rushed toward the hall.

He tried to stop her, but failed. "Wait!"

She paused at the threshold.

"The name is Willard. The only son of Jonathan Willard. At one time, years ago, he and your uncle were bosom friends."

"I never heard of him."

"No. Mr. Hood never mentioned his name again. Shall I proceed?"

"Go on."

"Willard and his son lived in a house in lower Park Avenue."

"But why didn't you inform the police?"

"When I learned that your uncle was going to offer the Blue Rajah for sale, I sent an anonymous note to the old house. When the young man came here as Berks, I was fooled. After he had gone, then I knew who he was. I did not inform the police because I believed they would catch him without help from me."

"Why did you warn him?" The blood in her was running high.

"Because the Blue Rajah is rightfully his, Miss Elsie."

"Rightfully his?"—thunderstruck. "Are you mad?"

"Nearly. I could not bring myself to hurt you."

"You have stressed that word. What do you mean by it?"

"I have always held that there was madness in collecting these stones."

"Will you come to the point?"

"I have said Willard and your uncle were once upon a time bosom friends. The friendship ceased when your uncle took what did not belong to him."

"What proof have you of that?" asked Elsie, chilled.

"A letter the boy wrote your uncle after his father died. A wild and threatening letter, for a boy of ten. He accused your uncle of bringing his father to his deathbed by treachery, of pretending to borrow the Rajah, having a paste copy of it made and substituting it for the genuine and swearing he had lost the historical document and the bill of sale in a fire. Oh, I warned you!"

"Where did you find this letter?"—her voice steady.

"Why your uncle did not destroy it I don't know. Every morning I empty the wastebaskets. This letter was all alone in the basket. Accidentally I saw a few threatening words. Then I read it all. Mr. Willard never attempted to recover the stone. He died too soon after. And the boy had no proof that the stone was his. I warned you."

"Let me have this letter."

The butler drew it out of his pocket reluctantly and gave it to her. She read it. But from her face he could not guess what her emotions were. In the end she drew a palm across her forehead.

"Did Uncle know that you knew?"

"Oh, never, Miss Elsie! Only, I couldn't destroy that boy's letter. It had all the strength of a man in it. I believe I know what happened. They met downstairs, and your uncle recognized him at last, for the boy's smile was like his father's. Your uncle seized him, and— It is a terrible stone, Miss Elsie. Death, death, death wherever it is."

"All this may be true. But with this letter I have him—I have him!"

"Will you discharge me, Miss Elsie?"

"No."

"Shall I serve the rest of the dinner?"

"No, no, no!"

She rushed to the stairs and up to her room.

That night the butler heard *her* tramping her room.

12

GERRY OWEN PACED THE ROOM while Willard sprawled in his chair, his face thin and haggard.

"Chick, I can't stand this inertia any longer. Every hour wasted is the other fellow's advantage. You did not kill Hood, but someone did. You can't stay cooped up here all the rest of your life."

"I can't think, Gerry. The old bean isn't working."

"You can go abroad."

"Why should I? I haven't hurt anybody."

"Let me do what I want to do."

"What can you do but become involved as accessory to the fact?"

"Look here, Chick; I have the detective instinct just as you have the flying instinct. There are two niggers in this woodpile—the man who sent you that anonymous warning and Roger Berks. My work in the secret service has trained my mind for sleuthing."

"But this fellow Berks—there's no motive. He merely came to warn Hood."

"Berks swore he got lost up a dirt road for hours. The statement was never thoroughly checked up because everything pointed to you. Of course he could get lost that way, but was he?"

"What purpose had he in lying?"

"That's it. On the face of it he had no purpose, just as you had every purpose according to the evidence. The man who sent you that note. Was he friend or enemy? He might have framed you."

"But nobody except Hood and I knew the story."

"Not so sure of that. There might have been a leak somewhere. I want to dig into Berks' testimony and learn something about this butler."

"That poor old gargoyle came rushing down with the others when Elsie screamed. Van Cleve in his testimony stated that."

"Elsie?"

"Yes, Gerry."

"Can't get her out of your head?"

"No."

"Now think. You were close to Berks for several days. Do you recall any striking fact about him?"

Willard rumpled his hair. "Nothing, except that he smoked cigarettes incessantly."

"Notice the brand?"

"Why, yes. That's what makes the picture stick. Smoked Laurens. Imported them from Switzerland, though I believe the company is owned by Germans."

"Chick, I caught a spy in Geneva because he used an unfamiliar brand of matches. Laurens—that's a starting point. Anything else?"

"No. But if you go, how will you get in touch with me? The telephone is off."

"You'll hear from me only when I've brought down the bird. I'll get Dodge, my chauffeur, to cook for you. You can trust him with your right eye. So there's Elsie."

"Yes. Two blows that utterly bewilder me. No use dodging it. A perfect crime. And a girl like that has to step into the picture. The cart's upset and the apples are all over the lot. But go, and God bless you, old-timer!"

"All right. I'll toddle over to the grocer's. Sugar and coffee's given out."

Alone, Willard began to pace. Memories. Jonathan Willard and Marcus Hood, friends from boyhood. They had taken the grand tour together, and during this voyage the collecting mania had struck them both. For years after there had been friendly rivalry, till the Blue Rajah, cobra-like, had lifted its sinister beauty into their gaze. Jonathan outbid Marcus, and Marcus became secretly obsessed. The man he had once loved he now hated. Pretending that he was writing a history of his gem-collecting adventures, he had prevailed upon Jonathan to lend him the stone and the documents. Neither the registered history nor the bill of sale had come back. There had been a fire. But the Blue Rajah had been returned later, to be discovered as paste.

"Never take the affair into court, my son," Jonathan had said on his deathbed. "His conscience will punish him as the law never will be able to. For he will always remember that I loved him."

The son had promised, but with reservations. He would never trouble Hood unless he offered it for sale. The son now remembered having written at the time a passionately angry boy's letter. No doubt, long ago destroyed.

Willard stopped his pacing suddenly. The butler! The butler had written that anonymous note. Henry had known the truth. And Henry had suspected his identity! Why, then, hadn't he denounced the pseudo Berks to the police?

Willard moved over to the piano and sat down.

On Gerry's return, in the act of entering the area door, a policeman hailed him:

"Hey, there! What a' yuh doin'? That house is vacant."

Gerry Owen took one deep breath. "Mr. Willard has just returned from abroad. He hasn't had the telephone connected nor has he informed the precinct. He is a great musician, sir, and is preparing concert work and does not wish to be disturbed."

"That's all right, but I'll have a look inside," replied the policeman.

"Follow me."

The policeman stalked into the basement. From somewhere above came the thundering chords of the Brahms Rhapsodie in E flat. Owen held a finger to his lips to command silence. He laid down his grocery bundles. When the music stopped, Owen shouted up the stairs:

"Mr. Willard, a policeman wishes to see you. Shall I send him up now or wait till your practicing is over? I've told him you were preparing for concert and had given orders—"

"Oh, send him up!" called Willard, snatching his cue.

He was a good guardian, this policeman. "You're Willard, the owner?"

"Yes."

"Got any proof of it?"

Willard showed him a passport.

"All right, Mr. Willard. We have to watch these houses where the folks 've gone abroad. You ain't been here in a long time. But y' oughta called up the precinct. I'll report your return before I go off duty."

"But promise me the newspapers won't get hold of my return to America. My friends will pile in on me, and I'll have to clean house."

"Sure. That'll be all right. The women—they drive you fellahs off the Carnegie stage. Play me a tune."

Willard sat down at the piano and played one of Grainger's rustics. The policeman kept time with his head and foot.

"You sure know your ivories. Thanks. That's my kind of music. I don't get this highfalutin' stuff like you was playin' when I came in."

"Gerry, the cigars."

The policeman helped himself. "Thanks. I'll smoke it after supper to-night."

"And be sure and close both the basement and area doors as you go out," reminded Owen.

"Trust me, sir."

The policeman went downstairs.

The two young men stared at each other. They waited in suspense till they heard the doors close.

"Pretty close," whispered Owen.

"Get your man to me to-night, and you go north. You're right. You're all the hope I have. The irony of it! I didn't even see Hood again after I went to my room. Check up Berks. And God be with you! I never thought of death during the war save as a fierce and glorious adventure. But death by the state, my name dishonored—"

"Hush!" whispered Owen.

Willard's body became tense. Steps—light steps on the basement stairs! His hand went into the pocket where the automatic lay concealed.

As the policeman opened the basement door to step into the area-way, he stood stock-still. And well he might. A young woman, regal and beautiful!

"Sh!" she whispered. "Let me in. I know. He's probably given orders to admit no one. But that would not include me, for he doesn't know I'm in town. Please!"

The policeman pushed back his cap and scratched his poll perplexedly. Sure, he had read about it—the women mobbing a famous pianist. If he turned this one loose on Willard—well, well; if he had been in Willard's shoes! Well, one of 'em couldn't start a riot call. So he winked and stepped aside for the young woman. He gently closed the area door. He recognized the type. They used to live on Fifth Avenue, now they lived on Park or on Long Island. There wasn't a good-looking fellow living who'd report a poor cop for letting in a queen against orders.

So it came to pass that Elsie suddenly confronted the two young men. There was no reading that calm, pale face of hers.

13

FOR THREE DAYS AND NIGHTS Elsie had watched the house. She had seen the red-haired young man depart and arrive with supplies, so she knew that Willard was hiding within. This was her affair; the police could enter it later.

Her obsession led her about in a kind of nightmare. She knew exactly the meaning of each move she made, her thoughts were diamond cut; but she could not have turned away from her project even if she had tried. There were little bursts of fury, each leaving her colder. She must confront the man alone, empty her mind of such scorn and loathing as would shrivel him; then she would force him to precede her to the nearest police station. Like the script of a play, all the lines and cues. The obsession was that this scene had to be enacted or she would never again possess herself.

She was not conscious of any excitement when she saw the policeman follow the young red-haired man into the house. Here would be her chance perhaps. If the policeman came out alone. She got out of the limousine and crossed the street. Luck was with her. As she slowly mounted the basement stairs she could hear the voices of the two men—sounds without meaning.

She held the tableau for half a minute. Her appearance was mesmeristic. Neither man had the power to move, his mouth loose with astonishment. She carried a capacious needle-point handbag. She broke the spell by drawing from this handbag a long envelope. This she calmly sailed at Willard's feet. He did not stir.

Still gazing at her, he said: "Leave us, Gerry."

Owen tiptoed from the room. There was no reason why he should tiptoe, but he did.

"That," said Elsie, referring to the envelope, "contains the documents which establish your inalienable right to the Blue Rajah."

She was here? What had happened? How had she found him? The hypnotic phase was gone out of him, but his astonishment had lost nothing.

"When did you learn the truth?" he asked.

Calmly and in level tones she freed her mind of its flaming diatribe. He did not interrupt her by word or gesture.

"Were you a prisoner," she concluded, "I could not say these things to you."

"I am a prisoner so long as I live. I did not kill your uncle," he said. "I never saw him again after I went to my room."

"No? Well, there is a court in which you may try to prove your innocence." Out of her handbag came a pistol. "I am quite expert with this. If your friend appears I will shoot and disable him. Put up your hands and come toward me."

"Dear lady, I shall fill your cup to the brim," he said recklessly. "I love you."

"Be silent!"—furiously.

"It is true. I knew it when I saw you across the piano. My plan to recover the stone was as perfect as human ingenuity could make it. But you had to enter the scene. Your uncle broke my father's heart as surely as if he had taken it in his two hands. It was not the stone; that did not matter. But that the man he loved and trusted more than any other human being should betray this love and trust—that made an end of him. I was only ten years old. But I became a man in that hour. I wrote and threatened him. If that letter is still in existence—"

"I have it! Do as I bid you!"

"To the end of the world!"

Something had gone wrong with the scene; she had wanted to see him cringe.

"Life isn't worth much now," he said. "But I am not the kind of man who permits the law to snuff out his life. You snuff it out." He smiled. "I am going to walk straight toward you, and if you do not shoot me I shall take the pistol away from you."

He began to walk toward her slowly. The pistol did not waver. One step—two—three—four. Her hand began to tremble. Five—six—seven—one step more! She threw the pistol halfway across the room and covered her face with her hands.

"I—I can't!"

He forced down her arms and pinioned them to her sides. Then he kissed her—her mouth, her eyes, her hair—but tenderly and loverly. He released her, recovered the pistol and offered it to her.

"Come!" he said.

"Come? Where?" Her thoughts were without coherency; her emotions were on the whirligig; her obsession gone.

"Why, to the police station! And you, Elsie, are going to take me there. Come, while I am in the mood for it. But I swear to you by the memory of the love I bore my father that I did not kill your uncle. We pay, don't we? Other people's bills along with our own. Follies—ten thousand of them—and we pay each time a stiffer price. That adventure into your camp was half sardonic, half rollicking. But fate had to appoint that moment for your uncle's tragic death. Come!"

But Elsie groped for the nearest chair and sat down. She knew that it was his voice; she knew that were she alone all her cold fury would return, all her will to vengeance. And the smothering rain of kisses, instead of filling her with loathing, filled her with another emotion which took away from her the strength to stand. Not to fight him, strike him; not even to want to strike him!

"Come!"

She did not speak.

So he knelt beside her. "You will not hold to your purpose? In a corner of your heart you know that I did not do it. I'm a madman; I have done crazy, impetuous things because I was trying to find you and couldn't. With a man of my temperament things ripen quickly. Elsie, if you really hate me, loathe me, then life isn't worth hanging on to. If you can look me in the eyes and say you still believe I killed your uncle because of a boy's crazy threat and a man's crazy caprice, then I will go and give myself up. And they will execute me. And that will be the end of it. Look at me!"

The voice, the voice! she cried inwardly. If only she could get away from this voice which seemed to disintegrate her will! She dared not look into his eyes. There was strange madness in this house, and she must fly from it. By a superhuman call upon her will she managed to pick up her handbag, dash into the hall, down the stairs and presently into the street, up which she fairly raced. . . . He had kissed her, and she couldn't strike him!

"Miss Hetherstone! Miss Hetherstone!" someone called from the curb.

She paused and turned bewilderedly. Her car and chauffeur, which she had forgot utterly!

"What has happened? Shall I find a policeman?"

"No. Take me back to the hotel. And do not ask questions."

"But your orders! Who was this man you were afraid of?"

"Return to the hotel. And if you wish to remain in my employ forget this day—all of it."

"Very well, miss."

Gerry Owen came running into the room. He saw Willard studying the chair Elsie had vacated. "She gone?"

"Yes"—listlessly.

"I heard everything, Chick. We must trek out of here at once. That copper didn't ask anything about me. So over to my ranch we go."

"No go. Gerry, I'm going to give myself up."

"In a pig's eye! Haven't you tumbled? That girl doesn't believe you did it. She's been under a terrific mental strain, and this was the crack-up."

"You heard what she said?"

"But she didn't shoot you, did she? And in the end she got scared and ran away. But the point is, she didn't come here without protection in the offing. And it's this protection I'm afraid of. Get what you need together, and I'll hunt up a taxi. Hop out of it! All I want is a week up there. If you give yourself up, good-bye. You haven't a

Chinaman's chance. You've said it and I know it. What the devil do you care what she said, considering the state of her mind?"

"You saw her?"

"With both eyes. I can see how easy it would be for you. She's a corker. But will she ever care anything for you if you give up without a fight? She'll be that kind of girl, Chick—that kind of girl. I know women. Because I'm red-headed and freckled and homely, they always come to me with their troubles. This girl's had two terrible jolts. She has lost her uncle and learned that years ago he committed a sneaky crime—something that wasn't done in her set. First shot, she believed you killed Hood. Anybody in like case would have believed it. Then she gets the true story. No matter. To her jingled mind, you killed her uncle. Vengeance. She would hale you into court by her lonesome. Then her brain would turn right side up and life would go on again. Now I believe that's just what made her run away—her brain has turned right side up. She won't give you away now. So look alive and get together what you need. There's a piano you can thump over in my joint. From now on I'm running this show. All I want up there is a week. Will you obey me?"

"All right, Gerry."

"Then I'll scout up a taxi. And what's more, I'm going to use five or six taxis. And it will be a whale of a flatfoot who'll be able to pick up my trail."

Gerry rushed from the house.

Willard remained before the chair. Things happened like this. The war had proved to him that nothing was impossible, no matter how absurd it appeared, no matter how incredible. While he had been racing to the highway, Marcus Hood had gone to his death in violence. He laughed, but caught and savagely smothered this laughter before it got too deep. He had kissed her. Why hadn't she fought him, beaten him in the face?

Elsie's chauffeur was not satisfied. Something queer about this adventure. Three days and nights, hanging around that house in Park Avenue. Finally getting inside, and then running out as if she had forgotten her name. Something connected with her uncle's

murder. So at nine that night he acquainted the police with his
suspicions. Later the police forced the doors of the Park Avenue
house, but found no living thing. However, they found a photograph of Captain John Murray Willard in uniform. One thing led
to another inevitably.

The Hood murder case broke out on the front page again because Captain Willard's description tallied exactly with that of the
unknown who had stolen the Blue Rajah and killed Marcus Hood.
A good-looking young millionaire. Human interest for everybody.

14

WESTWARD OF THE HOOD CAMP there were four parallel dirt roads, wending north of the state highway. Three of these roads Owen had investigated with microscopic carefulness. The result was zero. He had gone miles up each road but had found no evidence of a car having turned right-about, or evidence of a hiding place in the forest, or evidence of broken road shoulders. Berks had not got lost up any of these three roads. There remained the fourth, and upon what he found in this road hung the life of his friend.

Willard had not killed Hood. But somebody had, and nothing pointed to this somebody. He had left a path as invisible as a bird's in the air, and yet the path was there. A mad gesture on Willard's part; the peculiar and singular braggadocio of a brave man. Smoldering in his heart all these years was the treachery of the man his father had loved. To pay back Hood in his own coin. With this result! It made a man's brain wag a bit.

But he had got Chick out of that house in time. He had been a fox there. So long as the name of the Hood-case fugitive remained unknown, chances of discovery had been negligible. Now Chick's photograph was in the newspapers with his dramatic adventures under it. Seemed strange that the newspapers couldn't read the truth in that biography. Soldier, explorer, musician—more appetizing for the gum chewers. And his pal, Gerry Owen, must dig up a miracle to save him.

Hang the girl! She had upset the apple cart. But who had told her the truth about the Rajah? The old butler; no question about that. But twist it about as he would, Owen could find in the warning only good faith. In some mysterious manner the butler had fallen upon the truth and had tried to foursquare his conscience by warning Chick.

Owen's conviction that Berks had lied about getting lost went into the category of hunches—at least, so far. If the fourth road revealed nothing it would be a case of flight to foreign lands—Ishmael till the crack of doom.

As a base for his operations Owen had selected the hotel in the village twelve miles west. And this evening he got back to it at suppertime. In the dining room he found two state troopers—good-looking, hard-bitten chaps, one with chevrons.

"Good evening," he said as he drew out a chair. He was hungry, and his mind was busy.

"Good evening," responded one of the troopers.

The one with the chevrons stared at Owen peculiarly. "Well, I'll be tinker dammed!" he said.

"I beg pardon!"

"I say, is your name Owen or Owens?"

"Why, Owen!" Who was fair startled out of his boots. "You seem to know me, but I admit I don't recall you."

"We didn't meet socially. I may forget to get up in the morning or to go to bed at night, but I never forget a face."

"Neither do I," said Owen, sitting down. "I swear I never saw yours before."

"George," said the sergeant, turning to his companion, "remember the yarn I spun to you the other night? Well, this is the man. Twenty-odd thousand miles around the world, three or four billion people in it, and this man Owen has to drop into supper tonight! Get that?"

"I pass," said Owen, nervous and distressed.

"What are you doing up here?"

"Motoring about. Vacation. Maybe I'm going fishing. But do you think it's fair to quiz me till you've told me where we've met?"

The sergeant laughed. It was good-humored laughter. "Well, this is the bedtime hour on the radio. So here goes: Once there was a church. Its steeple was gone, the roof; the doors were still there and, funny thing, still locked. Someone was tapping our wires. We decided to stop it. I was detailed on that job. You and I stalked each other around that ruined church for an hour. I thought a mite quicker than you did. I doubled suddenly, and as you poked your head around the corner, I let you have it on the chin. Couldn't make any noise, you know. I knocked you cuckoo. I turned the torch on your mug. That's why I remember you and you don't recall me. To me you were a Heinie in a Yank's dress suit. So I took your gun, hoisted you on my shoulders, and got you back to the lines, announcing that I'd taken the wire-tapper alive. A week later I learned I'd knocked out one of the aces of the Intelligence, and that you had gone to the church to be captured. For what purpose I don't know. But I was almost laughed out of the army. They say that red-tops don't forget punches. There's a nice little plot o' grass out in front—"

"No!" Owen laughed and thrust his hand across the table. "You're right, though. The world is small. But I never knew who turned that trick."

"If we were in France," said the sergeant, "I'd stand treat. Wade into your chow and we'll talk afterward."

"The world's pretty dull now."

"Oh, I can't say as it is," replied the sergeant. "There's lots o' fun and excitement up here. Are you looking for trouble? If you were a trooper I could hand you a platterful twice a week. Bootleggers and murder and all that."

For a while speech ceased and food began to vanish.

"Where's this bootlegger's alley?" asked Owen.

"Around Malone. There's half a dozen alleys. Out of five bootleggers, we catch two, generally amateurs. Once in a while we chance on a real load of hooch, and then there's some pistol-shootin'. Gee, when you think of all the bullets that's been popped in ten years and nobody nicked! If you want any fishing, I know some good streams that aren't posted."

"Thanks. On some job to-night?"

"You might call it a job. Ever have a guilty conscience?"

Surprised by the question, Owen did not answer at once. "Probably I have had, but just now I can't recall the time."

"Well, sometimes a crime is committed. It's so darn cut and dried that you're prone to sit back with your thumbs in your vest. The whole thing is as plain as the nose on your face—motive and everything. So you let nature take its course. A little while ago a millionaire was murdered near here."

Owen reached for the sugar and dropped two lumps into his coffee.

"We did not know who the killer was for a while. But a couple of days ago the whole business came out in the papers. I mean, who he was and all about him. Aviator, traveler, musician, fine family, money galore. I took my thumbs out o' my vest."

"Meaning?"

"Not so cut and dried as it looked. Hunch. You've read about it?"

"Couldn't escape it. But where does the guilty conscience come in?" asked Owen calmly—calm outwardly. To maneuver this shrewd fellow into that fourth road!

"Suppose," began the sergeant—"suppose I just looked at the front door of the crime, seeing everything cut and dried. Suppose I'd looked at it from all four sides and found a hole in the wall. That's what I mean. This young fellow came up to rob Hood of a diamond. Something funny about that, when you learn that the young fellow is rich. He had an imitation stone which he palmed for the real one. And nobody would be the wiser till morning. Why should he go downstairs and kill Hood with the fire poker?"

"Have you found anything pointing the other way?" Owen wondered if his voice was steady, natural.

"No. This guilty-conscience stuff came to me too darned late. Maybe it's because I didn't take any particular shine to this bozo Berks. You know how it is. A hunch that kind o' sticks. You've followed the story?"

"Yes." Owen ran his tongue across his lips.

"Have you given the case any thought, Owen?"

"Well, it seems to me that you fell down on the check-up. You took Berks' word for it that he'd got lost for a few hours."

"Do you hear that, George, old-timer? Well, Owen, that's just where the guilty-conscience stuff comes in."

"And you're on that check-up to-night?"

"We sure are. Nothing may come of it, but I'm one of those guys who has got to be satisfied, by and large."

Owen breathed a prayer.

15

"HAVE YOU LOOKED UP BERKS?" Owen presently asked.

"Of course. No mix-up with the police, but the big jewel firms hint of shady transactions. All within the law, though. What you'd call ethically crooked."

"I see."

"He gets lost up one of the dirt roads. A stranger up here might have got lost just as he said he did. But on his ticket there isn't any motive. That's the hard nut to crack. No motive of any kind. This getting lost accounts for a few hours. Neither Hood nor his guests had ever laid eyes on Berks or had any business transactions with him. So the idea of revenge goes ki-yootin'. He just curled up on the lounge and slept till I woke him up for the coroner. That a man had been killed twenty feet away didn't trouble his dreams any. He's under surveillance, so we can lay our hands on him easily. He was the goat—Willard's goat."

A little while later Owen and the two troopers had their chairs tilted back against the clapboards.

"Did you ever stop to think," said Owen, "that justice gets hold of a lot of criminals through tobacco?"

"Sure. Berks smoked cigarettes. But, as I said, I wasn't paying much attention to him. To me he was just Willard's goat. But Berks smoked a lot."

"What kind of a place is this Hood camp?"—casually.

"All the comforts of home in a clearing. They've tried to make a lawn of this clearing. But the grass is dry and rooty, there being no real topsoil. Muck flower beds all around the house. But we found no footprints in any of these. But there's a girl over there that'd burn your eyes out. Eh, George?"

"Uh-huh."

"How about the servants?"

"The butler kind o' got me. But he hadn't any motive. Got anything to offer?"

"Did you examine this clearing?"

"No. Because we were all so sure of the other fellow."

"Let us suppose Berks had a motive. He would know well enough what Willard's game was. Let's say that it was his motive to make the camp and waylay Willard and frisk him of the diamond."

"Not bad. But to get into the house through the opened French window he'd have stuck one of his feet into the muck flower bed."

"He might have seen who killed Hood."

"Holy Moses! Man, you've said something. If he had frisked Willard of that diamond, he'd have— No, no; we're getting up a blind alley."

Owen's heart sank. "All right. Let's get back into the dirt roads. I'd begin with the one nearest the camp. When he found out his mistake—after two hours or more he had to turn around. There's been no rain and the turn will be visible. He'd have to back and break down the shoulder of the road. If he told the truth, good night to this Willard chap. But if he lied, there's a story to be dug out of him. One thing leads to another."

"Interesting. Go on."

"Well, if he hid somewhere, there'll be cigarette butts, naturally. And then you can ask him why he lied. Any traffic on the road nearest the Hood camp?"

"Seldom at night. . . . George, let's take a look-see at the road. Get it off our chests."

"Let me shoot you along in my car. I've a side light; you can swing it anywhere. And that will be better than using pocket torches."

"Fine! We'll give the road a couple of hours."

"But if we find anything leave me out of it. This is my vacation, and I don't want to hang around a country courthouse."

"That goes with me."

At four o'clock in the morning Owen's prayer was answered. They had gone miles up the road without success. But on the return Owen's eye caught the crumbled shoulder of the road.

"Here!" he cried.

They found the spot where Berks had hidden his car. The tracks were still visible in the muck. Eight cigarette butts, Laurens brand, in good condition, for all that the coals had been pressed out by heel. Near by they also discovered the old logging trail through which the trees from Hood's camp had been hauled when the making of the clearing had been in progress. From the road to the Hood camp was not more than two miles.

"Owen, I'm much obliged to you," said the sergeant. "If I hadn't had a guilty conscience, and if you hadn't turned up, that chap Willard wouldn't have had a ghost of a show. Now there's some doubt. Berks had some kind of motive. Cigarettes. What do you know about that, George? I guess you and I are only a couple of bum road cops. Want to go with us to the Hood camp to-morrow?"

"I'm going fishing," Owen declared.

"Well, let's shoot the car back to the ham and eggs."

When the troopers arrived at the Hood camp the next afternoon they found that the purpose of their visit had been anticipated. Elsie greeted them eagerly.

"I've found something," she said, "that puzzles me. I went over this morning to that lilac bush to trim off the dead flowers, and discovered these on the ground behind the bush."

She exhibited a small cigarette lighter and several cigarette butts. The lighter was initialed R. B.

The sergeant joyfully clapped his comrade on the back. "Well, George, that's that!"

"What does it mean?" she asked.

"That the real Berks did some lying about his time-table that night. He didn't go hunting for that lighter, George, while we were around. And when he saw that the other fellow's jig was up, he didn't take the trouble to come back."

"Do you think he did it?"

"Well, there's a chance now for an argument. Berks was hanging outside here half the evening. Either he did it or saw it done. And if it hadn't been for a chap we met in the village hotel last night, we wouldn't have had this fifty-fifty basis."

"What was this man like?" Elsie asked, feeling that her knees were going to buckle under her.

"We had a queer run-in during the war and I recognized him when he came into the dining room. Red-headed and freckled. . . . What's the matter?"

"Nothing, nothing! I was beginning to get used to it, and now it all comes back again!"

16

THE ROOM WAS ORDINARY, the desk, the table, the chairs, the streaked whitewashed walls, the chromos and hunting calendars—the office of the small-town deputy sheriff anywhere in the United States. But the scene this room enclosed was not ordinary; no scene of which Elsie Hetherstone was a part could possibly be ordinary. So thought Gerry Owen, who could not keep his gaze from wandering in her direction.

He had gone boldly into the office to sit beside the sergeant of the state police. He had known that she would be in attendance. If she recognized him and did not denounce him it would signify that she no longer believed that his buddy had committed the crime of which he was accused. She had recognized him instantly and had said nothing.

Poor old Chick was right. The one woman. In this motley gathering she looked, thought Owen amusedly, like Circe among her pigs. The two detectives who had brought Berks up from New York, Berks himself, the coroner, the deputy sheriff and the clerk—something piggish about all of them. As for the state troopers, with their trig uniforms and tanned faces, they stood outside the picture.

The New York detectives had confessed that they had been unable to get anything out of Berks. He had laughed at them and informed them that he would tell his story his own way when he stood before the coroner or the deputy sheriff. He had not been permitted to have a lawyer, for this was an examination and not a trial.

He sat at a deal table, indolently; the deputy sheriff's clerk, who was also the stenographer, sat at Berks's elbow. The gem runner seemed quite oblivious of his surroundings and of the semicircle of menacing eyes. For even in Elsie's eyes were unuttered threats.

The deputy sheriff cleared his throat. "Berks, you've been found guilty of perjury in your statements at the coroner's inquest. You were either inside or outside the house when Hood was killed. Where were you?"

"I was outside."

"You saw this fellow Willard, then, commit the murder?"

"First, just where do I stand here?" Berks asked thoughtfully.

"You are under arrest for perjury and we are inquiring into the facts before we present your case to the grand jury. You lied, and we want to know why."

"I see. Where are all the other men who were at Hood's that night?"

"We aren't answering your questions; you are answering ours. Why did you lie at the coroner's inquest?"

"I was in a confused state of mind."

"So confused that you could go to sleep coolly in the room where the body lay?"

"I was tired. I had gone through a good deal that day. I want you to let me tell the story my own way. If you keep shooting questions at me I'll forget some detail."

Cool beggar, thought Owen. The deputy was going to find Berks something like a porcupine. But what kind of a story was it going to be?

Elsie studied from memory the faces of Van Cleve, Morgan, Descamps, and MacFarlane. One could not corroborate the statement of the other; what each had been doing from the time they had entered their rooms to the moment of her alarming cry were statements which stood unsubstantiated. And yet she knew instinctively that none of them was guilty. Berks—the shady character of the man, the wolf which frequently shot from his bleak eyes. The man balanced on the wall, as it were. She heard the deputy's voice bellowing:

"You saw what happened inside the house! Tell it your own way, but watch your step! A man's life—perhaps your own—hangs upon the truth of this story you have to tell!" The deputy scowled.

"Well, the lives of two men hang upon what I have to say."

This bombshell held them all in the grip of such hypnosis that none observed that the door had been quietly opened and that upon the threshold stood a young man soberly but excellently dressed in summer gray, a bit of scarlet ribbon in his buttonhole.

"Which of you is the sheriff?" the newcomer asked quietly.

Double hypnosis.

Owen gasped but otherwise did not move. Elsie, however, covered her mouth with her palm. Here to give himself up! She wanted to cry out: "Fly!"

The expression on Berks's face went from astonishment to sardonic joyfulness. Company. The fool was giving himself up. Play with Roger Berks, would he?

"I'm the deputy sheriff. And who are you?"

"My name is Willard. I am under indictment for murder. Where do you want me to sit?"

"Get him!" yelled the deputy.

Two troopers, their guns out, started for Willard.

"Hold on!" cried Berks, rising. "I need this man's corroboration. He's a big part of my story. There are five policemen in this room. He won't get away. Bring him over here next to me."

The effrontery was too much for the deputy, but the coroner leaned toward him and whispered something.

"All right," said the latter. "But one of you boys guard the door."

A trooper thereupon marched over to the door and stood with his back to it, grimly ready.

"Welcome to our city!" said Berks ironically as Willard sat down beside him.

"You are John Murray Willard?" asked the deputy.

"That is my name."

"You have this diamond known as the Blue Rajah?"

"Yes."

"Where is it?"

"In my home in New York."

"Where it rightfully belongs." All eyes immediately switched to Elsie.

"What do you mean, miss?" asked the coroner sharply.

"That the diamond lawfully belongs to Mr. Willard."

"It wasn't your uncle's?"—bewilderedly.

"No. In a moment of madness my uncle took what did not belong to him. Mr. Willard sought to recover it by a most unfortunate method."

"Do you believe he killed your uncle?"

"No."

Berks's bewilderment was quite equal to the coroner's. The diamond belonged to Willard?

"Gee, what a case!" whispered the sergeant to Owen, who nodded mechanically.

"Miss Hetherstone," said the coroner, "you told a different story at the inquest."

"I did not know the truth then."

"How did you find out the truth?"

"I am not prepared to answer that question, but will do so when I am properly put under oath. It seems to me that the main business is to hear Mr. Berks' story."

The deputy sheriff rumpled his hair. "Go on, Berks," he managed to say without a crack in his voice. All this was just a little too big and too sudden.

"All right, Mr. Sheriff. No man ever made a fool of Roger Berks and got away with it, skin-free. This chap here made a prime fool of me, and I had to pay him out. Besides, as I proceed you'll see that I had myself to look out for. But in trying to pay him back I suddenly found myself pretty far out on a dead limb."

"Just a moment," interrupted the deputy. He turned to Willard. "You're the man who kidnapped Berks and took his papers?"

"I am the man. Everything Mr. Berks told about that at the inquest was perfectly true." Willard looked tired.

"That's all I want to know. . . . Go on, Berks."

"After I was knocked down and bound by Willard and his companion, I tumbled right away to what was on foot. Willard, or Bassett, as he called himself, was going to lift the Rajah. The light was so unexpected that I did not get a good look at the other fellow. The curtains were down."

The deputy spoke to Willard. "Where is your accomplice?"

"Here he is," announced Owen quietly, standing up. He smiled down at the astounded sergeant.

"Gerry!"—from the startled Willard.

Owen took his chair over to his friend and planted it beside him. He sat down.

Elsie's eyes grew blurred. She knew that eventually this was going to happen. Buddies. Both fearless and nonchalant; only one was not so masterful as the other. And would the other ever forgive her? What had she not said to him!

The deputy, quite dizzy by now, appealed to the sergeant of the troopers, "What'll I do with him?"

"Hold him for trial. If," the sergeant added under his breath, "there ever is a trial!"

"Get Berks' story," whispered the coroner fiercely. He and the deputy sheriff indulged in some whispering.

"Why did you poke your fool head into this?" asked Owen miserably of Willard.

"Handcuffs. Didn't like the idea of a big parade from New York up. How far is it to the jail?"

"Right under us, Chick—right under us."

Berks eyed them venomously. "Willard, if we get out of this, I'll hang your hide on the door. Don't forget."

"No use telling you I'm sorry, Berks?"

"No use."

"No talking there!" warned the sergeant. "Go on with your story, Berks."

"Well, I was bound and gagged in a chair. So when I got loose finally, I wasn't thinking pretty. To telephone Hood was not my idea of first-rate reprisal. Better, thought I, to walk in on Willard when he believed he had the game all bundled up under his arm."

Elsie shivered, though the room was summer warm.

"By the time I landed in Syracuse," continued Berks, "another idea popped into my head. I'd let Willard pull his stuff, and then hijack him on his get-away. What to do with the stone after I got it I hadn't figured out. I was mad—just plain berserker mad."

The sergeant nodded. He could understand that. He'd have been plumb mad, too, to be made a goat of like that. But he shot an admiring glance at the imperturbable Owen, who had adroitly if indirectly arranged this scene.

"Plain berserker," repeated Berks. "Put yourself in my place, Mr. Sheriff."

"You could have got the troopers and had Willard arrested for assault and battery and kidnapping," snapped the deputy sheriff; "and Hood would be alive to-day."

"But I want you to know that I wasn't quite hep to what I was doing. Brain storm. When a man is prompted by fury to do things, he's generally sorry after it's over."

For the first time Elsie's glance encountered Willard's. Perhaps the same thought had flashed into their heads. Prompted by fury.

"Well, I hid the car off the first dirt road, smoked a few cigarettes, and then found an easy trail to the Hood camp."

"You have those cigarette butts, deputy," said the sergeant.

"I saw Willard and Miss Hetherstone in the music room. I like music. I don't like Willard, though I'll admit he's good at the piano. Well, to pass away the time, I hid behind the lilacs and smoked. Funny, but I never missed that lighter. I was still boiling mad. You see, if I had premeditated a serious crime, I shouldn't have been so careless."

"Not all crimes are premeditated," observed the deputy. "There are crimes of impulse."

Berks ignored this. "By and by the house went dark, and I got ready to trip up Willard. All I thought of was to get even with him."

Elsie felt her body gathering into tenseness.

"After a little a light popped up in the living room. I hurried to the window, but saw nobody. Then the piano began to play, and I thought Willard was at it. To my surprise I saw Hood come out of the music room. I didn't know who he was at the moment, but I soon guessed it. He crossed over to the wall safe, and then—"

"Stop!" shouted the deputy. "Who killed Hood?"

"Lots of time," drawled Berks. "I saw a car heading for the main road. I knew it was Willard, making his get-away. All right, said I. Stew in your own juice."

Elsie was on her feet. "Who killed my uncle, since Mr. Willard could not have done it?"

"Nobody killed him," said Berks gently. Stunned, all gazed at Berks. It was his hour, and he smiled thinly.

"What!" simultaneously barked the deputy sheriff and the coroner.

"Just what I say. Nobody killed him. He died a natural death. There wasn't any murder, but neither I nor Willard had a ghost of a chance of proving it." Then Berks shook a finger at the dumfounded coroner. "Small-town booster. Name in the papers and all that. Election in the fall. You fell down on your job. You emphasized the poker and the cracked skull and muted the condition of Hood's heart."

"The evidence pointed to murder and robbery!"

"It certainly did! Well," said the stormy Berks, "as Hood opened the safe—for then I knew it to be Hood—he suddenly clutched at his chest and staggered toward the mantelpiece, which he fumbled. Then he pitched headlong into the fire rack. He was dead probably before he struck. And that's God's truth!"

"You skunk!" cried the deputy sheriff. "And you let another man be hounded for murder—for a crime you say wasn't committed!"

"Willard," said Berks, "you understand, don't you?"

"Yes. When we are angry we do things we're sorry for after."

Berks turned upon the deputy. "You country bumpkin, what would have happened to me if I'd rushed into the house? I'd be right where Willard is now. I saw the whole mess clearly. One or the other or both of us would be accused of murder. The circumstantial evidence was a mile high. Look at the newspapers. Not an item anywhere giving Willard the benefit of a doubt. If I opened my mouth before the right time, it would be my funeral. And how about the prosecuting attorney linking us together? He'd have missed a shot like that, wouldn't he?"

"The right time—what do you mean by that?" asked the coroner.

"Till every mother's son would have believed Willard had done the job. Till there wasn't a loophole left. On the first day of the trial, Willard, I'd have cut in with the truth. You believe that?"

"I begin to see. Did you have gloves?"

"Yes."

"So did I. A perfect case against either of us, with all those gems in the safe."

Berks faced the coroner. "I acted as I have to save both our lives. . . . Coroner, wasn't Hood's heart in a bad condition?"

"Yes"—reluctantly. "But there isn't a coroner in the world who wouldn't have accepted the evidence which appeared to the eye. . . . Sergeant, am I right?"

"Yes, sir. It was always murder till just now. But I wasn't quite sure who did it."

"Well," said Berks, "there'll be another autopsy. My lawyer in the morning will demand it."

"Very well," agreed the coroner.

"Willard, you see I had to let it ride this way?" said Berks.

"Yes. I gave you rather a raw deal. But I went berserker too. How much do I owe you?"

"Fifteen thousand, my commission."

Rough, tricky and all that, thought Owen, but this fellow Berks was a man.

"Well, gentlemen," said the sergeant, "the coroner can't discharge you till after the second autopsy. So downstairs you go, if you please."

As Willard passed Elsie she looked down. She remembered her furious accusation. Besides, her eyes were blinded by tears. Impromptu. Impulse of the moment—deadly or joyous.

Three blind angers. And all this muddled horror as the result!

Owen was last to enter a cell.

"From a punch in the jaw to this Ritz bridal suite," said the sergeant. "Owen, you're a pretty good scout."

"I am his friend."

"Well, that goes for me too." And the sergeant shut the iron door and locked it.

17

THERE WAS A TREMENDOUS POWWOW in the newspapers. Reporters and cameramen flocked to the obscure village. Three times the Hood case had broken into the front page, as craters break out on the slopes of volcanoes—the final eruption being the state's decision that it had no case against Willard, that there had been no murder, that Hood had died from what is known as a wandering blood clot, that he had been dead two or three seconds before his skull had struck the poker. The case collapsed with the suddenness of a parachute.

The state also decided to ignore Berks's perjury on the premise that a man had a right, in such peculiar circumstances, to make what defense he could.

Even the most blasé reporters got a kick out of the case, there were so many odd angles. Back files revealed no comparison. There were serious editorials, too, on the uncertainty of circumstantial evidence. In this case it had been easy to cry murder. No one censured the coroner. It was agreed that his deductions had been humanly logical. Ten thousand coroners would have made the same mistake.

The case was featured two or three Sundays. Then city editors leaned back and waited for the aftermath—Berks versus Willard, assault and battery and kidnapping—waited in vain.

Willard, Owen, and Berks left the jail together. It was raining.

"Buzz saws are tricky things to play with. I haven't forgiven you, Willard," said Berks. "I accept your check without thanks. I take fifteen thousand when I could have taken a hundred. But to me there's been eighty-five thousand dollars' worth of rope around your neck. You'll always owe me something. Good-bye and the worst of luck!"

"Gerry," said Willard as he stared at Berks's diminishing back, "do you know, I rather like that beggar."

"Cured?" asked Owen dryly.

"If you mean cured of being a fool, I don't know, Gerry. See you at the hotel later."

Owen laughed.

Suddenly Willard became lost in the crowd.

Elsie remained hidden till the reporters and cameramen disappeared. When she started for camp it was raining pitchforks, as they say in the North Woods district. No thunder and lightning; just rain, cool and sweet, but thick and monotonous. It would rain all day, for there was no break in the drab bowl above. Mist, like steam, rose from the parched earth. One could see only a little way into the forest.

The deputy sheriff's umbrella covered her to the car.

"We all make mistakes, miss," he said.

Elsie nodded and got into the car. To get back to the camp, to wander through all the rooms, no longer filled with sinister shadows. She peered through the rain-lashed windows. When she saw the trout run, boiling and swirling at flood, her fingers sank into her palms.

"Faster, faster!" she called to the chauffeur, who had betrayed Willard's identity to the police.

"All right, miss, but it's mighty slippery."

When at length the car rolled under the porte-cochère and Henry came down to open the door for her, she brushed him aside and ran into the middle of the clearing, and stood as straight as a pine, her arms tight against her sides, her hands shut, her face tilted to the rain, which presently saturated her. There was ecstasy in this tattoo upon her body.

All at once she sensed a presence near by. She turned. Willard, hatless, stood beside her. She had known from the beginning of things that this moment must arrive, from the hour he had entranced her by the magic of his fingers. She had fought other men with her wit and invisible stratagems, but there was no will in her to fight this man.

She loved him! All the torture, all the agony, the incredible madness, because she had known all along that she loved him! And had begun to a few minutes after he had started to play. To have read of such a situation, to have seen it enacted upon the stage, would have aroused in her only cynical amusement. In her world men and women did not fall in love at first sight. Too canny to be fooled by moonshine and poetry and lutes. He had kissed her like a madman, and she had not struck him! Oh, she would not lie to herself. She had believed him guilty; believed him capable of everything base and despicable, but neither could she shoot him nor surrender him to the police. The human eye that often saw not what the eye of instinct always saw—the truth!

"An eye for an eye is Biblical but unprofitable," he said. "All I intended was to pay back your uncle in his own coin. I did not know that he loved anybody or that anybody loved him. That would have made the adventure impossible. I'm sorry."

"All my life I have known only the kind and loving side of him. Obsessions."

"I have always been a creature of impulse."

"And see how far the ripples of this one have gone! I had my obsession, too," she admitted. "I entered your house that day with the single murderous thought in the whole mad business."

"Will you forgive me?"

Instinctively—and she was determined to let instinct guide her—she knew to what he was referring—that mad embrace. "For what?" she asked.

"Don't you remember?"—uneasily.

"Remember what?"—smoothing her hair from her forehead where the rain had driven it.

"That unforgivable act in my own house, believing I should never see you again."

"What act?"

"I—I kissed you!" What a sophomoric sound it had!

"Did you?"

He understood. She had wiped the whole affair off the slate. Quite right, too. But how lovely she was, her eyes sparkling like sapphires and her tanned cheeks shining like beaten gold! Well, presently he would go.

"It will rain like this," she observed, "all day." She turned her face to the rain again. "How clean everything has suddenly become! Naturally—he died naturally. His heart stopped. We human beings—we think we know so much! . . . Yesterday I found a letter addressed to me. That operation in Paris—he thought perhaps he wouldn't pull through. For two years, immediately after the war, he had agents hunting all over the world for you. But you were in mid-Africa or the Himalayas. You see, he dared not write. He never wished me to know. He couldn't find you; then the old obsession returned. All men become mad, at some time or other, upon some one subject."

"Yes."

"And what is your madness?"

Suddenly the breath was shaken out of her. Another kind of rain fell upon her face.

"Good-bye!" he said, flinging her roughly aside.

But she ran at him and took hold of his sleeve.

"It seems to me," she said breathlessly, "that you are always kissing me good-bye forever. Won't you stay to luncheon? After all, you came here because you love me or because you are hungry, or both."

"Hungry!"—seizing her again.

"Luncheon is served."

Astounded, Elsie and Willard turned, to behold Henry, the butler. The smile on his saturnine face was hidden by the shadow of an enormous cotton umbrella.

Part II

Presto!

1

THE SHADE DID NOT QUITE REACH the windowsill; so the man outside could see into the room easily and clearly. The room was in the rear of the old Park Avenue house which three generations of Willards had occupied and sometimes lived in. Sometimes lived in because the second and third generations—son and grandson—had been wanderers.

There was a backyard—rather a sorry thing, as most New York backyards are. There was so little sunshine that even the grass had hard work to survive. Along the sides there was evidence that some-one had attempted to start a garden and had been defeated. Be-sides, there would be no privacy in such a backyard, there being so many staring windows in the business skyscraper on the adjacent street.

The man outside arranged his body as comfortably as he could, for he knew that this would be a long vigil, probably as fruitless as the vigils of previous nights. It was cold and starless. The watcher knew that this job must come to an end before the first real fall of snow. No tracks to be left behind; and the order had gone forth that there was to be no rough work—outright burglary. A case of rare gems, reputed to be worth half a million. It was worth patience.

So the man, this chin resting lightly upon the chill brownstone window ledge, waited and watched. Slung around his neck was a pair of field glasses, which he used from time to time. He knew the walls of the room better than the lines on his palms. Old fashioned wallpaper, of white and red roses; dim outlines of rows and rows of books; small paintings—priceless, he had been told; the top of the bookshelves littered with Oriental masks, war helmets, the tail-mark of a German airplane; pieces of trout rods tacked fanwise to the wall. Yes; he knew the room. But where Willard had the wall safe—not any more than he knew the geological characteristics of the stars which blinked coldly down upon him. It would be a trick safe; he had been particularly warned in regard to this; no ordinary affair just stuck into the wall. Even if he located it, all his ingenuity would be required to open it. Alarm wires, high voltage wires, and the devil knew what else!

He sighed. It wasn't the waiting that tortured him so much as the infernal craving for a cigarette. Just because he was ordered not to smoke.

Inside it was a man's room, swimming with strong tobacco smoke. All four corners of the room were deep in purple shadow which lightened into a silver-blue mist as it reached the desk in the center of the room. Light from an amber-tinted lampshade flooded the top of the desk, once upon a time a bridal chest. A collector would have pulled his hair over the mutilation of the exquisite piece. But the young man—Willard was thirty-two—seated at the desk was in no wise to blame for the sacrilege, nor his father, who had purchased the chest in its present condition years ago in Switzerland.

Pipe smoke drifted hither and yon, buffeted by a draught of air imperceptible to Willard, who was playing with one of the strangest games in the world. Upon the desk lay a square of white velvet; and upon this lay a dozen of nature's riddles. For, after all, precious stones are riddles which nature has not yet fully explained to science. (If you want the truth, nature has never fully explained anything to science!) She has permitted science to label these stones, but she has never given any reason for their existence. Perhaps her reason is that she believes humanity hasn't enough ordinary trouble and threw in, for extra fermentation, these colored transparent and translucent objects. A king's ransom lay upon that square of white velvet. Emeralds, pigeon-blood rubies, cornflower sapphires, a single glorious diamond, and a pink pearl so lovely and perfect that the first woman who saw it must have gone mad.

A woman—a strange woman who possessed a million in gems—entering this room and gazing at the collection, at the man entranced by it, would have frowned perplexedly. A man, playing with precious stones! That would be completely out of her orbit of deduction! For women may possess any quality and quantity of gems without knowing anything about them except that they glittered and shone and that all women coveted them.

But there were men in Amsterdam, London, Paris, and New York who would have known instantly what these stones represented—a priceless collection: gems which rarely came into the market. Curios. Indeed, only death or financial disaster brought this quality of gem within reach of other collectors. There was a queer, grim warfare going on—millionaire against millionaire—for the possession of such stones as lay upon that square of white velvet.

Humanity is well leavened with men who turn a hobby into an obsession; and all obsessions are but degrees of madness. There is no obsession quite like that of collectors, and there is none more desperate than the obsession of a gem collector. He will sometimes shut his eyes to theft and murder. What's that to him? A man offers him a gem and he pays the price. Perhaps on the morrow he will endow a university with a million for biological research. Conscience is never entirely dead in any of us.

Nature, who is an inexorable and malevolent dame, gathers a great deal of sport out of her creations. Wonderful nature! Poetical imagery! The chemist, the biologist, and the physician, however, they will tell you she is only interesting and terrible. She creates a colored crystal: and men will thieve and kill, and women end in the gutter.

The young man who studied her manifestations in crystal had a fine hand, lean, brown, and sinewy, with closely clipped nails: the hand of a man of dynamic energies, eternally restless. Those who have entered into and come through great dramas never accept peace with any substantial philosophy. Willard had seen war from and in the air; the jungles of Asia and Africa; he had climbed—as

far as ever man will—the Himalayas. The adventurer, married and
settled down, with all these burning energies blindly striving for
an outlet—an outlet which must not overflow the conventions of
domesticity! He had always been an ardent lover of color, particularly in music; and it had not been difficult for him to fall in love
with these stones, part of his too plentiful inheritance. It was a
kind of outlet, because there were sinister aspects. The whole underworld knew about the Blue Rajah—the great Asiatic diamond
of antiquity—and that it was in this house; and that merely to possess it was a bold challenge.

Gem collecting—gem frenzy, you might call it—is acquired as
the taste for caviar or Strawinsky is acquired. It isn't in the cor-
puscle; the descendants of a gem collector rarely carry on, but sell
out as soon as the inheritance laws permit. Museums will no longer
accept such collections; curators like to sleep well o' nights. The
Morgan collection in the American Museum of Natural History
contains no collector's stone; it merely presents to you a sample of
all known precious stones in their everyday values, in line, a good
lesson in crystallography.

Willard was not only a lover of color, he was also an inarticulate novelist: for he never played with his gems that he did not
build romances. He reveled in the authentic tales of battle, murder, and sudden death, and these tales he would elaborate fiction-
ally. He was not aware that his interest had drifted from admiration to passion. Seldom is any human aware of this transition till
the thunderbolt reveals it. The gems were lovely objects which
soothed him as music did, as lordly mountains soothed him, and
the clouds over which his airplane flew.

He still rode the air, but now with lethargic interest. Perhaps
this was because there was no longer any wartime enemy to seek
out up there.

A strange thing was happening to Willard, though he was totally unaware of it. From interest to fascination is but a single step,
and from fascination to obsession is a winding road. We are fasci-
nated instantly by an object, animate or inanimate; but an obsession has to grow somewhat before it is recognized, not so much by

ourselves as by our friends. These gems had captivated him: he had to go back to them again and again, always to discover some new beauty, always to reconstruct the fabulous histories he had created out of the registered facts.

Was there somewhere in the back of his head the subconscious notion that eventually some outlaw would attack him? Perhaps. And was it because of this, despite the protests of his wife, that he stubbornly refused to take the gems down to the bank Vaults? Perhaps. What was his he would defend: which was the Willard legend. Besides, it would have been an admission of cowardice. But the bravest are equally the most cautious; and Willard had forgotten this homely military truth.

It is true that the devil finds much for idle hands to do; and Willard was both idle and rich.

Perhaps Willard's main trouble was that he was not creative; he was interpretative. Could he have created he would have found the outlet for his vital energies. A truly great pianist, the urge to composition was lacking in him. He dreamed melodies, but could not hold them: no more than he could write the thrilling romances he built around the gems. He could improvise for hours, but could not recall these improvisations. Perhaps, after all, he did not lack the ability to create; he lacked incentives. A dusty garret would have forced this flower. *Must* does all the great things.

The air, the mountain peak, the jungle war: a man who had been born lonely, with the spirit of the eagle caged in conventional wool and linen. What to do with a man like this? His wife often wondered.

He loved her, she knew, beyond all other mortals; but always in her heart was the abiding fear: when love became the accustomed thing, he might break the chain and fly away. There were no manufactories to interest him; the bulk of his fortune lay in New York real estate, and old reliable agents handled this so competently that it would have been folly to meddle. She could read his thoughts when he was thinking of Tibet, the far places: he looked through crowds and walls—and her. A man who hadn't found himself, who saw the great fields of adventure dwindle to the size of his palm, figuratively. Other people's adventures, those crystals he dandled in his palm, not his own. How to capture truly this soul and hold it without chains? She sighed, for she had been standing in the empurpled doorway at his left for a long time. She never interrupted him; she always let him tire of the game before she spoke.

How she hated them, those glittering baubles! Fear. She could not account for it, but it was abiding. Not for herself—no, no—but for him. A fear which had grown into an obsession. She was conscious of possessing a savage pride and admitted to herself that jealousy tinctured this fear. Wanting music sometimes, she would come to this door hopefully, only to find him deeply immersed in his gem dreams. Her stormy pride often threatened to burst forth verbally; but her innate dignity abhorred scenes; and if she spoke as she felt there would be a scene. And yet he loved her better than other living thing on earth—any *living* thing. Pebbles, dead, inanimate . . .

She had had great ambitions for him: to triumph on all the famous concert stages, in recitals and with symphonies. To show them that her man could stand up beside the great in his particular field. But crowds bored him to extinction. They came to recitals and symphonies to have something to chatter about on contract-bridge afternoons—not for the sake of music. He would play to her friends and his, at all times, but he would not play in public for any purpose. He was sorry; but that decision was final.

And she knew that it was inevitable that soon he would begin the search for other gems to add to this collection.

Love. Well, that would go on forever; but in the pleasant amenities of daily contact there appeared a rift.

The man outside the window could see the dim outline of her. He had discovered her there more than once. But always, when she broke the silence, Captain Willard would put the gems into the case and turn out the light. Even his wife did not know where he hid his toys! The watcher crumpled a cigarette in his pocket and sniffed his fingertips. Ordinarily he could go half a day without tobacco, if he had to, but here the temptation to break orders was almost insupportable.

2

WILLARD WAS IN FULL EVENING DRESS; and in the lapel of his coat was the ribbon of the Order of Leopold. He had fought and flown in Flanders, having a preference for all underdogs. He wore the order, however, only to please his wife. He had been this night to the opera with Elsie; and from time to time he hummed bars from The Love of Three Kings. Stage jewels and stage love! He chuckled; struck a match and set his pipe going afresh.

He rolled about, with the tip of a finger, an emerald in matrix, the crystal, flawless and perfect in color, jutting out at an angle of forty-five degrees. A fifteenth-century gem, alleged to have come out of the lost Somondoco mines. His father had found it in a pawnshop in Peru. Pizarro, and all that, perhaps: or it was really an ancient emerald and nothing more. But it was a great stone to muse over. To Willard it was always burgeoning with the secrets of a thousand crimes and had come to a peaceful end in a pawnbroker's den.

Next, he played with a great pigeon-blood ruby. Queer; whichever way he turned the stone it never deepened in color at the center. A miracle in refraction. Another of nature's riddles. Atop the bookshelves stood a small gilded Tibetan Buddha. Out of this Buddha had come the ruby, wrapped in a scroll of prayers. His father's particular find at Prome in Burma. The old boy had dug out the prayer scrolls of a thousand metal Buddhas, always with the hope of finding something like this.

A great game, a great game. And there you were; that was the thing that got you by the throat. You hunted the lion and killed him, and that was the end of it. You came out of a dogfight in the air with your enemy whirling down in flames, and that was the end of it. But to the tale of these gems there was no end, and never would be till humanity ceased to speckle the earth. For every gem on that bit of velvet had a *to-morrow*.

And the outraged little Buddha on the bookshelves knew it: the man outside the window: the woman in the doorway.

Willard reached for the single diamond, the size and shape of a large pecan nut, strangely blue, with a thousand rainbows imprisoned in its flawless transparency. The Blue Rajah. From the ancient sands of India: durbars and strange gods and mutinies. The gem of all these gems. Willard did not have to build a romance here; he had lived one. Here was a gem to the history of which he himself had added somewhat. The Marcus Hood camp in the north woods; Hood and his niece Elsie Hetherstone, and Henry the butler, good old Gerry Owen, and the redoubtable rogue named Roger Berks. And John Murray Willard, wanted for murder!

The spice of that adventure would never die out. Marcus Hood, stealing in a moment of gem-frenzy the stone from Jonathan Willard, his lifelong friend: substituting a paste copy which defied all but experts: breaking the heart of his friend by treachery. Twenty years after, the son, burning with vengeance, going boldly into the Hood camp and posing as Roger Berks, palming the paste for the real stone. The Fantasie Impromptu (Chopin) and Elsie, leaning against the piano as he played! The mechanical piano-player playing the same piece as Hood died of heart failure, cracking his skull against the fire-irons as he fell. Murder, said the coroner, because motive and circumstantial evidence appeared indubitable. A hair-raising time! And love that had struck the avenger, thunderbolt-like. Hunted for a murder that hadn't happened!—and only by the sheerest luck escaping a dishonored death!

Roger Berks. Willard pressed a thumb over the bowl of his pipe. A rogue, yes; but, hang it all, a man, brainy and fearless. A year and a half, and no sign of him. Well, that was that. He had given Berks a raw deal; no question there. Playing cat and mouse with him and assuming his name: Berks, who had believed he had been engaged to go to the Hood camp to barter for the Rajah. Crooked as a corkscrew and as brave as a lion. Gem runner, trickster, but a man: for Berks, escaping from New York, had been witness to the manner of Hood's death through a window, but had not dared give evidence till the whole land had damned an innocent man as guilty. Yes; he owed something to Berks. His life. A good deal of sweat on *that* adventure. Vengeance, just or unjust, was a prickly thing to handle.

Berks had not pretended he had forgiven; he had taken what would have been ten per cent. commission on the sale of the Rajah, without thanks and without threats, but with an eye and a chin which were implacable. Something of a sportsman. He could have gone to court and sued for thousands, for kidnapping, imposture, and violence. He had gone his way, contemptuously. Yes; Willard often thought of Roger Berks.

But certainly there would be a to-morrow for the Rajah. A stone like that did not remain permanently in one man's possession. Keen Elsie! Vaguely sensing some impending bolt, Elsie wanted him to sell the diamond. A bit of a rift because he wouldn't. No. What if the publicity of that adventure had informed the underworld that he possessed such a gem? Sinister? What of it? Wasn't he man enough to defend his own? Wasn't he as clever as any crook? Yes; a bit of a rift, but so it must stand. If only she could be made to understand the game! To go hunting for gems together—what sport! But she would have none of it. Her fear was an obsession. And because of this he dared not let her know where the wall safe was, and had warned her of the shock-volt.

She was the most beautiful, the most alluring, the most valiant woman he had ever known; but she was granite when it came to her dislike for trinkets. She could not be got to wear jewelry; even her wedding ring was a simple band of gold. If she had been a timid woman, he might have understood her better; but she feared no living thing. She was like a young woman who had been listening to an old-wives' tale. If he could but impart to her the fascination of following each gem along its twisted path to the present hour: madmen, lovely women, palaces and hovels, strange lands and strange seas. But always she saw only the cruel and bloody hands that had, at some time or other, touched these gems—and her uncle's treachery. He regretted now that he had permitted her to sell her uncle's collection, particularly the Mogul emeralds.

By George! Willard stiffened in his chair. Suddenly he saw adventure of a sort hard by. Why not? Instantly was revealed to him what had been going on in the back of his head for days: to hunt down that collection and buy it back. Here was a notion with an active thrill in it. And there was one man who could help him— Roger Berks!

Willard replaced the gems in the red Morocco case and locked it. The man outside became intensely alert. Willard folded the square of velvet and put it away in a drawer.

"Man-child, do you know what time it is?"

Shocked, Willard jumped to his feet. "Elsie? What time *is* it?"

"Nearly two in the morning."

"Good Lord! And how long have you been there?"

"Several years. But you were so interested I didn't have the heart to disturb you."

Nevertheless he was disturbed. "I'm sorry!"—contritely. "I thought you had gone to bed."

"Those funny old stones! Supper has been on the dining room table since twelve. I sent Henry to bed. And you ordered the supper, remember."

"I forgot."

The combined notes of irony and weariness in her voice confused him, and he thereupon committed the act for which the man outside had been waiting and hoping these many nights. Willard took the jewel case and crossed the room to a small Rembrandt hanging above the bookshelves. (Had the man outside but known it, that foursquare of canvas was nearly as priceless as the Rajah!) The painting was swung aside. The watcher, through his opera glasses, dimly saw Willard press two spots—two roses, to be exact—and a door popped open. He understood the meaning of the two pressures. They freed the outer casing of the safe. Presently the door to this swung back. Into the black hole went the Morocco case, and shortly the wall became blank again, the Rembrandt dropped to its usual position.

Suddenly Willard caught his breath. He had never wanted her to know, for her own sake. Hitherto he had put out the light before going to the safe. Oh, well; the damage was done.

And so it was. For the man outside the window stepped quietly off the empty box, carried this to the side of the kitchen porch, and then climbed over several walls and fences till he reached the garage alley to the street which bisected Park Avenue. He took good care that no one in the garage saw him. Gaining the street, he lit a cigarette, hailed a night-roving taxi, and was driven to a hotel in lower Broadway. The curtain had rolled up.

Elsie threw her arm across her husband's shoulder and drew him into the dining room, pushing him into his chair.

"Champagne and foie-gras sandwiches!" he cried.

"I made the sandwiches and brought up the wine."

"Where was Henry?"

"I told you I sent him to bed. He looked so old and tired. Man-child, we kind of belong to him, and we must be careful. He is sixty-seven."

"Henry. Yes; we kind of belong to him. If he hadn't secretly warned me that the Rajah was to be sold. . . . How beautiful you are! Your hair always reminds me of the ruddy dried pine needles on the floor of the forest. 'Member how you caught me poaching? Hooking your exhibition trout?"

"And I, hoping the black flies would smother you!"

When he looked at her like this she knew that she would have forgiven him murder. She was first; she would always be first; but in her heart she knew that she had a sinister rival. She would really have preferred a woman; she could have defeated any woman, annihilated her, by the strength of her mind and the beauty of her body. But little inanimate pebbles!

Her heart sickened. It was like shaking her fist at the Matterhorn. Besides, that terrible example was always before her—her uncle's base treachery because the Blue Rajah had once driven him mad. The gentlest and kindest man she had known—a liar and a thief all in one mad hour. Then twenty years of secret shame!

The man she loved no longer played the piano as he used. Till recently, wherever he had come upon something so beautiful that it struck him inarticulate, he had gone to the piano for expression. Music was in the very bone of him, and he had begun to neglect it. This gave her thought for serious meditation. Yesternights, when they had returned from concert or opera, he would always go to the piano. Now he got out his colored pebbles.

She was afraid. Not of visible things; she could, with highest courage, cope with anything she could see or understand. What she feared was something stirring in the Unknown, something yet to be born. It was printed indelibly on her mind that the possession of the Blue Rajah was an invitation to disaster.

"What has become of Gerry Owen?" she asked, suddenly.

In all walks of life there will be two men who will meet and amalgamate spiritually. Each lacks something the other has, and together they are complete. What this lack is neither knows. They come together not by anything purely intellectual but intuitively. One can only obscurely explain this human phenomenon. The phase is not within the orbit of feminine actions, because women are more like cats and men are more like dogs.

Willard had the gift of music; Robert Owen—Gerry to his intimates—had the gift of observation. He could walk along a strange gravel path and at the end tell you where the pebbles had come from—glacial pit or the sea; and if there happened to be a pebble of odd shape, he could lead you back to the exact spot. And all the while, as you walked the path with him, he would be chatting pleasantly about the latest novel or play.

He was freckled and redheaded and rather shy of women because he thought himself ugly: when the bright kindliness of his eyes and the joviality of his smile never failed to catch the interest of women. But they found it difficult to get through the barriers he threw up around his true individuality. He had the body of a young Samson, though he wore his clothes so modestly and correctly that the breadth of his shoulders and the depth of his chest were not particularly noticeable. Added to this was the grace of a leopard.

He was a little older than the man whose Fides Achates he was; but he was younger because he had been born not lonely but gregariously. He liked the fellowship of men, a round-table with a bit of grog on it; liked to elbow crowds and study faces; and appeared restless when he was only curious and observant.

Willard had fought in the air. Owen had burrowed underground and fought in subterranean passages. One the ace in the air, the other the ace in the ground. Owen's gift of languages had naturally sent him into the Intelligence; and peace-time hadn't changed his activities much. He still prowled o' nights.

"Gerry?" Willard set down his wineglass. "That reminds me. I haven't laid eyes on the beggar in more than a week. I'll call him up to-morrow and ask him to dinner. I wish the right girl would put the barb into him. But you can't get it out of his coco that he's ugly to look at. And half the girls we know are crazy about him because they can't get a line on him. All the money he needs, too."

"Perhaps the war keyed you both a little too high," Elsie suggested, wistfully.

"Elsie, old girl, the world isn't the same as it used to be, and that's a fact. But men will go on loving and fighting till the old top cracks up and blows away. I wish it were May instead of November."

Her heart leaped. May. Together, with their rods, whipping the wild trout runs, living in dogtents, bathing in icy pools, and, oh, dear God, the perfume of the saps!

The bell rang—the doorbell. The two looked at each other surprisedly. It was a prolonged ring—a vigorous demand.

"Two o'clock," said Willard. "Who the devil! . . . Well, somebody wants to see me."

"I'll go with you," Elsie declared, her heart beating swiftly.

So together they went to the hall door. Willard threw off the chains, unlocked the door and drew it back boldly.

A man, who had evidently been leaning against the door, stumbled heavily into Willard's arms.

"It's Gerry!" cried Elsie, her voice high-pitched.

"Ye-ah," said Gerry Owen, trying to grin.

Willard stared bewilderedly at his friend, diagonally across whose face ran a thin trickle of blood. Gerry, in a velvet smoking jacket and a pair of slippers—his head cracked!

3

WHAT NEVER CEASED TO AMAZE ELSIE was her man's instant acceptance of a mishap and his soldierly manner of handling it. In these times, when he gave an order, she obeyed it instantly, without question, knowing the order to be the correct one.

"Run upstairs and get the guest room next mine ready."

"Shall I call Henry?"

"No. Toddle, old girl."

She flew up the stairs but hesitated at the landing and looked down. Gerry was already hanging over her husband's shoulder and the limp body was being shifted to the proper balance. Then Willard lurched toward the stairs. By the time he reached the guest room, Elsie was ready to help him to lay his burden on the bed.

"On the third shelf, in the butler's pantry, behind the old punchbowl, are three first-aid kits. Get them. But before you come up, phone Dr. Keen."

Elsie rushed away. A terrible resolve flicked through her head. She entered her own room first, then ran downstairs. When at length she returned to the guest room, Willard eyed her rather grimly.

"Could you get Keen?"

"He'll be right over. I kind of lost my nerve for a moment—couldn't see the numbers on the dial."

"Now, now!" protested Gerry. "Don't go fussing about like this. I wanted a quiet place to think in; that's why I headed in here. A slug of that old brandy of yours will do me as much good as old Doc Keen; though he may have to take a stitch or two."

Elsie fetched the spirits; and Gerry emitted a shudder and a *ha* as she took the emptied glass from his hand.

"Gerry, what's happened?" asked Willard, seriously.

"Chick, somebody tried to kidnap me to-night—right off my own doorsteps."

"But why?"

"I ain't never ben nowhere and I ain't never seen nuthin'," Gerry quoted. "That's all I know about it."

A shudder struck Elsie's spine. It was queer; but she *knew*. This was the beginning of something. Gerry was the first episode.

"You mean to say—" began Willard.

"That the bell rang and I went to the door. I found a darned pretty girl crying. At the curb was a taxi. The cabby had insulted her, and she wanted to telephone."

"And you, of course, ran down to punch the cabby."

"Good egg. That's it exactly. This crack on the coco was luckily only a side swipe."

"But your knuckles are raw!"

"So they are. I had to lay out two roughnecks. It was all a frame-up to land me in captivity. But the why of it, only the devil knows, Chick."

"Reprisal?"

"I don't know. If they had tried to bump me off, well and good. I could understand that. But I don't know why they should want to cage me. There isn't any smell to that. My mind's clear, but what it's all about is not. There are men who would like to bump me off if they got the right break. Those fellows are not in on this. To-night the bump-off would have been easy, the get-away perfect. But they wanted to carry me off somewhere."

"Gerry, why will you play this dangerous game?" asked Elsie.

"Because I get a kick out of it, Elsie. Besides, there's nobody to care."

"We care!" she returned vehemently.

"I mean, no widow and orphans"—grinning.

"The trouble is, Elsie," Willard offered, "Gerry doesn't know that the war is over."

"That is possible," replied Elsie, her voice subdued. The war. After all these years! To neither was it over; so long as they lived the rags and tatters of it would cling to them. Gerry, still the secret-service man with his life in his hands; John, with his soul wandering among colored pebbles and losing itself.

"You see, Elsie, it's this way," Gerry submitted: "I get a thrill out of studying these poor moron minds. Sometimes I let a poor devil go—give him money enough for a new start. And only one out of twenty has failed me. Now listen. I can't go back home via your front door. So I'm going to take to the roofs, the way we did when we were kids. Remember? Make that garage alley, go to Dr. Keen's, then some more back fences to my own rear door. I'm all right. Feels like a hangover, that's all. But if anyone followed, they'll be watching from over the way. And whatever this business is, I'm not going to have your house mixed up in it."

"Anything you say, Gerry.'

A figure appeared in the doorway: a kind of gargoyle with a human and friendly eye. Striped vest, tailcoat, and black cravat marked him as a servant; but Henry was more than that in this house.

"Anything I can do, sir?"

"No, Henry. Someone tried to hold up Mr. Owen; but he escaped and got as far as our door. There's the bell. That will be Dr. Keen. You might let him in."

"Yes, sir.'"

Henry looked at his mistress for a space. He recognized Willard as the master of the house, but his body and soul belonged to his mistress. This is not to say that he wasn't fond of his master; he was; but his mistress in her childhood had often crawled upon his knees.

Dr. Keen had come and gone, after putting two stitches in Gerry's scalp and ordering him to keep quiet for two or three days, at which Gerry grinned.

"Chick, I'm no Adonis with the ladies. But what's the procedure when a chap finds a peach of a girl on his doorstep and crying her eyes out?"

"You might have kissed her."

"What do you know about that! But all I heard was blub-blub . . . taxicab man . . . blub-blub insult . . . blub-blub . . . telephone."

Willard laughed. "Why didn't you escort her to the phone? You'd have blown the whole business sky high."

"No women in my house, Chick."

"No go, Gerry. You saw a chance for a fight and jumped in. And now you'll go and hunt for the girl."

"That's whatever. For that little gal will know what all the shootin' was about."

"Where was she during the fight?"

"Ringside, by the corner lamppost. If I had had shoes it wouldn't have been so bad," Gerry remarked ruefully. "You can't set yourself properly in loose slippers. Which makes me think. Get me a cap, a pair of golf shoes, and a sweater. I can't go prowling the street in these togs. I'm going to lie still for an hour. If, later, you hear me stumbling around in the garret, don't pull the burglar alarm."

Elsie bent and kissed his bandaged head, Willard gave him a pat on the shoulder; and the two of them left Gerry in the dark.

Owen knew the plan of the house as well as he knew his own, if not better. Most of his boyhood had been spent either in the upper rooms or in the backyard where he and Willard had played pirates and circuses. He would lie perfectly still for an hour, rest. His head would ache for some time to come; but he had managed to get along with headaches before from poison, gun butts, and drink, all in the line of duty.

He was going to leave this house. The cap would hide the bandages. The point was, no one must see him leave. Some funny business was toward, he did not know what; but unless he had absolute freedom he might never find out what this whirlamagig signified. Kidnapping. But why the devil should they want to suppress Gerry Owen? They could have put a bullet into him and made a perfect get-away. But they had only intended to kidnap him. Why? A peach of a girl, too, and a crook. Lord, Lord; the town was filled with pretty girls who were crooks. He had got one good look into her face, in spite of the hanky with which she had tried to hide the upper part. But he would know her again, out of a million. She had been too sure of the result. And there was that ring—a square opal, probably imitation.

Then Owen remembered something else. He had left the front door wide open! He chuckled silently—and then swore under his breath. The patrolman would be likely to notice it and investigate, and there would be a hullabaloo, which was the last thing he wanted. Well, it was spilt milk. It had been the most natural thing in the world to go down to the curb with the notion of punching the cabby's jaw.

He settled himself comfortably. There was still a star or two that wouldn't go down the horizon. If that cabby had been on his feet when he had struck, Robert Owen, alias Gerry, would, to-mor-row, rest quietly with folded arms under pale lilies. And yet they hadn't come to bump him off. Something deep; but where did he come into it?

An hour later he slipped out of bed. His head throbbed pain-fully but he felt steady on his pins. He put on Willard's coat, then the cap—which act caused him a stab of pain in the eyes. Never-theless, the cap completely obscured the bandages. Then, picking up the golf shoes, he tiptoed out of the room toward the door which led to the upper servants' stairs.

He remembered the scale of the vast garret perfectly; but there would be many new trunks—Elsie's. Chick, the lucky beggar! His knee touched a trunk and he stopped shortly. The roof trap was on the other side of the chimney. Now then, Mr. Golightly! Was the grandmother's old Saratoga trunk where it had been twenty years ago? Owen proceeded. He was used to the dark. He had in his time got safely out of many dark holes.

Ha!—Grandma's trunk, all right. He mounted the trunk care-fully, stood full height, and fumbled around for the trap latches, found them and pulled them out. The freedom of the roof was his.

His head ached abominably, but no matter. The ancient tin roofing might strike a note; so be. He pulled himself to the roof; it was a tough job. He let down the trap and sat on it, to rest. Then he groped about for Willard's golf shoes, which he had had to toss to the roof. Nice job, bending over, the roof apparently covered with sparks. Shoes on, he maneuvered lightly to the street parapet and peered over.

Right! He had been right all along. Someone across the street, watching the house. But what the devil was it all about? It was his job to find out. After a while a taxi came along and drew up alongside this watcher and carried him away, but leaving another man. They wanted Gerry Owen for some specific purpose.

Owen carefully crossed three roofs. The old Pemberton place had rear balconies, down one side of which ran a heavy drain pipe. Gerry made silent use of these and presently got to the backyard. Lord, but he had a head! Fences and stone walls came next. He followed the exact trail of the man who had watched Willard through the window, and presently came out into the garage alley. He slunk through this. But once in the street he had to lean against a wall—more sparks and vertigo. These sensations died away and he made for home. It was the dead hour before dawn.

He entered his own home by actions similar to those by which he had left Willard's. To the engineers of this queer night's frolic he must suddenly become elusive and mysterious, at least till he had a clue to what it was all about. The first thing, after entering from the rear, was to examine the front door. It was locked, but the chain wasn't on. Shut from the outside. And where was Dodge, his man?

"Dodge?" he called. "Hello, Dodge!"

Silence. Hang the idiot! He had gone to the police, the last place Gerry Owen wanted anybody to go in this queer business. To be sure, however, he ran upstairs and banged on his chauffeur's door. "Dodge!" He tried the door, and it opened easily! Knowing where the light switch was, Owen turned the key. Then he leaned against the door jamb—another round of spinning stars.

On the bed lay his man Dodge, trussed shipshape and a handkerchief over his mouth. Owen freed him.

"Dodge, when did this happen?"

"About eleven, sir. They got through some back window. You said you didn't need me any more for the night. But what's happened to you, sir?"

"A piece out of the same pie. They didn't get me, however. I left the front door open. It was shut when I looked at it a minute gone."

"Well, it wasn't me that shut it," said the chauffeur, working his jaws, his wrists, and his ankles.

"They got in, tied you up, and I never heard a thing! Got you out of the way so you couldn't help me. Did you struggle?"

"No chance. I was dead to the world. What's the racket, boss?"

"Search me. One of them came back and shut the door before the patrolman made the round."

"How about the safe?"

"All right; let's go down."

The safe was under the lower stairs. Nobody had touched it.

"But where have you been?" asked the chauffeur.

"I got to Willard's, where Keen patched me up. They tried to kidnap me. That's all I know. They weren't trying to bump me off." Owen reached for the handkerchief which had been used to silence Dodge. "It's a blank. Ten million of 'em in town. There are some folk who, if they got the chance, would bump me off. These chaps could and didn't."

"Fight?"

"Uh-huh."

"They picked on a Mills bomb; huh? Any line?"

"No."

Gerry knew that he wouldn't let this chap leave his service even if he stole the house. A figure of speech, since Dodge was as loyal and as honest as a servant possibly could be. Good head on him, too. Later, they sat before two cheerful tumblers. Owen stared at the rug and his man stared at him. Dodge was a perfect servant except in moments like this, when he knew that Owen accepted him as an equal and a comrade.

"Now, why should they try to kidnap me?"

"What do you know, boss, that they might want to know?"

"Hang me, if there is anything!"—explosively. "She was as pretty as a peach, too, Dodge."

"Who was?" Dodge's eyes bulged. A skirt in the picture?

"The girl who rang the bell and lured me into the cornpopper. But I'll see her again, boy. Now, listen. How much food have we in the house?"

"Including the canned willie, enough for a week."

"Good enough. For three days we are not at home. Detach the phone. We'll sleep all day and watch all night. Then we'll sneak down to that joint of ours in Fourteenth Street."

Whenever Owen attacked a serious criminal problem he changed his residence to a flat in Fourteenth Street. It secured his incognito extremely well. Another point worth mentioning. When his crossword puzzle was solved he would hand the solution to Detective-Sergeant Arthur Heller, headquarters. The detective got the glory and Owen got the sport. This queer partnership was based upon a first-rate friendship.

Owen sipped his grog. Suddenly he raised his head.

"Come to think it over, Dodge, we'll have to roost right here. For the present, anyway. Got to stay here for the first clue."

"Maybe someone has got loose and wants to torture you."

"Blah! A gun would have led me right into the car. But they didn't point any gun at me. Someone who knew me and where I lived. Yes, and what I'd do! Someone who wanted me out of the way, temporarily. Damn funny!"

"How many?"

"Three men and a girl."

"I'd like to have seen it."

"It was merry while it lasted. Dodge, is it easy for a woman to cry?"

"Easy as falling off a log, boss. That's their one best bet."

"Well, I'll make that little lady cry again, some day."

4

IN ANOTHER PART OF THIS CITY of troublous nights, some time previous to the hour Owen opened his door to the weeping lady, the man who had peeped into Willard's study window knocked on the bedroom door of a hotel in lower Broadway—a relic of the nineties. The man was bidden to enter. As he did so he sailed his cap jovially across the room into the lap of a middle-aged man who looked as if he had lived well but not wisely. The *bon vivant* impression you got of him was somewhat modified by a pair of eyes as bleak and gray as the ice of the Rhône Glacier. He made no effort to touch the cap but spread out his knees and let it fall to the floor. The hooked nose suggested a pride which was very inflammable.

"Well?" he said.

"Done it!" cried the visitor.

"A wall safe?"

"Behind a picture. I could find it in the dark. Wallpapered. His wife came in. Something she said must have given him a jolt, for he forgot the usual routine. That's where I came in."

The middle-aged man hove himself out of his chair and went to the telephone. He called a number, waited, then said crisply: "Start the ball rolling, and report." The man went back to his chair. "A wall safe."

"Easy as cheese!"

"Oh, you think so, do you? I've told you that the wife's uncle was one of the greatest safe builders in the world. Only a ton of dynamite can open most of the safes. The small ones are all full of tricky devices. I'll wager that the girl can open any ordinary safe. The old boy Hood taught her all he knew for amusement. Still, in the Willard house, it may be an old-fashioned safe. Could you see anything?"

"With opera glasses, yes. Captain Willard has the bug, all right. He fiddled with the Blue Rajah for fifteen minutes. I can open that safe when the time comes"—confidently.

"All right, Joe. But you're going to treat it as though it had all the General Electric inside. Maybe I'll be with you."

"Got a snifter? Getting cold outside."

"Lower bureau drawer; and don't guzzle it."

Joe sipped the whisky slowly and with relish.

"Here's your cap."

"I see it, boss."

The man called Joe set down his glass and walked over to the bell button and pushed it.

"What do you want?"

"Bellhop. I'm not picking up that cap, boss, in front of your knees. Not me. You may have your thumb in the eye of the other guys, but not mine. Anyhow, not yet."

The man with the bleak eyes recovered the cap and sailed it into the owner's hands. He had made a mistake, and, because he wasn't a fool, corrected it.

"I wasn't trying to humble you, Joe. You see, my vest is getting ahead of me. And anything on the floor that doesn't belong there annoys me."

"All right, boss."

"I'm running this affair on a fiddle string. One mishap anywhere, and we're done. So I have what the French call a crisis of the nerves."

Joe nodded appreciatively. But his thought was: Fussy? A man who never lost his poise, who never said a word too much, whose comfortable body belied the strength hidden therein—nerves? A cold, ruthless man, who might become terrible because he feared nothing. Fussy? Joe put on his cap thoughtfully.

THE BLUE RAJAH MURDER   135

"Have another snifter?"

"No, boss. I'm off that stuff till this job is done."

"Good boy! Sleep all day to-morrow. So long. Need any money?"

"A hundred wouldn't put a crimp into me."

"Here she is." The man with the bleak eyes wadded a bill and filliped it into Joe's outstretched hands. Then he lit a Laurens cigarette. "I don't know, Joe, but it would be a good idea for you to run down to Atlantic City and stay till I need you. The other business may take four or five days."

"I understand," replied Joe, smiling.

The older man smiled back, but the smile had a wintry cast. "You'll find two hundred more in your mailbox by noon. Three hundred ought to take care of you down there—if you lay off cards and hooch."

"Believe me!"

"I picked you all carefully. You're the only man I haven't got anything on. But this I want you to understand. I'm not a crook; I'm a humorist."

"That goes with me, boss."

"Well, then, skedaddle!"

After the puppet was gone, the master reached for another cigarette, the printed ends of which had been snipped off. Previous to the arrival of the tool, he had passed the time snipping off the cigarette ends. The box labeled Laurens he now ignited; and when the ash lay complete on the tray, he milled it with the end of his pocketknife. This done, he eyed the door. The fool!—let him go on believing that there was no thumb in his eye, as he had expressed it. A few scratches of the pen, and Joe Rossi would go up the river for a ten-to-twenty-year stretch. The man chuckled. Not half bad. It was true. Certainly he was a humorist. He should have been a dramatist, for he had the constructal talent that went with play-writing.

Cigarette after cigarette went up in swirling, thinning plumes.

He was now utterly sure of everything but one—a single man. Lay this chap by the heels, and the play would be perfect.

Steps in the corridor, approaching; a hand against the door. The man went to the door eagerly. Three men and a young woman with red eyes and swollen lips entered. The door clicked behind them. Two of the men were somewhat battered up. The third, in the get-up of a chauffeur, was scowling.

"You got him?"

"No, boss." The man with the purple eye spoke. "Why didn't you tip us off that he was a light-heavyweight and as fast as they go?"

"You didn't get him—the three of you?" demanded the man with the bleak eyes, bleaker than ever now.

"No, boss," said the chauffeur. "He laid out Mike and Louis so quickly that my think-box didn't work till it was too late. Anyhow, I gave him a side swipe with the blackjack he'll remember. Almost got him."

"Where were you, Jenny?"

"By the corner."

"How'd you get those swollen lips, then?"

"Louie struck me."

Bleak-eye whirled upon the offender. "If you ever lay a hand on her again, I'll break you. I mean with my hands."

"She's my niece"—sullenly.

"I've warned you. What made you strike her?"

"I laughed," said Jenny, her black eyes spitting fire. "Why shouldn't I? He was in a velvet smoking jacket and wore a pair of old slippers. He threw Louie into the gutter and knocked Mike cold; and it was only by a fluke that Jimmy hit him with the jack. I think Owen was off his bean, didn't know what he was doing; for he did not run back into the house but beat it down the street. I ran back and closed the door. The cop would have noticed it."

"Would he know you again if he saw you?"

"My hanky half-covered my face."

"Take off that ring and don't wear it again."

"It was my mother's."

"I'm not telling you to throw it away, Jenny. Don't wear it till we're out of the woods." Bleak-eye turned to the chauffeur. "Why didn't you chase him?"

"I was busy hauling those bozos into the cab. When that was done, this Owen had turned the corner. Probably looking for a cop.

Boss, the show just busted up. You should have told us this guy was a mauler. And then, you said no gun-play, just kidnap him. You gave us all the dope about his line o' thought. He came down just as you said he would. But you didn't wise us up to his fists. At that, I don't think he went for a cop but for a taxi. He didn't know a thing, except that his own house wasn't healthy just then."

"I know where he has gone," said Bleak-eye. "You're the only man with brains, Jim. Take off those puttees and beat it to the Willard house. Hang around till dawn. I'll have another man take your place then. Owen is dangerous; so we must put him on the shelf. The very fact that he didn't try to get back into the house is enough for me. He won't go to the police. He'll want to find out what's going on all by his lonesome. Jenny, there's a new job for you. Go back to the night club. He'll be looking for you in one of these. Let him find you. But never wear that ring. Puzzle him; then lead him into a trap. I'll take care of the trap."

"But you've told me he's afraid of women."

"Not in a case like this he won't be. He will be out to learn what interest we had in kidnapping him, Clumsy fools!" The voice cracked like a whip. "Jenny led him right into your hands, and you let him get away. Well, the game must go on, just the same. Clear out! Louie, I want a few words with you."

Alone with Louie, who, twirling his cap and waiting for what he supposed would be a private tongue-lashing, Bleak-eye said: "Is Jenny really your niece?"

"She is, boss. She gets high-hat once in a while and needs a crack."

"What are you trying to make out of her?"

"Who, me?"

"Are you going to make a crook out of her or put her on the street?"

The veins in Louie's neck swelled.

"Well," said Bleak-eye, "she isn't going to be either. When this game is over, I'm going to take her away from you."

The huge paws of the ex-prizefighter clamped down on Bleak-eye's shoulders. "Listen to me, boss. I'll play your game because I haff to. But I'll bump you off as sure as hell if you start any mon-key business with Jenny. She's clean an' straight. An' I'll kill her, too, if she ever gits to be anything else."

Bleak-eye pushed Louie aside. "That's all I wanted to know, Louie. Vamoose!"

5

THE FOLLOWING MORNING Willard said to his wife: "Now don't worry about Gerry. He knows what he's doing. And he has hinted that he wants to be left alone for two or three days."

"Men!" She uttered the word wonderingly.

"We are a troublesome lot, aren't we?"

"Troublesome and lovable. Why is it we women always go crazy over men who are always hurting us in some way? And yet, I suppose we couldn't live with a model husband."

Willard laughed. "Lots of funny things in this world."

"Lots," she replied.

Drunkards and loose-living men could be reformed, so she had heard. But how to reform a man gone drunk on beauty?—something which left the moral fibre intact? She heard Willard speaking and let down the shutters over these rambling thoughts.

"Gerry never takes anybody into his confidence till he's got the fourth side to the square. All over the world the police hate the amateur, and basically with good reason. But Gerry is on the war records in Washington as a man at once brave, patient, and cunning, who performed miracles. He is a real detective. He has one of the finest criminology libraries on this part of the globe, and he follows the Viennese methods rather than the Anglo-Saxon. He'll tell us the yarn when he is ready. So sit tight, beautiful lady, sit tight."

Sit tight, she thought. Sit tight. Elsie felt a strange tingling at the roots of her hair.

"Man-child," she cried impulsively, "let's spend Christmas on the Riviera!"

Astonishedly he faced her. "The Riviera, for Christmas? We couldn't make it. What's the matter with little old New York?"

"It is cheerless, cold. It's a whim. Let's go. We haven't any aunts or uncles or nephews. Sunshine and the blue Mediterranean. We haven't had a real honeymoon. I was in mourning."

"Really want to go?"

"Yes."

"All right."

But when he returned from the telephone he shook his head. "Only one boat before Christmas, sailing the nineteenth of December. All the others are full-up. You don't want Christmas at sea?"

"No." The eagerness had gone out of her voice; it was dull. To get him away from New York, without any reason which she could define! She felt like a child who had unexpectedly entered a dark room and was afraid. Madness. Was she, too, a little mad? Did she possess a prescience which was blind?

"But," said Willard, "there's one curious phase in last night's work. Why did he come barging hitherward? Why didn't he go back into his house?"

"He wanted to be among friends in case his injuries should turn out serious. Came here instinctively. At any rate, his affairs keep him active and interested in the world outside."

Which left her man mulling this over with the uncomfortable suspicion that this subtle barb had been aimed at him. He felt a touch of annoyance. The Riviera for Christmas! What had put that notion in Elsie's head? He had a sudden longing to fly. He crossed over to a window. Clouds and high winds.

The doorbell rang. Presently Henry the butler entered the living room.

"Mr. Berks wishes to see you, sir."

"Berks?"

Willard and Elsie exchanged startled glances. Berks! What would he be wanting?

"Show him in, Henry. Do you wish to see him, dear?"

"Why not?"

Berks came in, dressed in morning gray; everything about him was sartorially correct. He bowed to Elsie and smiled pleasantly at Willard. But into the minds of all three there came a vivid flash of memory.

Berks saw Willard entering the dingy village courtroom, up north, the red ribbon in his buttonhole, his manner debonair: to give himself up for a murder which hadn't been committed! Berks suddenly came upon a fact. He was the real adventurer and this man was only adventurous—a line as definite as the horizon. He was driven by necessity, Willard by choice.

Elsie saw the motionless Thing on the floor by the fireplace— what remained of the human being she had once loved—and re-spected!

Willard saw the man in front of him contemptuously telling the truth about what had happened that night—what he had seen through the camp window. Compelled to admire the man, though instinctively he disliked him. Homage to courage, no matter what kind of case the jewel lay within.

This tableau was but momentary.

"Well?" said Willard, smiling.

"I am here upon a peculiar errand," began Berks.

"Be seated. We had quite a time of it, didn't we?"

"Yes. And whenever I think of it, my few hairs stand up. If I hadn't been outside that window—"

"Please!" interrupted Elsie.

"I beg your pardon! To go straight to the mark, I have a client who will give you two hundred and fifty thousand for the Blue Rajah."

Elsie covered her mouth to suppress a gasp; and both men turned astonished glances upon her.

"It always comes back—the horror of it! Mr. Berks, I do not like that stone. There is too much sadness and tragedy behind it. But I'm quite sure that my husband will not sell it."

"She's quite right, Berks."

"But fifty thousand more than that chap from Holland was ready to give!"

"No, Berks. It isn't for sale. In the first place, it was my father's; in the second place, a million would not tempt me."

"Can't you get him to see it my way, Mrs. Willard?" Berks pleaded.

"I'm afraid not, Mr. Berks. He doesn't quite understand my antipathy to it. And yet it does seem nonsensical that I should feel as I do. It draws evil, mesmeristically. It brought evil to his father, to my uncle, to Mr. Willard himself. It isn't through yet."

A rift in the lute? Berks wondered.

Willard smiled. "Perhaps that's what makes the stone so hypnotic. But, after all, why should there be evil? The stone was lawfully my father's, therefore lawfully mine."

"Was it lawfully the man's who sold it to your father? Was it lawfully the Rajah's, who gave it its name?"

"My dear, were those three magnificent Mogul emeralds lawfully your uncle's? But they came to him through the lawful channels of commerce."

Berks lost none of these shadings.

"That's the queer thing about these uncommercial gems, Mrs. Willard," said Berks, thoughtfully. "I understand how you feel. But most of us, like your husband and myself, do not believe in curses or banshees. How far does a curse reach? Actually no farther than the sound of the voice. Curses are of no utter use"—and a humorous glint beamed in Berks's eyes—"unless you stub your toe in the dark."

"You see, Elsie?"

"Yes, I see. But I wish you would sell the Rajah."

"Out of the question."

"That is final?"—from Berks.

"Absolutely final."

Berks rose. "Sorry. Of course I didn't know that you had taken to the game the way your father did and Hood."

"Wait a minute," said Willard. "I will not sell the Blue Rajah; but I'll buy back the three Mogul emeralds, fifty thousand beyond what they were sold for, and ten per cent commission."

Elsie's hands fell listlessly in her lap. There was a slight perspiration where her forehead joined her hair.

"The three Moguls?" said Berks. "They are in Paris. A Place Vendôme syndicate owns them."

"Will you accept the commission?"

"It's a bargain. I'll leave for France immediately after the New Year."

"And this time," said Willard, "I shan't creep upon you in the dark."

Both men laughed.

Roger Berks departed.

"You trust that man?" demanded Elsie.

"It's a sporting proposition, Elsie. To square a debt. Once I manhandled that chap pretty roughly."

"You know how I hate these gems."

"Elsie, it's the only amusement I have."

"What about the piano?"

"I simply can't play in public."

He stepped over to the piano and played the Scherzo from Mendelssohn's Midsummer Night's Dream. He had scarcely finished it, when Elsie appeared in the doorway, dressed for the street.

"Going out?"

"Shopping a bit"—giving him her first lie. "I'll be back for lunch."

She wanted to be kissed and he wanted to kiss her, but both were conscious of a barrier to be got around.

"Got the car?"

"No. To-day I want a top seat on a bus."

"Got all the money you need?"

"Oodles! By-bye."

The bright November morning sparkled perhaps too brilliantly, for it set tears trembling on the lids of Elsie's eyes. She was mad; and the strange part of it, she knew that she was mad.

Five o'clock that afternoon. Bleak-eye sat in his hotel room, smoking and musing. No one answered the telephone in the Owen ménage. It signified that Owen and his man were off and away somewhere, which was a blotch on the escutcheon. Smelt a rat, but did not know what sort of rat it was. Nevertheless, it was not

pleasing to contemplate Owen being at large and boiling with curiosity. All the same, the thunderbolt was forming rapidly; and
when it was launched Owen would not know what hit him. The red-
headed sleuth would not have *time* to find out anything.

Presently a thin little man came in.

Bleak-eye barked: "I told you to keep an eye on the Willard
house till relieved!"

"I know it, boss. But something darn funny has happened."

"What?"

"Well, this morning, about eleven o'clock, this Willard dame
comes out in furs, an' o' course I follows. I had a hunch. I know I
disobeyed orders."

"What happened?"—the bleak eyes boding no good to the de-
linquent.

"Well, she makes for crosstown; an' I think mebbe she knows
where this Owen has his hide-out. But all she did was to get into
the Jersey City ferry—me near by, watching."

"You fool!—while Owen may have walked out of or into the
Willard house and nobody the wiser."

"Just a minute, boss. She leans against the rail, never turns
her head. Watching tugs an' ferries an' ships. But here's the point.
When she gets to the Jersey slip, she stays right where she is, never
looking at nobody."

"What next?"

"Why, when the ferry gets back to town she slips into a taxi
and beats it back home. If that ain't rummy, what is?"

"You shrimp! A bit of air and sunshine, which she can't get in
her car. You're a fine specimen of a watchdog!"

"But she'd been cryin', boss."

"Crying?"

"Ye-ah."

Bleak-eye stroked his chin musingly. "Go back to your post till
you're relieved," he ordered. "I'll overlook it this time. Don't bother
to think. Do as I order. Beat it!"

Bleak-eye dined well that night, in a small, choice but illicit
grillroom. The Corton Charlemagne wasn't half bad.

At nine o'clock Willard sat reading a book on the varieties of green beryl. Elsie sat near by, doing needlepoint. The doorbell rang. They saw Henry, with dignity and assurance, pass the door. They heard the door open and close. Willard laid his book on his knees and Elsie stuck her needle into her pattern, expectantly. A minute passed; two. Curious, Elsie called.

"Henry?"

No answer.

Willard got out of his chair and hurried into the hall. No Henry was visible. He wrenched open the hall door.

Henry was nowhere to be seen. He had vanished inexplicably.

Presto!

6

HENRY THE BUTLER HAD VANISHED, as completely as if, a bit of dust, the wind had blown him away. It was early in the evening. In the avenue there were streams of vehicles riding north and south. Henry might be in any one of these, but only an unearthly eye could have told which cab held him. Vastly puzzled, Willard returned to his wife.

"Elsie, something strange has happened."

"Where's Henry?"

"The Lord only knows! They may have thought him Gerry. For somebody's after Gerry."

"Henry gone?" The tocsin of fear rang in her head. "But they couldn't have mistaken that old man for Gerry! I am going to notify the police."

"Wait a moment. That's just what Gerry would not want us to do. And nobody in God's world would set out to kidnap Henry."

"What do I care for Gerry's detective orders? What are the police for?"

"Give it half an hour. If we hear nothing, then we'll notify the police."

"Half an hour, then, and no more"—resolutely.

Then, with an appealing gesture: "Will you take the gems down to the bank in the morning? John, so long as they are in the house, I shall be nervous."

"Elsie, what's the matter with you? That wall safe is impregnable. It will fairly knock out anyone who does not know the trick of it. I wish you would drop the subject. This is my home, and I can defend it."

"Suppose someone has kidnapped Henry to force him to disclose where the safe is? Torture him, when he knows nothing?"

"Aside from yourself, who knows of the existence of the safe?"

"The man who put it in."

"Who knew nothing of the purpose for which it was built."

"How do you know?"—quietly.

Willard laughed. "Elsie, if I bowed to your inexcusable fears, I should be a coward."

"Is it a sign of cowardice to be cautious?" she countered. "Did foolhardy generals ever win a great battle?

"What astonishes me is that a woman of your poise and intelligence should act as though she'd been attending old-wives' meetings."

"That isn't fair, John."

"Maybe not. But, Elsie dear, I have known you to be a woman without fear. You never had any fear like this while you lived with your uncle."

"I did not know then that he had committed a crime and betrayed a friendship and was about to add to the original crime another. Selling the Blue Rajah in private, miles away from other habitation. It is you, John. I care nothing about the gems themselves, or what might become of them. I'm afraid for you."

"And that's the point I insist upon. I can take care of myself."

"If Berks hadn't been outside that window, could you have taken care of yourself? Look at me! I, I knew you had killed Uncle Mark!"

Here the telephone interrupted; and both of them hastened toward the tingling bell. Willard took up the receiver, while Elsie listened in.

"Who is it? . . . Gerry? . . . Yes; this is Chick. . . . What? Not to worry, no matter what happens and under no circumstances call in the police? . . . Yes. Your house wire is cut and you'll be away three days. Yes. Now, where is. . . . I say, Gerry!" Willard waited a moment. "Confound the beggar, he's rung off! But it means he has called in Henry for some reason."

"I don't believe it. Why should he act mysteriously over Henry if he wanted him?"

"Why should he call us at all, then? You leave it to Gerry. Henry's all right. And you know Gerry; there must always be a mysterious slant to the work he does."

The two of them returned to the music room. The fierce pride which was Elsie's burned brightly. No more pleading. It would only harden his resolve. The family row should not go any further. They had been so happy!

Both of them were sensible and resolute persons. There would never be any petty squabbles, pinpricks; the subject would have to be vital to arouse them to argument. In the present argument—the only one they had ever had—the queer thing about it was, they were both right.

She would give him one more test; from another angle.

"Please don't buy back the Mogul emeralds. I'll admit of your right to do anything you please with the collection. But don't buy the emeralds."

"I made a verbal agreement with Berks."

"But if I wrote him?"

With slow strides Willard began to pace. All at once he faced her. "All right. If you can get me out of that bargain, go ahead. If you wish that I should never buy another gem, that goes too. I will do anything you wish so long as my sense of property rights is not infringed upon. You women are funny."

"I suppose we are." He would do anything on earth for her except the one thing she wanted him to do.

"Superstition!"

"Well," she said, "when we have it we have it. And it isn't anything you can laugh away, John."

But the bitter anger in her heart did not subside. Suddenly she made up her mind. A live woman or a handful of colored stones; sooner or later she would force him to make his choice. She had been so happy till these gems had insidiously intervened! Very well. She would never, now, be sorry for what she had done. Yet, when she tried to analyze it, her superstition was an elusive thing.

Before that tragic night at the camp, superstition had been something to laugh over. Perhaps he was not conscious that he was crooking his finger and bidding murder, battle, and sudden death to cross the doorsill. Portents—omens of evil—she could not dissipate the feeling that something dreadful was to happen. A live woman or a handful of stones: he would have it so.

He on his side was bitter that he could not eradicate this nonsensical old-wives' feeling. She was so big in soul and mind that it did not seem possible that such an obsession should lay hold of her. Evil out of stones? Bah! There might be danger and excitements. . . . Pshaw! Why, it was out of the medieval; and he must cure her of it, once and for all.

The little Tibetan Buddha, in the dark of the study, reading these two minds, must have smiled. He was a god, and his honor had been stained by the shadow of a theft. It would seem that another tithe of Buddha's vengeance was to be garnered. Through how many centuries had men fought and died, and women. . . . This diamond was not directly his affair, but nevertheless he would profit by it.

"Shall I play for you?" he asked, melting suddenly.

"The Impromptu." Elsie's face brightened.

"Don't you ever tire of it?"

"Why?"

"You know"—lowly.

The Tibetan Buddha began to frown—to keep up the illusion. The rift was drawing together. All at once he smiled again. The musician was playing the Impromptu Fantasie with frills which did not belong. Elsie reached out and caught Willard by the hand.

"Please! You know I love it better than any other piece of music. Always play it for me as you did that night."

Swiftly he bent and kissed the hand. How lovely she was! But she must be cured of this nonsense. "I'm sorry. I'll play you Grieg—honestly."

So he began the Ballade with variations. He played exquisitely, up to the final movement, when he broke down. Three times he went back; three times he broke down.

"Something the matter with my fingers to-night. Funny. I never broke down like that before, not anything by Grieg."

"You don't practice as much as you used to"—gently. "Play something light. It will restore your confidence."

He played Dohnanyi's Marche Humoresque; and he played it with all the drollery of the master himself. Elsie began tapping the floor and nodding her head. It was one of those irresistible compositions: you *marched!*

He wanted to seize her in his arms and kiss her, and she keenly wanted to be seized and kissed. But the same thought came into the minds of both. An embrace, given and taken, would have taken on the color of surrender. So, with only a friendly goodnight, they proceeded to their separate bedrooms.

The little Tibetan Buddha winked at the wall safe where his ruby heart lay concealed. For the first time in his recollection the Sahib and the Memsahib had separated without the good-night kiss.

At this very moment Henry Granger—the butler—sat with his head in his hands. He was in a dark room, and his nose and lips burned with what he knew to be chloroform. Presently he peered about him. He was on a cot. But where? What had happened? Bewilderedly he staggered to his feet. Light. A window. But it was many stories down to the street. Next, he dimly saw a door. He found this locked. He groped back to the cot and sat down. He must wait till his head cleared. But what could it mean? As he opened the door, three men had seized him before he could shout. . . . Then this cot, this locked room! Why should anybody kidnap poor old Henry Granger?—who had neither money nor enemies? He began to sob, senilely. Well, someone would come in the morning and he would learn what it was all about. Carefully he stretched out his aching body and fell asleep.

7

GERRY OWEN AND HIS MAN DODGE sat drinking forbidden beer and munching ham sandwiches. It was ten o'clock, the same night.

"Dodge, I've got an idea."

"Spill it, boss. Say, you wouldn't believe I could make home-brew's good as this, would you? Call it beer, if you want to, but it's up to any Scotch ale I ever had over there before they brigaded me with the Froggies."

"Don't call them Froggies. The French are a fine people."

"Well, they started calling us Sammies."

"That's your mistake. They meant *les amis*—the friends."

"So that's what it meant? Well, spill the idea."

Gerry leaned back and crossed his legs. "Dodge, what did we do over there, when we wanted to move our right against the enemy's left?"

"Why, we shelled hell out of Heinie's right."

"To keep them from coming to the assistance of their left."

"Sure."

"Well, maybe that's it."

"Is the beer getting you, boss?"—anxiously.

"Want me out of business before the big push. Now, I'll stake everything that they never followed me over to Willard's." Gerry paused. "Yet there was a watcher posted there when I left by the roof. Saw him over the parapet."

"Oho!"

"I don't know. When they saw me running away, they may have tumbled to the fact that I was headed for Chick's. An anticipatory mind in the woodpile. I studied my private records to-day. There are three men just out of prison. One of them is as clever as the devil, and I think he's got it in for me. But he wasn't in that bunch the other night. Still, crooks have queer minds. He may have wanted to have a little personal chat with me before giving me the deep end. He liked filigree work. What I've really got to do is to find that gal. She'll be the serial in book form."

"A peach, you said."

"That, too, makes it interesting. I want a real good look at her."

"How's your head?"

"Sore as the devil to touch, but otherwise all right."

"Uh-huh. Maybe you're right."

"For three days we are not at home. No doorbell to be answered and the phone wire to be cut. Don't want any outsider to come in and do any telephoning. Dodge, there's something in the back of my head trying to tell me something, and it can't work its way to the front. Your job is to stand guard here. We'll sleep in the day-time and do patrol at night. If they're after me, bub, they are sure to have another try. So I'm not going to be home nights. What bothers me is the ease with which they got you, without either of us hearing a sound. They got into the backyard somehow."

"Where do you think you'll find the skirt?"

"Night club."

"Gee, boss, there are seventeen thousand that I know of! But what'll I do when you're out?"

"Get your gun license. Shoot to cripple. The license is in case the police butt in."

"But will you recognize her?"

"She had her face pretty well covered up. But I'd recognize those eyes of her ten years from now. Lovely!

"Boss, are you hunting the gal, or just falling?"

"Atta boy. You'll never learn anything if you don't ask questions. Ask the question a week from now."

"She'll cry on your shoulder and tell you her daddy beats her and sends her into the street. Ye-ah. I know, boss. You may not be no Valentino; but you can sit right next this guy Menjou and still look like a million dollars. In your glad rags, I mean. You could stand in a line of a thousand head waiters, and any smart dame would pick you out. And so will this bootlegger's daughter."

"Maybe so, bub. But this girl is going to know a heap. And no woman has ever put the comether on Gerry Owen."

"Well, boss, I'll give you that much handicap."

Owen went up to dress.

The medico—a strange one—would have confined him to bed for three or four days. But Gerry knew himself. His head was all right, except that it was sore. Kept in the house, he would have fretted himself into the very condition a medico would have wanted to avoid. Inactivity was the curse of him. His vitality had never ceased to astonish Dr. Keen—hale at sixty-four—who had brought both Owen and Willard into the world.

Owen and Keen lived on streets which bisected Park Avenue, several blocks below where Willard lived. Owen lived on the north side of his street and Keen on the south side of his. The doctor was in Gerry's complete confidence, and gave the young man the run of his house. By climbing fences, it was easy to make Keen's rear door. When engaged upon one of his adventures, Owen always used Keen's house for his entrance and exit. The doctor's servants had long since grown accustomed to Owen's passage to and fro, at all hours.

Old houses, flat-roofed, with parapets, honest chimney pots. When Park Avenue became ultrafashionable south of the Grand Central Terminal, the pleasant skyline of the present would become harsh and ragged. What Owen loved about Paris and London was the uniform height of the buildings. With such as partially enclosed the Place de la Concorde, Central Park would have been almost as lovely. Now the Park, it seemed to Owen, presented a timid, half-hearted garden aspect, growing almost clandestinely, surrounded by myriad eyes which glittered in the daytime and burned snugly and reprovingly at night.

His overcoat kept his shirtfront immaculate, and he could give himself a brushing at the doctor's. "The thing that worries me," said the doctor, "is that someone will pot you climbing over fences."

"Some of them know. Anyhow, it's my funeral."

"What's it this time?"

"Not sure. But I'll tell you when anything breaks."

Gerry quietly let himself out the front door.

The girl would be the key. Queer thing, he had never found it difficult to get himself into the graces of women—when he was hunting them. In his secret service work his homely mug—for somehow women trusted homely faces—had helped more than once.

Clever stroke. A girl crying at the door, a supposed brute of a taximan at the curb. Sherlock himself would have fallen for it. The chauffeur could have finished the job had he joined the mêlée instead of staying at the wheel. But naturally he believed that the two plug-uglies could handle the victim. Funny thing, though: heading for Chick Willard's. He must have been half cuckoo. All the same, it had turned out right.

He stopped a cabby and got aboard. Something buzzing in the back of his head and trying to project itself upon the screen of his consciousness. The way you remembered a chap's face but not his name. You brought up a lot of objects; you mulled over the alphabet: bang went the bell. You had the name. But to-night that process did not arrive anywhere. It had something to do with this business, or it would not have awakened to aggravate him. Soon or late, it would of course come into the open; but he wanted it now. His common sense warned him that this affair was going to move fast. He did not want to find his ticket after he had paid the fare to the conductor, as the saying goes.

He would drop into the Capitol and witness the wind-up of the last show. Theaters would be emptying themselves then and the gin-mills waking up. He would look in at the best, to begin with. Such a good little actress would not waste her talents in the lower order of dancing clubs.

By three o'clock in the morning he had sniffed enough terrible champagne to have gassed the Hindenburg Line. First-class bombs. And the hostesses really drank some of the stuff. But nowhere had he seen any girl even vaguely resembling the tearful one. And all his eyes required was a vague resemblance.

Three o'clock. Well, let's see what Popolopoulos had to offer. Greeks, Dagos, street-walkers, gunmen. Street-walkers who no longer had to walk the streets because the nighthawk cabbies steered the moneyed inebriates into their claws, and their profits were enough on wine alone.

Owen was clean, both his body and his mind; and the two resented some of the atmospheric effects he had to encounter. Maybe he was wrong. It did not seem possible that such a girl as he was hunting for would act as hostess in any of these portals to hell. Cheap tobacco, liquor that was neither corn, grain, nor potato. As he did not know how to peddle pencils, he pretended that he already had drunk enough. (One glass of champagne to taint his breath sufficiently.) Histrionic talent, he possessed that, too. He spent his money freely. Girls sang for him. One dollar each. The musicians collected a dollar. When they learned that he was about broke, he was told they were closing. And when he got to the street, two chaps in top hats were struggling to crowd into the lift. Owen drank the air for a couple of blocks. Fun! They called it having fun. His head ached. It would have ached even if it had had no bump.

Another cabby—who got his split for bringing in the soft money—and three more of the increasingly repelling places. What struck Owen was this: he had been in nearly all these places months before. Not one familiar face remained. All this Walpurgis going on because the Government wasn't strong enough to catch the bootlegger, or if it was, not strong enough to hold him.

The last place on the list was dim-lit, purposefully. You would not be able to recognize your friend across the dance floor. For everybody danced or tried to. About ten feet away was a little coupe in which sat four musicians, with faces from the ghost-brush of Doré. Owen walked over and dropped five dollars into a cigar box.

From the dancing floor to the bar was a darkened corridor.

A man and a young woman were watching the guests from the vantage point of this corridor. Suddenly the man seized the girl by the arm.

"The gray fedora! It's him! The boss was right. He's on the look. Sing. I'll get back t' th' bar."

The girl shivered, but not from fear.

8

WHEN THE DANCING WAS OVER and Gerry, weary, rather nauseated by headache and visions, was about to leave for home, the orchestra began a Mammy song; and the young woman stepped under the spotlight. Owen stared at her. Something about the eyes and nose . . . But what a voice! He wanted to put his hands over his ears. Poor kid! She sang dreadfully. All he could understand was the *whang-whang-whang*. As a wife she would have to have other talents. The eyes and nose. . . . He must have a good look at her.

He beckoned to one of the waiters. "Hey! Bring me that girl—the one that's singing. And bring a bottle of Pommery, 1919."

"Ye-ah, 1919. Say, are yuh kiddin' me?"

"Well, if you haven't that, bring me the best, brother."

The waiter grinned. "What other label wouldja like? Pommery's th' on'y thing we ain't got."

"Go to it."

"Girl an' a bottle o' Hell's Bells." The girl had finished her song by the time the waiter reached her. "The Grand Duke o' Roosha has thirty iron men he'd like tuh spend on yuh."

"Where?"—indifferently.

"The guy with the kelly like an Englishman's."

Jenny strolled over to Owen's table and sat down.

"Hello, Big Boy! The waiter tells me you're a wine-hound. How come you're out so late?"

Owen received a shock. He wasn't sure of the face, but the voice was the one he sought. His ears memorized as well as his eyes. All

157

the voice needed was the whimper. Her fingers were ringless. The speaking voice was sweet. *Whang-whang-whang* had been pretense, because the customers would not want Just a Song at Twilight or any other tear-starter.

"I'm a writer," he said.

"For the papers?"—in mock horror.

"No. I'm a novelist. I'm out looking for color."

"Have you tried Harlem?"

He laughed genuinely for the first time that night.

"Boy," she said. "I like your hair. It isn't henna-red. And where did you ever buy those teeth? Ever try anything for freckles?"

"Grammatical as well as musical."

"What's that?"

"I was making a mental note aloud. What made you sing like that?"

"Like what?"

"That whine? You can do better than that."

"What makes you think so?"

"Your natural voice is sweet."

"Dear me!"

He took out a ten-dollar bill and gave it to her.

She accepted it. "What's the name of this act?" she wanted to know.

"Company. Here comes the wine."

His gorge rose. To keep the game going he would have to drink this time. For this was the girl; and she knew perfectly well who he was. The cork popped, far too loudly. Where *did* they make the stuff and what *did* they make it of? He raised his glass at salute, and was about to take a swallow, when her hand staid him.

"All you have to do is to buy it. You don't have to drink it." All the mockery had gone out of her voice. "Lay down the bluff. You've been drinking, but you're as sober as I am."

"You don't drink?"

"Ginger ale. You men are queer. You always want to get us girls blotto."

THE BLUE RAJAH MURDER

"Are you a good girl or a bad one?" he shot at her, rather cruelly. Well, this was a sordid dump.

Her dark eyes flashed. "Would I be likely to tell you one way or the other before six o'clock, when we close?"

"What's your name?"

"Jenny." She looked down.

Jenny. Owen thought of Herrick and the sweet ever-memorable ballad. Jenny. No name for a dump like this. Devil of a world!

"May I see you home?"

"No go. We're not allowed to go home—to our homes with strangers. Come, come!"—impatiently. "You know as well as I do that the whole business is a stall to get rid of this fermented garbage."

"What if your boss heard you talk like this?"

"He won't hear me—not this time." She smiled.

"What would you do if I kissed you?" Now why the devil did he ask that?

"Why," she replied, "with this bottle of wine on the table paid for, I'd have to stand for it." She leaned toward his ear. "But I'd wash my mouth the moment I got home"—savagely.

"Am I as ugly as that?"

"All men are ugly—here."

So they would be, thought Owen. "I've three hundred—"

"Sh! Don't let anyone but me hear that."

"Why you?"

She looked into his eyes suddenly. A glorious Latin eye, as steady as his own. He reached out and covered her hand with his.

"You're strong," she said. She felt of his arm. "Y'know, I'd like to see you in a mix-up with these Greeks and Wops. They are all yellow."

"Guns?"

"Some of them."

"How did you fall into such a life?"

She smiled dryly. "What if I told you I'm safer in this dump than in a broker's office? I tried a broker's office once."

"I understand. You can stay straight if you want to. And you've stayed straight."

"What makes you think that?"

"You do. Is there anything I can do for you?"

"You can kiss me, if you want to. I won't mind—or rub it off when I get home."

So Gerry Owen kissed Jenny Lavina—as he might have kissed a child.

"You're straight, too," she said, as she drew back. "What are you doing in a joint like this? No man ever gave me that kind of kiss before. Do you want me to sing, honestly? All right"—as he nodded. "Come to-morrow night, about two, when I'm not too tired. Good-night."

Owen, as he went down the dark stairs, was conscious that he hadn't asked the girl one leading question! The puppet of a bunch of crooks, and straight. No; he didn't know a damn thing about women, even when he was hunting them, lawfully. Straight. How could he prove that she hadn't played him from the start? Yet she had wanted that kiss, that kind of kiss. Sixes and sevens—he couldn't say which alley he was in.

Louie Lavina caught his niece by the shoulder. "Is he coming to-morrow night?"

"Yes."

Louie peered down into her face. "What are yuh blubberin' about? Did the boob insult yuh? Come across."

"He kissed me."

"Kissed yuh? Well, what the hell's a kiss?"

"I don't know, Louie, I don't know."

9

WILLARD DID NOT CONSIDER himself stubborn. To be wrong and to refuse to admit it—that was true stubbornness. A man had to stand firm sometimes. Superstition had got Elsie, somehow. He could see her point of view, but it was such an infernally silly one. To lock up those stones downtown because her imagination had got out of hand! To prophesy battle, murder, and sudden death, simply because the stones had lively histories! If he surrendered, her notion might become permanent and cause all manner of petty friction. Elsie was basically a most sensible woman; if he held out, she would soon be coming around to his side of the tent. Only a few months gone she had admitted that if it hadn't been for the Blue Rajah, they would never have met! And now this unreasoning attitude!

Anything else in the world, but those gems were going to remain in the house, indefinitely.

There was in each of these two persons a pillar of steel. Not the gay rapier type, to bend quickly and brightly at a pressure and then to flash back. This steel was rather the stuff out of which the Crusaders' double-handers had been hammered. A lot of queer swords leap out of hidden scabbards—after one is married.

On her side. If a great business had taken him away from her, she would have accepted his daily absences as one of the immutable facts of married life. But a case of precious stones—she would not abide by it. She *knew* that something would happen. It was inexplicable, but the fear stood up in her mind as a beacon stands up in a storm. Suppose the *Thing* got him as it had got her uncle? Second fiddle. She would not play it to any man on earth.

Her uncle had carried the stones—the great emeralds—wherever he had gone. But the public had never known about it. But every rogue in New York knew that John Willard possessed one of the most beautiful diamonds known.

Two swords, then, which would not bend; and perhaps a little too much money on each side.

"Elsie, I'm going over to Dr. Keen's. I'm frankly worried about Henry, and I might as well admit it. Of what use is Henry to any but us? He can't sit down without sundry creakings."

"I'm worried, too. There isn't any handhold to his disappearance. And why shouldn't Gerry have told us over the phone?"

"Darn his mysterious stuff! Well, I'll see Keen."

"Will you be home to lunch?"

"Probably not. But I'll be back to dinner."

Elsie followed him into the hall and watched him get into his coat.

"If anything serious is up, I'll telephone you. By-bye."

Elsie's face was expressionless; but after the door closed her face fell into tragic lines. He hadn't kissed her, even perfunctorily. In a burst of fury she ran into the study and beat the wall behind which lay the safe. And immediately became ashamed of herself for this futile and childish gesture.

At Dr. Keen's Willard wanted to know things.

"Gerry ambles verbally," said the doctor. "All I know is, he's climbing over the back fences on the way home. That's always the sign. He hasn't said anything about Henry. Certainly he didn't bring him through this way."

"Mind if I go through the rear?"

"Go ahead. You know the ropes. That devil of a Dodge of his is brewing ale in the cellar. Good stuff."

"What's he on?" asked Willard.

"He doesn't know yet. But just before he passed through this morning, he told me he had located the girl. The one he found crying on his doorstep. Bang on the cellar door four times. That's the latest signal. Gerry makes me smile. He just *has* to be mysterious. But he's never fallen down yet."

"Why not the front door?"

"You can ring the bell from now till Christmas, but you won't get in that way."

"All right."

Willard felt something of a fool as he began to climb the fences across the block, wondering if anyone saw him and what they would think of him if they did. He reached the cellar door—or to be exact, the rear basement door. He signaled.

"Who is it?"

"Willard. Is that you, Dodge?" Willard got a refreshing whiff of malt as Dodge let him in.

"Howdy do, Mr. Willard? Have a glass? I'm bottling twenty gallons, but I've some six months old."

"All right. Crack a bottle for me. But first, tell me what Gerry wants of old Henry—the butler?"

"Henry?"—astonished. "You mean your butler?"

"Isn't he here?"

"Why, no, sir. The boss tells me plenty, but he's never mentioned your man. Has he left your house?"

Willard recounted the incident of Henry's evanishment, emphasizing the bewildering suddenness of it.

"Gee!" said Dodge. "I don't know when the boss will be back. My orders are to stick inside the house. He went out early in a business suit. No sleep at all. I'll get you that beer."

Willard sat dumbly upon a crate. Henry, kidnapped, by the same forces that had tried to kidnap Gerry. But why? That poor old duffer, with his gargoyle face—how was it possible for him to fit into any scheme which might concern Gerry? Willard heard a pop at his elbow.

"Swig it out of the bottle, sir."

Willard emptied the bottle, his throat stinging pleasantly. "Dodge, what does someone want of Gerry?"

"Search me, boss. Nobody's trying to bump him off. They just want him out of the picture. And he's trying to find out why. But leave it to him."

"But where does my butler come in?"

"Don't know. Somebody's after something. What? Who? Maybe the backfire of an old job of the boss. Johnny-Get-Even stuff. Mr. Willard, the boss is a great detective, and I don't mean maybe. We got blotto together Armistice Night in Armentières. He took me on after I was demobbed. Say, he's cleaned up fifty police jobs in this town. He helps out a dick down at Central. Now, when you get home, stay there till you hear from the boss. Wandering around, you might be accidentally mistaken for him. See? Sit tight."

Willard waited till one, then decided to go home.

"Elsie?" he shouted, after his own door closed behind him. Silence. "Elsie?" He ran up the stairs. Servants' day off; so if Elsie wasn't home, he would be alone in the house.

There was no Elsie. But in her room nothing seemed to have been disturbed. He opened various bureau drawers, the cedar chests, and the hanging closets. So far as he could see or remember nothing was missing except the short sable coat she usually wore. He was frankly alarmed, nevertheless.

He hurried down to the library and opened the safe. The combination was of deadly preciseness. If you did not whirl the knob completely around to zero, you were partially electrocuted. If you stopped at any even number, you summoned the Burns and the Fiaschetti agencies. This, if you were lucky enough to turn the knob completely. If you then reversed and did not stop at seven, you shot up all the lights in the house and they winked for several minutes. It was a safe full of the ingenuity of the devil himself. Willard had warned Elsie never to meddle with it, this warning having been uttered the night when she discovered where the safe was.

The jewels were in their accustomed depressions. Carry them down to the vaults? No. That was final. He would give in on any other point; never on this one. Why, good Lord, the Sub-Treasury wasn't any stouter. It was all nonsense.

Suddenly the house had the feel of a barn about it. He wandered through room after room. Her touch everywhere, but strangely no longer warm. With a violent gesture he sat down at the piano and began the Grieg Ballade. Again he stumbled at the end.

He burrowed among the sheets in the case, found the composition, and began to play it by note, not with feeling but with accuracy and with slower tempo. He repeated this performance five times. Then he tossed the composition off the rack and played the whole thing faultlessly—but emptily. He could not put any soul into it.

"That's better," he said aloud.

He glanced at his watch. Half after two! Where was Elsie? He ran out into the hall, to the telephone stand. She hadn't said anything about going out to lunch. There ought to be a note. There was none; but the pad was covered with her pencil scrawls—half-thoughts, subconscious pencil-work while listening. All at once a phrase caught his eye. "A live woman or some dead stones."

He put the pad down, sick at heart. She took it as seriously as all that!

What about Elsie? This. She had gone forth angrily. Women do sometimes, leaving the house and not even returning for dinner, and not a line of information as to where they have gone. Let their hubbies squirm a little. Let them suddenly note what a big hole had been left behind. It is human nature for Mr. Husband to dash about, telephone, and if he has a locker at the club, eventually turn to that.

This notion popped into Elsie's mind, and impulsively she acted upon it. The first big thing she had ever asked of him, and he called it nonsense! She could not tell him outright that she was being confronted by the most terrible rival a wife can have—a hobby in which she has no share; and in this case—because she had experience to know—a menacing hobby.

He called it superstition, when it was only an unacknowledged fear for him. The newspapers, during what they had called the Hood Murder Case, had stressed the jewels; and trust the underworld to put away the clippings. Not once in a great while, but nearly every night, after she had gone to bed, he had gone into the library—that one hour when a woman wants her man all alone to gossip with over the events of the day.

So she had ordered the limousine from around the corner where Willard kept the cars.

Ever take real note of a spider?—the skill and boldness with which he weaves his net? And then, the inconceivable patience of him! The wind cannot rend this net, the rain cannot drag it down, the sun dissolve it.

Elsie was so busy with her mental bruises that she did not take any particular notice of her surroundings. She became alert and curious only when she saw that they were outside the city and on the way to Thunder Mountain.

She did not return to Park Avenue that night. And the terrified husband could not find Gerry Owen.

10

GERRY DID NOT RETURN HOME that day; in fact, he did not return home till the middle of the following day. When whirlwinds and thunderbolts pop out of a blue sky, the schedule breaks down. His first visit, around about noon, was to Police Headquarters, where he was fortunate to find his friend Detective-Sergeant Heller.

"Hello, Sherlock!" hailed the professional. "What terrible crime have you brought in to-day?"

Heller was a bulldog hard to shake loose. He was a man-hunter because he liked the job; and this made him like Gerry. But the trouble with this first-rate amateur, in the mind of the professional, was that he flew too high. That is, he generally gave the crook credit for being far more astute than he was; and in rounding him up got tangled among the brambles of theories. But Gerry could find things, even if sometimes it was too late. Give him the breaks, and he got his man. But he wasted time in trying to be mysterious. Heller recognized the basic trouble. Gerry had stalked Germans with superbrains and could not be made to understand that ninety-nine per cent of the crooks had brains only half-baked. Soup instead of super.

"Art, I'm up a tree," Gerry confessed.

"What kind of dogs are chasing you?"

"Nary a dog. But the other night somebody tried to kidnap me. Now, going over my record, I can find nobody who'd want to shanghai me. There are two or three who'd like to bump me off. But I don't see the kidnapping part."

"Give me the low-down," said the detective.

Gerry spun the tale, omitting only his discovery of Jenny.

Heller scratched his chin. "Did you know that Potowski had escaped from Dannemora?"

"What?"

"And not a line on him, anywhere. Got out and vanished. Been loose for a week. You put the skids under him. There's a criminally insane guy who wouldn't bump you off cold. He'd want frills—the way he did in that poor little boy he held for ransom. You did a good job there."

"No; that won't do. If Potowski was after me, there'd be no woman in the party."

"That's true. Why don't you find the jane?"

"Just what I'm going to do."

"Where do you expect to find her?"

Gerry smiled and shook his head. "Nothing doing, Art. I don't want you butting in till I've found something."

"So she's pretty, is she?"

Gerry laughed again. "What makes you think I've found her?"

"You didn't describe her."

"Art, I was very busy."

"There are just two things in this detective business—hunches and good luck. And I've the hunch that you've located the girl, but that she hasn't spilled anything yet. Gerry, don't be too slow. Round her up; get her in a cell. I'll dig up what you want."

"Don't believe in any third-degree stuff."

"You wouldn't. But that's the only way to handle a crook. Watch out for this Potowski guy."

"Funny thing, but that chap doesn't ring anywhere. The bell doesn't strike. But, dang it, there's something in the back of my head that's trying to give me the low-down and won't come through."

"The way you forget a guy's name when you've known him for years. Uh-huh. Well, keep your stuff; but don't loaf. Say, why don't you hook up with some jane?"

Gerry blushed. "Haven't had the time."

"Better start hunting, then. Some morning you'll wake up just forty years old."

"What are you on now?"

"Dope ring. I want the middleman, and his name is Louie Lavina. Oh, I can put my hand on him, but I can't get the goods on him. Big guy. Tin ear and broken nose. Middle lower tooth gone. If I can land him, it's bigger and better shoes for the kiddies. This guy couldn't make the grade in the ring because he always lost his temper. Uses perfumes instead of bathtubs. Keep an eye open for him. Louie is my mugful of bad luck. Did a bit ten years ago, but nothing on him since. Deaf in his tin ear, so he got out of going to war. Bouncer is his open job. But he peddles dope, and I want him. Look out for this pretty jane, though. She may trim you. Y'know, they trim as many wise guys as they do boobs. Twelve o'clock. Come along with me and hang on the nosebag."

"All right. But I wish that buzzer in the back of my head would come through. Maybe that crack on the dome paralyzed its legs. I'm sure that it will make this abduction stunt click."

It did, when it arrived—too late. But this time it was through no tardiness on Gerry's part. All the breaks fell to the enemy side.

At two o'clock that night Willard went around to the garage for the fifth time.

"No news, Mr. Willard. Your chauffeur took the car out. And he's as good as there is in town. And from what he's dropped about you people, he'd drive through hell for you. There's been no accident or we'd have heard of it," said the manager of the garage. "Nothing yet has turned up at Police Headquarters; but every cop in the city is on the lookout for the car. That silver-eagle water cap makes the car noticeable, sir. Maybe she's gone into the country to visit friends."

"My man would have telephoned."

"She have any jewels on?"

"She never wears them," answered Willard, patiently, his nails in his palms.

"Well, I don't know, sir. Your valet's disappearance, too. Come into the office and smoke."

Willard accepted the invitation. If anything happened to Elsie! . . . Those damned stones! One single straw held his head above water. She might have gone away in a huff, to spend the night at some hotel in the country, to teach him a lesson. . . . Had he kissed her that morning? Torture.

The business of the garage went on. Cars came in to abide for the night. Horns tooted. Cars rolled out, probably to return in the morning. The whole town was going on as usual . . . as usual! But Willard sat stonily still, without gestures. He was conscious of the manager's frequent entrance and exit. At a quarter to twelve the manager dashed in.

"The car is here, sir!"

"My wife?"

"No, sir. But your man is back, with a detective at the wheel."

Willard rushed out, his mind on fire with the old instinct to kill.

11

"You're Willard," said the detective who had brought in the car. "Perhaps you remember me. I'm Owen's friend at headquarters— Heller."

"Yes, I'm Willard. What's the matter with my man? Where is my wife?"—rather wildly.

"Your man has been drugged a couple of times. A policeman discovered the car on East Fourteenth and got Headquarters." Heller turned to the garage manager. "Get some coffee; not a cup but a pot—strong and bitter. No cream or sugar. Hike! There's opium here. Sit tight, Mr. Willard. We'll get both your wife and your butler. How old was he?"

"Nearly seventy."

"That let's him out. Have you any idea what the game is?"

Willard lied grimly. He was going back to the house—alone. He wouldn't need company. "No."

Half an hour later the chauffeur was able to speak coherently.

"I was out in front, waiting. . . . A cab run up behind. . . . Fellow dressed like me. . . . Wanted to know if I'd seen the new windshield. I leaned forward. . . . Gun. Jabbed something into my arm. . . . I came to, tied up in a dark room. . . . Before they put me back into the car, they gave me another jab. . . . What time is it?"

"Twelve-thirty."

"That's all I know. . . . The Missus hadn't come down yet." The chauffeur reached for more coffee. "Mr. Willard, I'd go through hell for you and yours. You know that. But I can't tell you anything more. I don't know anything more."

"Did you see Mrs. Willard at all?" asked Heller.

"No, sir."

"All right, Jack," said Willard. "I understand."

"I'll have to take him with me, Mr. Willard. We'll fix him up all right at the precinct. He may remember something later, and I want to be on hand. Did the disappearance of your butler alarm you?"

"I thought my friend Owen had taken him."

"I see."

"Do you believe this chauffeur of mine?"

"Story sounds good. But a chap, in a case like this, has to look around a bit. I want an eye on him. Any letters—Black Hand stuff?"

"Nothing."

"Any money of her own?"

"About two millions."

The detective, who had had odd experiences with robbed and kidnapped wives, released a whistle.

"Ransom," he declared. "You'll get a letter tomorrow."

"Do you know where Owen is?" asked Willard—so calmly that Heller eyed him carefully.

"Gerry's trying to locate the bunch who kidnapped him, or tried to. He will probably be out of touch till morning. Shall I set a man to watch the rear of your house?"

"No. But if you should want me for anything, ring the front bell three times. That is, if you bring any news. Don't telephone; send someone or come yourself. Even Gerry's man Dodge will not answer."

"Leave everything to me," said Heller. "After I've got your chauffeur comfortable, I'll make my report and go over to Gerry's. I have a key. You go home. There's nothing for you to do but sit tight. There's a brain back of this. We don't know a thing yet; we're only guessing. The kidnapping of your old butler is a kind of herring across the trail. But to-morrow morning there'll be light. So go home and sit tight."

"I'll sit tight"—quietly and grimly. Willard squared his shoulders.

Ay, he would sit tight: in the study, without lights; and, before God, he would shoot to kill any or all who entered secretly. Ransom! He laughed inwardly. To get him scurrying about town so that the house would be empty! He marched out of the garage. His gems. Well, they could be had, at a price.

Heller watched him disappear and was somewhat worried. There went a killer, if ever he had seen one!

12

INTERIM.

Elsie could not tell exactly what had happened to her after her discovery that the man in front was not her chauffeur. She called through the tube.

"Where are you taking me? Where is Jack?"

The car came slowly to a halt. The driver got out, opened the door, and, with a hand cupped to his ear, as if deaf, asked Elsie to repeat the question. As she leaned forward to do so, her arm was seized.

"Oh!" she cried, as a stab of pain came into her arm.

The strange chauffeur got into the car and seized her by the shoulders. The man's face slowly faded on her sight. The next thing she knew, she was in this semi-darkened room, and it was night. She felt slightly nauseated.

Beyond the window were the millions of city lamps. It took her considerable time to make out where she was. The moment she tried to concentrate she grew dizzy. But at last she got the outlines of the Brooklyn Bridge. She was near the waterfront, either in New York or Brooklyn.

She lay down for a while. Her head ached violently and her tongue was thick and dry. Drugged. That much was clear. But why? She could hear no sounds except a ferry's occasional bleat or a tug's piping; there were no near-by sounds. Her left arm ached dully, continuously. Morning—and now it was night. What had they given her to keep her senseless all these hours?

Light! Oh, she knew what had happened! Elsie Willard, in exchange for the Blue Rajah—the whole collection! And John would not give them up. All her fears, come to the thunderclap. A brave man, he could not understand her fears; he could not even have patience. And now, for his blindness, he might have to pay with his life. Had he but taken the gems to the bank as she had urged him! If he could but show the thieves an empty wall safe! She had known: from what source this information had come she could not say: nothing, except that she had *known* that this hour would come. She sat up.

The Blue Rajah, the inanimate crystal—a thousand years of havoc. She began to laugh hysterically and rock her body. She had run away from the house to punish him. Anger on both sides. Dear God, they might never see each other again! Again her shrill wild laughter rang out.

A hand began to pound on the east door of her prison. She stifled her laughter.

"Who is there?"

"Is that you, Miss Elsie?"

"Henry?" she screamed.

"Yes, miss." To Henry Elsie was still the child who had played about his knees.

"Are you hurt?"

"No, miss."

"What do they want?"

"God knows, miss. They have treated me well. When they come to feed me they wear yellow rubber masks and carry guns. We are on the Brooklyn side. I imagine the building is empty. I hear no human sounds till they come with the food. Is the collection safe, Miss Elsie?"

"Yes." Elsie paused. "How are the doors?"

"Too thick for me to break."

"The windows?"

"Straight down into the street, miss."

"You have tried to attract attention?"

"Oh, yes; but nobody seems to look up; and if they do, they can't see me."

"Can you open the window?"

"Only by breaking the glass. Then they might put me in a worse place. So I've just waited. Don't worry, Miss Elsie. They are not going to hurt us if we don't interfere seriously. In two or three days they'll let us go. You'll find a cot in your room. Mr. Willard should never have kept such things in the house. I was always scared when your uncle carried his with him. I told him so, more than once. But it doesn't do any good to warn certain types, miss."

"No, Henry, it doesn't."

"Don't worry."

"It's good advice, Henry."

But as Elsie's face touched the unfresh, musty pillow she began to weep silently. Nothing would happen to her if she kept her head. But her man, angry as a lion and as bold, full of wrathful impatience—when they tried to take him, what would happen?

"Oh, my man, my man!" she whispered. "They will hurt you. I feel it!"

She heard Henry stirring about, and eventually the creak of his cot as he wearily stretched his old bones upon it.

Over in the Owen establishment Dodge awoke about seven and proceeded to prepare his supper. The beer that noon had made him sleepy. Good thing the boss hadn't come in and caught him. He would have got Hail Columbia. His duty was to patrol the house, basement to garret, till the boss returned; and he had been A.W.O.L. for six hours. As he finished his second cup of coffee a brilliant idea star-shelled itself into his vision.

This detective business had got into his blood, but so far he had done nothing more than to run errands, keep the house in order, and stand by. He was minded to go over and stand guard over the Willard ranch. You never could tell. After all, he wasn't in the army or on the police force. The boss couldn't send him metaphorically to clink for a bit of initiative. In Dr. Keen's office he heard news.

"Dodge, where's Gerry?"

"Don't know."

"Bad business. Henry the butler has been kidnapped, and now Mrs. Willard hasn't returned. Willard is frantic. He has notified the police, for he is sure that she's been kidnapped, too."

"Gee!" gasped Dodge. "Then my hunch is right." He exhibited his small-arm. "I'm going over to watch the Willard place. If the boss returns, tell him where I am."

"And if anything happens, get to the nearest telephone."

"Willard's missus!"

"Yes; and Willard's inside that house, and probably full of murder. Any notion where Gerry is?"

"Some bootlegger's dump. He's located the jane who lured him to the door the other night. I'm off. If anything breaks, I'll phone."

But Dr. Keen received no telephone message from Gerry's man that night.

A series of oil-and-water expeditions, which did not mix very well, as will be seen.

It was ten by the clock when Dodge took his stand across the street from the Willard house.

Gerry did not return home at all that day. The farther away he stayed, the freer his actions. After leaving Detective Heller, he went uptown to the University Club, found a comfortable lounge, and slept like a log till dinner time. He dined at the club, cashed a check for two hundred, saw the new Guild play, then was ready for the night's work. For to-night would solve everything or the riddle would continue.

Gerry decided not to change. Something might happen, and a stiff shirt and collar would be distressfully in the way, either in a fight or in a race. She had said about two o'clock. He would walk about town, in the meantime, clear his head and digest his beefsteak. His head no longer bothered him seriously.

As the sailor smells rain, Gerry could smell trouble. He felt it in the air to-night. Well, he was ready. If anything broke in the line of rough-house, he would lose a good overcoat and about three hundred dollars.

He could not put aside the notion that he had been soft last night. This time she would probably try to get the grappling irons into his hide. Eyes. He could always get something out of a man's eyes. But what the devil did he know about a woman's? He did know that a woman could lie beyond any man's ability to trap her. Moreover, she could remember last week's lie. Pretty as a peach, too. Jenny. It was such a decent, old-fashioned name. Devil of a world!

As he entered the evil-smelling dive she discovered him instantly and ran toward him, smiling. She drew him down into a chair.

"So you've come back?"

"Sure. You asked me to."

Out in the country, among chickens and cows and clover, she would develop into a raving beauty, he thought.

"Hey, boy!" he called. "Wine—Canal Street grapes." He turned to Jenny. "You're good to look at to-night."

"Don't ask me to sing."

"Leave it to me."

"If he brings in the bottle open, don't drink it," whispered Jenny.

"Why not?"

"Don't drink it. . . . Laugh, now, as if I'd said something funny."

Gerry laughed and patted her on the shoulder. Mentally, very alert. Something doing, then? And she was quietly tipping him off! Hang it, maybe the kid was good.

"You haven't told me your name."

"Robert Owen. They call me Gerry, though."

"Gerry Owen." She piped the old melody. "You're Irish!"

"Irish and Scotch. And what's all of your name?"

"Jenny Lavina."

"That's pretty." Figuratively his bones began to sing a warning. He stood up and threw off his coat. Louie Lavina, and perhaps the kid was his. But it was a queer game she was playing.

The wine came, foaming.

"Put it back in the lamp," cried Owen. "When I pay thirty bucks for wine I want to hear the cork pop.

"What's the diff?" snarled the waiter, a sleek-haired, sly-eyed rascal.

"Twenty-nine dollars different. One dollar for this or thirty for one corked."

The manager approached. "What's the row?"

"I want my wine opened in front of me."

"Bring him another bottle, Hank," said the manager. "You'll have to pay for it just the same, mister."

"All right." Gerry had felt Jenny's foot touch his.

The war cloud died away. The music began. One of the girls began to *wah-wah, whang-whang.*

"Who is that ex-pug out there in the hall?" Gerry asked, grinning widely. "The one with the shiner?"

"Louie Lavina—my uncle. He handles the souses."

Louie Lavina. Owen laughed loudly and emptied his wineglass because he must.

"Trouble for me?"

"When you leave. Laugh often. Now, kiss me the way you did last night. They expect it. Don't do anything to make them suspicious."

Stunned, Gerry stared at her. A boy of nine could have knocked him out of his chair.

"Quick!" she panted, her eyes desperate.

He bent toward her and kissed her. She pushed him away, and his elbow knocked over the wine bottle. It wasn't exactly the same kind of kiss they had exchanged last night; and they stared at each other astonishedly. The music stopped. The girl who had sung came over. Gerry gave her five dollars.

"Sing something else, lady; something else."

The flattered girl beckoned to the orchestra. *Whah-whah-wah.*

"Now, Jenny," said Gerry under cover of the music, smiling, "Come across. You're the girl who rang my bell—"

"After the waiter goes."

The waiter set down a fresh bottle and pulled the cork. Gerry took out a fat roll and handed a fifty-dollar bill to the man.

"Keep the change, Hank."

Hank, his eyes sparkling, started off for the bar. He had seen a roll, a cow-choker.

"Give me the rest of that money," whispered Jenny. "Under the table."

Gerry grew cold. "I'll keep it," he said. He smiled, but ironically.

"Laugh, but listen."

He laughed, but it was beginning to be very difficult work.

"You know who I am," she said. "You recognized me last night. My Uncle Louie is the man you knocked out. All I know is, you're in the way—somebody's way. I don't know what his real name is. We none of us know. We just call him Bleak-eye. You are not going to get out of here."

"How many?" Bleak-eye, thought Gerry. Bleak-eye.

"Five, just outside the street door. You can't possibly get through. And Louie will beat me if he finds I've talked. I can take your money home for you. I must sing now."

He slipped the roll along with his night key. "Front door. Stay there till I come." He banged on the table for another bottle. The waiter flew to the bar. "My name is Robert Owen. But you don't know my middle name, Jenny. Outside they'll know it."

"Dear God, you're not going to put up a fight?"

Gerry laughed. It was the same kind of laughter she had heard from him the other night.

"Hey!" he yelled to the orchestra. "Give us a dance."

He swung Jenny to the floor.

"What's it all about, anyhow?"

"I like you," she answered. "You're *right*. Have you a sister or a mother?"

"No."

"All alone in your house? Well . . . all right."

"You don't like your uncle?"

"I hate him! He's a beast. But he'd kill anyone who mishandled me. Yet I hate him."

"Tell my man Dodge everything. Keep dancing, and smile. Have you ever seen this chap Bleak-eye?"

"Oh, yes."

"Where have you seen him?"

"No. He's been kind to me. I won't give him away."

"He laughs with his mouth and never with his eyes?

"That's it."

"Well, good-night."

"Don't fight. Run!"

"See you later. I like you too, Jenny."

Gerry started for the door which led to the hall and the two flights of stairs.

"Hey, mister, here's your coat!"

Chagrined, Gerry returned for his coat, which he did not want.

"An' thirty bucks for the new bot."

Gerry counted out thirty-five which was loosely gathered in a pocket.

"Night, everybody."

He gained the hall, the coat over his arm. Down the first flight he went, noisily. Then he paused.

Bleak-eye. The thing in the back of his head burst through like a magnesium flare. Maybe too late. An eye, gray and bleak as upper Alpine rock. Oh, he knew such an eye. A genial Falstaff, till you looked into his eyes. All day long the memory of Roger Berks had been trying to burst through; and if Jenny hadn't said Bleak-eye, open sesame, as it were . . . !

The door of the club closed with a bang. No doubt the signal. He dropped his overcoat, ruefully. And began the descent of the second flight. No one was in sight. He took the last step.

Then he rushed!

13

TWO THINGS A MAN DOES when he enters out upon a street. He steps forth briskly, then lags for a moment to look up and down, at the sky, anywhither, then proceeds toward his destination. It is probably one of the most common acts we humans perform, common and natural. However, if a man be somewhat suspicious, the natural act is to peek out before stepping out.

In ordinary circumstances, Gerry, upon leaving the cabaret, would not have had one chance in a thousand. But he had been forewarned. As he shot out of the doorway, as if catapulted, only one hand lightly touched his shoulder as the five closed in behind him. He was across the street before his would-be assailants got themselves untangled. Then they raced after him.

One thing Gerry always carried—a police whistle. Heller had given it to him. Still running, he put the whistle to his lips and blew a shrill blast. To an eyewitness the whole affair would have assumed the jerky revolutions of a movie camera in a comic scene. The pursuers halted, ran back and piled into the doorway. Trick or not, they dared not risk it. One bull or twenty; you never could tell what that whistle might summon forth out of the deeps of the night.

Gerry kept right on, turning the first corner and then dropping into an easy stride—apparently easy. In the distance he saw two policeman coming on a run. Gerry chuckled. In his mind he could picture those hold-up louts scurrying for their funk-holes, still dazed by the suddenness of his dash and escape. He would have stopped the police and given them the story but for the fact that he did not want harm to come to Jenny Lavina—a square little shooter. Louie Lavina. Bleak-eye. Willard's jewels. Things began to hook up.

"All right, Jenny," he said. "I shan't forget. By the Lord Harry, you *are* straight. But what you see in Gerry Owen . . . !"

He must warn Willard at once and anticipate Berks. He soon found a telephone and called up the Willard home. He made three separate calls in ten minutes. (Each of which Willard heard grimly.) The house was empty, then? thought Gerry. So be it. He himself would be in the house to meet Berks when he arrived. And every minute now was worth its weight in emeralds. For a second or two he thought of calling headquarters for Heller; but Heller would want a troop of plainclothes men, and Berks would probably see them a mile off.

To get Gerry Owen out of the way so that he could not help his buddy. So that's what all the shootin' was for? There was a brain under Roger Berks's hat. Louie Lavina and a lot of crooks under his thumb, to obey his slightest order, or suffer for it. Poor old Chick!— what the devil did he want of such deadly truck in the house?

Bleak-eye. Loot and reprisal. He had never underestimated the man, but he had almost forgotten him.

All right. Gerry Owen would be there to receive Roger Berks. A taxi drove Gerry within two blocks of the Willard place. He got into the house by the old route through the garage alley, over walls and fences, up the Pemberton balconies, thence over the intervening roofs to the Willard trapdoor. He had his pocket flash but no weapon. No matter. Nobody was going to loot Chick Willard's safe this night.

The Blue Rajah. Funny, about the blamed things. Chaps went gaga over them and robbed their best friends and lured thieves and let murder be done. Not for Gerry Owen. He wouldn't have given a hoot for all the crown jewels of the Romanoffs.

"Berks," he murmured, "some bean, yours! What seemed a patch out of Bedlam's quilt was only a novel style of plot. But Roger, old scout, you should have netted me first. I'm telling you."

Gerry bent to the roof trap. If it were latched! He put his fingers under the edge of the trap. Free! Then he took off his shoes.

This time he wouldn't have to maneuver around Elsie's pile of trunks in the dark. He had his light. All there was to this detective business was hunches and good luck. Art Heller was right.

Noiselessly he laid back the trap and shot down a lance of light. He lowered himself to the trunk which had lately been his stepladder, out. Presently he put his hand on the knob of the garret door. It swung open soundlessly.

Gerry, in his war adventures, had learned all about stairs and their hidden voices. You let your weight down slowly and waited; you repeated this maneuver till the bottom of the stairs was reached. Particularly old stairs, which always resent quick steps. The lower door was also unlatched. He rested for a moment in the upper hall. No flashlight now. He would have to depend upon his ears and his knowledge of the house plan.

He remembered that this was servants' night off—the cook and the maids, who generally spent the night with relatives in Yonkers. A little shocked, Gerry frowned into the dark. Where was Henry the butler who had an extension phone in his bedroom? Odd. Why hadn't the old boy answered the calls? Henry hadn't any nights off; he hadn't any relatives. He knew where Henry's room was. . . . Good Lord!—bound and gagged in his bed, and Roger Berks already below!

He stepped toward the stairhead. But before his foot touched the floor it came into contact with something else—a Dutch brass milk can. It clanged and banged its way down the stairs to the main hall. Gerry flattened himself to the floor, cursing under his breath. A fixed barrier—an alarm bell, as it were. This time he waited five minutes. No sound in answer to the racket. One of those fool maids, probably: they left things everywhere.

He rose. The house was empty. Chick had once told him that the safe was in the library. Thither he would proceed and lie doggo. The weak point in this business was that he had no shooting iron. But he had dependable fists and legs.

He was half way down the stairs, when there came a crash like thunder and a blaze of white flame. The bullet came so close that Gerry felt the wind of it. He was instantly convinced that the second attempt would be a volley in spray. And that would be the end of Gerry Owen. One chance, and he boldly accepted it. He dived headlong down the stairs.

His shoulder hit the thigh of the man below, and together they crashed to the floor. Gerry was first to recover his faculties, and his right hand swarmed over the unknown in search of the gun. The other, with an upheaval of astonishing power, considering that the wind had been knocked out of him, threw Gerry's body aside. But ere the gun could be focused, the two were at grips, and they rose simultaneously. No Louie Lavina here, thought Gerry. Steel. With a superhuman effort he managed to get hold of the other's arm—the gun arm—and threw it back. From the metallic clatter which followed, it was evident that the hand had hit the wall. The gun lay out of reach, in the dark. The contest now had some equality.

The two slithered across the hall floor, their shoes clicking, their breaths hot and quick. After a little it came to Gerry that he was just a shade the stronger of the two. He suddenly shifted his grip. He would lift up the fellow and smash him down upon the marble. But as he proceeded about this coup, the other broke away by giving Gerry such a smash in the ribs that had his heart been the target he must have gone down and out.

Blows—half of them futile, half of them terrible. Soon Gerry knew that one of his eyes was closed and that the thumb of his left hand was broken. He did not mind the temporary loss of sight in one eye, the hall being dark; but his left hand was almost useless. Filled with fury and chagrin, he bore in, fending with his left and banging away with his right. Suddenly he knew that a blow had gone home—to the point of the other's chin. In the dark, a chance straight jab. Quiet for a few seconds, then he heard the fall of a body. Warily he waited. Stertorous breathing told him the story. His man was down and out. With shaking hand he fumbled in his pocket for his flashlight. The beam roved.

"God!" whispered Gerry. "Chick? Oh, my God, what have I done to you?"

Gerry laid the flashlight on the floor and knelt beside the man he loved best in the world. Old Chick Willard—boys together,

man-comrades. Defending his own home! Why hadn't he chal-
lenged? The bloody face . . .

Gerry heard a chuckle behind him.

"My word, the most amusing thing I ever heard of! . . . Give it
to him, Joe!"

A flash of excruciating pain; and Gerry Owen slumped across
the body of his friend.

14

Sounds and movements and a spot of light moving inquisitively about.

"Bind their mouths with their hankies, Joe. That damned pistol shot!"

"We better get a gait on, boss. They've picked up the car and the chauffeur by this time."

"And, if you stop to think, Joe, that's how-come we've got our birds right to hand. Perhaps the shot wasn't heard. It's late, and the walls are thick. That can I put at the top of the stairs! Joe, we've just made it. All along I was afraid of this fellow Owen. Did you hear anything before Owen hit the can?"

"Not a sound, boss."

"Willard did, or he wouldn't have left the library. Our luck to be here first. But we wouldn't have been lucky if Owen hadn't dropped in. Willard would have stuck to his post till dawn. And then, we would have had to hurt him. Do you get it, Joe? Those two trying to kill each other! Ever hear anything like it? I thought I had a perfect case. And pure luck let me through!"

"There they are, boss; all tied up."

"Then let's get to the safe. Do your cutting exactly where I pencil-mark the wall. Been looking at wall safes lately, and so I've a pretty good idea how these fancy ones are protected. The girl's uncle was one of the greatest inventors in the business. Two things this safe will have—a shock wire and a burglar alarm. But there may be something else. Get the safe free from the plaster, where we can dope out the wiring. Follow me."

In the library the man called Joe set down a grip, which he opened—out of which he took a rubber suit, shoes and gloves, and the sundry tools of his calling. His companion drew a square about the safe, the position of which had been pointed out to him.

"Fast is the word, Joe."

Joe was a master workman. In less than half an hour the safe stood in full view, with half a dozen wires radiating from it. Each of these wires he snipped, with all the caution of a linesman. The live wires he bent into a safe position, beyond accidental human contact; then, with a pull and a heave he staggered back with the now harmless safe in his arms. He deposited it on the floor and began to manipulate the tumblers, while his companion watched him from the comfortable folds of an easy chair, from time to time studying the Rembrandt (which had covered the safe) under the glare of a powerful pocket lamp.

"Do you know, Joe, those two chaps? Born New Yorkers. Neither could find Broadway without a man from Cook's. You see, on this racket I didn't want anybody hurt. But if they had to have a war all by themselves, no fault of mine. No getting around it, I'm a humorist. When anything's funny, I see it right away."

"Sh!" hissed Joe, his ear flat against the safe. "There she is, boss!" Joe opened the safe triumphantly. He passed out a red Morocco case. "Pretty good job, if I do say so. Now, let's beat it. No use crowding our luck. For, believe me, we have been lucky."

"Run to the door and see if the car has come. We're only five minutes over the schedule."

The speaker opened the case and stared at the exquisite pebbles. He touched the Blue Rajah and chuckled. After all, it was humorous. All along he had wanted Willard beaten up. He had been—by his best friend!

"All clear, boss. Jimmy across the street would have whistled otherwise. George the Greek and Hugo have the car outside."

The Morocco case vanished. "We'll take them out as if they were a couple of souses, Joe. You on one side and I on the other. Have you bandaged their eyes, too? I don't want them to recognize each other—yet."

"All serene."

"Wait a minute, Joe. You have in your pocket ten thousand for this job."

"Ye-ah."

"And your get-away as well placed as mine."

"Uh-huh."

"Well, don't look back over your shoulder when you blow."

"What do you mean, boss?"

"Did you ever kill a man, Joe?"

"Kill a man?" cried Joe. He stared at the other, whose face was only a dim patch in the light of the lowered torch.

"You have been anxious to learn who I am. But your tailers, Joe, weren't clever enough. You thought I had nothing on you. Bank murder, Joe. If I die suddenly and violently, so will you later. In other words, no blackmail. You named your price and I've paid it. You and I alone knew what this job was. The others work blindly because they must. The only man I want hurt is Louie Lavina. He beats that niece of his. That's all."

"You've got the say, boss," replied Joe, evenly. "Let's get these bozos in the car."

"Give them both a shot first."

It was done.

It was a man's job to get Owen and Willard into the big limousine; but that, too, was done. The exhaust barked, and the car rolled swiftly down the street; but not too swiftly for Dodge's agile legs.

Dodge was no mean pupil. It was true that only rarely did his Gerry Owen call upon his powers, mental or physical; but he had learned and memorized enough points in the game to carry him on his own two feet—sometimes. He knew that whatever he did to-night must be crowned with success, or he'd be looking around for another job.

The first act, when he found himself near the Willard house, was to seek a convenient area-way, from which he could watch the Willard door obliquely. Arriving, immediately he felt something small and hard pressed into the middle of his back.

"Stick 'em up!" someone spoke in a snarling whisper.

Dodge stuck 'em up. He could have burst into tears. Done, the very first thing!

A hand went expertly over Dodge's body, relieving his pocket of gun and handcuffs.

"A dick!"—venomously. "Put your paws behind your back."

Dodge obeyed promptly—but sent his body backward heavily. For it had come into his startled mind that the gunman wouldn't shoot if his pals were in the Willard house, and he would not be on guard if something wasn't going on over there.

A snarling dogfight ensued; and it pleased Dodge presently to learn that he was twice as strong as the crook. He soon got the upper hand and stoutly maintained it. He found the crook's gun and gave him a thump on the head with it. He then handcuffed the fellow's ankles, gagged him and tied his hands behind his back, using handkerchiefs. In all, Dodge felt very well pleased with himself. Gerry couldn't have done any better.

Hunches and good luck never stayed in any one place very long. But they stayed with the neophyte.

The crook had a light gray cap. Good. Dodge put it on. Pleased as he was, he was being pulled two ways. Should he seek the police or go forward on his own? This balancing was short-lived. The boss never went to the police till the very last moment.

He wondered seriously, even nervously, why no one had come to the area door. The shindy must have made some noise.

Hours. He began to grow cold—infernally cold. He had never given much thought to the flatfoots who patrolled the streets at night, in the winter. Poor dubs! Dodge shoved his icy hands into his pockets. From time to time he could hear the clink of the handcuffs, as the crook twisted and writhed—like a viper with a broken spine. But he never took his eyes off the Willard door. Something like the old days, when there was a war going on in "La Belle Frang." Ye-ah. The cognac had been good, but the beer! Why, Mr. Dodge, with a brewery in France, would be a rich man in a few months.

A big limousine! It came to a stop before the Willard house. It made the door impossible to see. He would not be able to note who went in or who came out. Bad. Devil and the deep blue: Dodge did not know just how to act.

Fifteen minutes. The car began to move, and as it began to gain headway there came to Dodge a subconscious urge. He caught the empty tire holder and hung on. But he was so tired and numb it was a question how long he could hang on. For all he knew, there might be a ton of T.N.T. inside the car. They hadn't seen him, or, if they had, deduced that he was the other fellow. There was no fear in Dodge, but there was a deal of anxiety. Wherever they were going there would be some cops. If a cop hailed the car and it didn't stop, there was Mr. Dodge a perfect target at a hundred yards! Not so good. Well, he was on the way to somewhere. Let 'er ride!

It is ancient history (among newspaper paragraphers) that when you want a policeman you never can find him. This chanced to be one of those nights.

15

Ransom, thought Detective Heller, as his stride carried him to Dr. Keen's. Ransom. A rich and beautiful young woman: a hundred thousand, to be placed in such and such a spot, or Mrs. Willard would never be seen again. The toughest of all police jobs. For abduction for ransom half the time turned out to be murder and flight. And there were worse things than death. It was natural that Heller, having no clue, should fall back upon theory, generally so despised by Police Headquarters.

Dr. Keen greeted him gravely.

"Gerry may need me to-night, Doctor. So I'm going to his house to wait. There's a queer job going on."

"Any news of Mrs. Willard?"

"None. Got the car and the chauffeur, but no sign of the wife."

Keen never thought to express his opinion—that Willard's gem collection was at the bottom of everything.

And Heller thought it best not to scare the doctor with his own forebodings.

It is like that. It comes every so often when we do the right thing at the wrong time.

"Will you return this way?" asked Keen.

"No. Gerry's front door when I leave. Goodnight."

Grumbling, Heller scaled the intervening fences. Moving-picture stuff, and he disliked it. Somebody wanted Gerry on the shelf; well and good. But this fence-climbing and chimney-pot

dodging read like Gaboriau. When he reached the cellar or basement door, he signaled and waited a reasonable length of time. No
answer. He signaled four times. The result was minus. Owen's man
Dodge, supposed to be on duty, was evidently playing hooky. Fum-
ing, Heller was forced to return to Dr. Keen's. From there he ran
around to Owen's, applied a key to the door, and silently entered.

He drew his gun and his flashlight and prowled upstairs and
down. He even took survey of the garret. Downstairs he found the
telephone disconnected. Heller carried on his person a flashlight,
small tools, a bunch of picklocks, and a gun under his left arm-
pit—his marching kit, so to speak. Within a few minutes he had
the telephone in order. He called the detective bureau, notifying
them where he was.

All these actions—the two trips to get into the house, the ex-
ploration, and the telephone call—took considerable time, precious
time. (He had had a hunch to join Willard's vigil, but he had dis-
missed it.)

He had not looked into the library, where there was a remarkable collection of books on crime, psychology, pathology, and bi-
ology. London, Paris, Berlin, Vienna, and St. Petersburg; Naples,
Palermo, New York, and Barcelona. So he went in, turned on the
reading lamp, and soon became absorbed in the chronicles of the
Chief of Police of Vienna.

For all his interest in the Viennese methods, his ears were open;
and he heard the hall door open. In a flash the reading lamp went
out. He heard a light step in the ball. A pause. Then the steps proceeded down the hall, toward the kitchen. He silently followed.
Master or man, he would not have paused; he would have turned
on the hall light, with hearty sounds. A match was struck. Heller's
hand drew out his gun. Suddenly the kitchen was revealed by electric lights.

He beheld an amazingly pretty girl. He saw her approach the
kitchen table, take up a plate to inspect it.

Heller advanced. "Hello!" he said. "Where'd you come from?"

She whirled. Tableau. "Are you Mr. Owen's man?"

"That depends. I'm his man if he gets into trouble. But as for being his chief cook and bottle-washer, no. I am Detective-Sergeant Heller, from Headquarters. Now, who the devil are you and how did you get in?"

The plate the girl was holding crashed to the floor.

16

THE GIRL PUT HER HAND to her throat. There was less fear than astonishment in her eyes. A dick! And how could she answer his questions? Despair took hold of her.

"Well," Heller said, affably. "What's the answer?"

"Mr. Owen gave me his key."

"Oh, he gave you his key, did he? Where is he?"

"I—I don't know."

"Where'd you leave him?"

"He had to leave me, and sent me here. I was to stay till he could find a place to send me."

"Maybe I can help him out. Come along. You're the skirt who rang his bell the other night. Come."

"Where to?"

"For the present, in the study, where we can chat more easily."

His amiability did not deceive her. A dick from headquarters. She followed him listlessly into the study. She did not care what happened. Owen had framed her in this fashion! His key and his money! Heller indicated a chair, and she sat down.

"Now, come across. Give me the story. If you lie I'll be sure to find it out. Come clean. What's your name?"

"Jenny Lavina."

"Lavina? Any relation to the bouncer who works at the Pink Oven?"

"I am hostess there. Louie is my uncle."

"Oh-ho! Where does Louie get his coke?"

"Coke? Coke? I don't know anything about coke."

"Come across. We're all alone; and it looks like we'd be alone for some time yet."

"Mr. Dick"—her eyes blazing—"if you lay a hand on me, Mr. Owen will break your neck. I'll tell the truth, but you keep your paws off me."

"Well, break the news."

"You're right. I'm the girl he was looking for. But I don't know why they wanted Mr. Owen. Neither does my uncle. Mr. Owen wasn't to be hurt. He was just to be locked up for a few days. My share in the game was to get him to the door. But he got away."

"Ye-ah. Where was this place he was to be hidden?"

"That I don't know either. They tried to get him to-night; but I tipped him off, and he got away. There were five of them, at the street door. There wasn't a fight; he got through. He gave me his key and his money, and I was to wait for him."

"Where is the money?"

She rose and turned her back to him. "Here it is. And listen. I'm not one of those girls. Louie takes care that men don't get too fresh. I average about sixty a week."

"The Pink Oven is a helluva dump for a decent girl to be in."

"I'm decent." She tossed the roll upon the table. A thousand dicks didn't matter now. Warmth was in her heart again. Her faith in one man went back to its pedestal. This meeting was pure accident; she hadn't been framed.

"So he ran the gauntlet!"

"He blew a police whistle. And the crowd came scurrying back like a lot of rabbits. They closed the club for the night, and in the confusion I slipped away and came here. And that's all I know."

"Owen trusted you?"

"Yes. He knows that I'm straight. Would I have come here with his three hundred if I'd been crooked?"

"We dicks always judge people by the company they keep. Don't blame me if I doped you wrong. Girl, for all that, you're in dutch. Even attempted abduction is a serious crime. You can't even play it as a practical joke. But I'll lay off till I get in touch with Gerry and hear what he says. Your uncle is a bad egg."

"I know it. I hate him."

"You hate him?"—frankly astonished.

"Yes. He beats me after he's been drinking. They give him my earnings. He saves it and doles me out a little at a time. Oh, he's wise. If I could get a couple of hundred together I'd beat it where he'd never find me. But, except for the other night, he'd never asked me to do anything wrong."

"You may have heard some of the talk. Did you ever hear the name Willard spoken?"

"No."

"Well, I'll tell you what's happened. Mrs. Willard has been kidnapped for ransom. They wanted Owen out of the way so that he couldn't help his friend Willard. But Owen didn't have time to pick up a clue to what was going on. Now, if nothing happens to Mrs. Willard, why, you can blow the scene. But if she's injured, Jenny, you'll have to stand your chance."

"Abduction for ransom!"—bewildered. "I don't understand!"

"I've been after your uncle for a long time, but I've never found any dope on him. And that's what he is, a dopester. He passes it to the peddlers."

"I don't know a word about it. But I've seen the dopes. Poor things! But I never knew where they got it."

"Well, if that red-head says you're all right, it goes with me. What you tell me sounds like him. See? It's the way he does things. A philanthropist, trying to make the world free for democracy by hunting down crooks and then handing them over to me. A couple of wildcats in one suit of clothes. Jenny, something big is on."

"There's a strange man none of us knows," she said, staring at the floor. "We've seen him only a few times. Middle-aged, red cheeks, but with eyes like ice. He's been kind to me—threatened Louie if he ever struck me again. He laughs often, but his eyes never do. He was the man who wanted Owen out of the way for a week. Something about the stock market. A joke. It all comes back now.

We were all afraid of him because he seemed to have something on all the men."

"Where's his hangout?" barked Heller.

Jenny named it reluctantly.

"We'll call it state's evidence, Jenny. I'm going to forget all about you."

Then she saw, for the first time, a professional detective at work. He called headquarters again and gave orders. Next, he called up the hotel Jenny had named. Here he received a buffet. Mr. Jones had checked out that morning for parts unknown. But Heller knew his men, already on the way to the hotel: bellboys, manager, clerks, maids, waiters, porters, and taxicab drivers.

"A little late, Jenny; but it will help a lot. In half an hour I'll have the number of hairs in his eyebrows. Now, I've got a hunch that Willard will have seen this man at some time. Anyhow, I'm going over. Dodge—that's Owen's man—will be back any time now. Tell him who you are and how you came and where I am."

"I shan't run away," said Jenny.

"You won't be afraid to stay here alone?"

"No."

"So long, then."

Heller let himself out into the night.

Jenny saw a book on the table. It was autographed: "Gerry Owen, his book." She hugged it to her heart. It could never be; but she would always have these two nights to remember.

Red-headed and freckled and kind.

17

As he went along the deserted street, Heller regretted that he had not put a couple of men on guard, not to protect Willard but to protect others from him. He had seen the killer look on Willard's handsome face.

How to get in? He felt that the doorbell wouldn't be answered. And it was odd, too, that Willard would want to stay in the house alone. What was he expecting? Or didn't he want folk to see the condition he was in? Heller decided on the roof method; for he knew all about these scramblings of the playboy detective. And where the devil was he?

Twenty minutes later he stood on the Willard roof. As Heller approached the trap, which he saw was flung open, there rose from silent Park Avenue the pant of an auto. Heller ran to the parapet just in time to see a big limousine begin to race downtown, fifty miles an hour, when not one cop in a hundred would give it any attention. He thought of his whistle. No go. From where he was he doubted the blast could be heard or located.

Was Willard in the limousine? What was all this about? Every step something queer popped up. The wife and the butler. But why the butler? What was a decrepit old butler doing on a ransom case? Or was it ransom?

Heller pulled his gun and dropped through the trap. He had the highest authority to act as he thought best, and he could shoot straight. He banged into trunks and the usual garret lumber, but he did not care how much noise he made. A cold dread fell upon

him. Willard was downstairs somewhere dead. A deadly enemy—
Willard had a deadly enemy. Kidnapped both the wife and butler to
clear the decks. And Willard had *known*. That killer look on his face!

Resolutely Heller turned on any light he could find. He found
a master key in one of the bedrooms and flooded the house. Then
he started down the hall stairs. He discovered a huge brass can
and an overturned chair: Willard had put up a fight.

Room after room Heller entered, and at last the study. He sat
down, limply. He saw the whole story. Loot. To kidnap everyone
so he could extract a deadly safe without interruption—this Mr.
Bleak-eye of Jenny's. A new kind of job.

Why hadn't that fool Owen told him that there were jewels in
the house? No, no. He couldn't blame Owen, who'd only been trying to find out why anyone should try to kidnap him. Gerry Owen
had been utterly in the dark.

Ships. Heller sought for and found the telephone, got Headquarters and gave the story as he saw it. Ships, railway stations,
airplane fields: soon men would be hurrying in all directions. From
Bleak-eye's hotel would come a complete description. He wouldn't
get far.

But Heller cursed the luck that had led him to Owen's house.

This is largely a story of regrets.

All at once he became alert. The doorbell! It rang authorita-
tively several times. He waited. Then came a tinkle of glass and
later the banging of a door. Dicks or cops: he could tell them a
mile off.

"Hello, boys!" he shouted. "This is Art Heller, Headquarters."

Four men came rushing into the study. One of them knew Heller
and nodded gloomily.

"How'd you get here so quickly?" Heller asked.

One of the newcomers jerked his thumb toward the hole in the
wall. "That's a part of this trick safe. That rear wire gives the alarm
only when cut. We've often warned Willard not to keep those stones
in the house. How late were we?"

"Ten minutes. And they took Willard along with them in the
get-away."

"Probably didn't cut our signal wire till the last. Ten minutes. Hell!

Agency detectives, but Heller knew them as good ones, all of them having served on the regular force.

"What's the loot?" asked Heller.

"One of the finest private collections of jewels in the country. The diamond called the Blue Rajah is known all over the world. He would keep 'em in the house."

Heller shook his head dismally. "I thought it was a ransom case. They kidnapped Mrs. Willard today. Anyhow, she won't be hurt. I'm going to telephone."

But from Gerry Owen's he got no reply. For the simple reason that Jenny Lavina had found a sun parlor off the dining room, found a wicker lounge with abundant pillows, and had stretched herself out on it. It was exactly four rooms removed from the telephone; and Jenny's sleep was profound.

In the rising winter's dawn Dodge entered home by the front door. He was nearly frozen. His fingers were bruised and bleeding. His bones ached, his muscles cried out. He walked straight to the kitchen, his feet dragging like those of a deep-sea diver. He was all in. The boss wasn't back, evidently. If he went to the police, they'd take all the credit. All right; he'd wait till Gerry Owen returned.

He found two bottles of beer in the refrigerator; he emptied them and curled upon the study lounge for a short snooze.

We all make mistakes.

Dodge awoke because a beam of sunshine had struck his eyes. He sat up, blinking, not quite ready to swear where he was, till the muscles in the back of his neck loudly proclaimed the adventure of the preceding night. He must get the news to the boss. He pulled himself up figuratively by his bootstraps. Holy mackerel!—two o'clock in the afternoon!

"Boss!" he yelled at the head of the stairs. "Hey, boss!"

Silence. Dodge ran all over the upper part of the house. No Gerry. Then downstairs again, to discover in the sun porch a girl asleep on the wicker lounge—a girl as pretty as they came. A kind of momentary trance held him. Something darned wrong! The boss had evidently come and gone without discovering his aide. The trance fell away. He stepped forward and shook the girl. She awoke.

"Where's Gerry Owen?"

"I don't know. He sent me here to await his return. You are his man Dodge?"

"Ye-ah." Dodge sat beside her, his head in his hands. "Then they've got old Gerry, too!"

"What?"

"Anybody here last night?"

"A detective named Heller. He fixed the telephone."

Dodge rushed out to the telephone and got Headquarters, Jenny Lavina at his shoulder, gone white with cold. Dodge began to stutter his information.

"I tell you, I don't know the street or the number. . . . You dumbbells! . . . Send half a dozen men and Art Heller. . . . Of course I can take you to the place. . . . Brooklyn, but I can't tell where. But everybody's there. I can lead you to the spot. . . . Did they see me? Would I be telephoning to you if they had? . . . For the love o' God, get busy and can the questions!" Dodge turned to Jenny. "They'll be right up. . . . What are *you* crying about?"

18

IN THE ENEMY COUNTRY.

Elsie was asleep, but lightly. All at once she sat up, listening. From the window she could see that it was still dark outside. She had heard something fall—it might have been two heavy bags. A door slammed. She had noted particularly that the rogues were indifferent about noise. This would be an unoccupied building. It puzzled her, however, how she had been carried to this height. The noise had taken place in the room at her left. Henry was a prisoner in the room at her right.

She rubbed her arm tenderly. There was a large inflamed spot above her elbow: where the sleep-producing needle had entered. Presently she slid off the cot and approached Henry's door.

"Henry, are you awake?"

"Yes, Miss Elsie. There was a noise."

"In the room at my left. Couldn't you possibly break in this door?"

"I am too weak and old. I think the men meet in the room at my right. I've heard someone laugh two or three times. What did the noise sound like?"

"Something heavy, falling to the floor."

"They may have got Mr. Willard this time."

Elsie flew to the other wall, beating upon it with her fists. "Hello! Hello!"

"That you, Elsie?"—faintly.

"John, John!" she cried, frantically.

"No, no! It's Gerry. Chick is here with me, but he hasn't come around yet. They gave him more dope than me. We are both bound. Where are we?"

"In Brooklyn, near the river. Tell John, when he comes to, that I'm free and unhurt."

"Buck up!"

"How did they get you?"

"That'll keep, Elsie." Gerry grinned painfully in the dark. Ay, it would keep. Better never tell either the truth—that Damon and Pythias had tried to kill each other in the dark. "Get all the rest you can," he advised. "There'll be a scene or two in the morning."

"Gerry, is he badly hurt?"

"No. He just got one more punch than I did."

"Do you know what it's about?"

"I do now. That dear Mr. Roger Berks has joined the Welfare Club. Reprisal. Wanted me first—and got me last."

"Roger Berks! Why, he came to the house and asked John to sell the Rajah!"

"He likes a joke, Elsie, even if it takes a year to spring it."

"Berks." She spoke the word levelly. "Then this is his revenge?"

"Evidently. We didn't give Berks his right measure; but he had ours. One thing: Chick will never see the Rajah again."

Elsie shuddered. Then she laughed, wildly.

"Hey, there!" called Gerry. "No hysterics, now! Get yourself together. The show isn't over yet."

Gerry—for all his splitting headache pushed himself along by the heels of his stockinged feet. For his shoes were still on the Willard roof. He came into contact with Willard's body. Alive, anyhow. They had probably given him a big shot of the stuff. A belt on the head hadn't been sufficient for the quietus of Gerry Owen; they had stuck the needle into him, too. Having a head of cast iron, wood, and ivory, he had come out of it more quickly than Chick. But what a head it was! Gerry groaned softly. Still, he was in luck. In ordinary circumstances he would be in a hospital, with a nip-and-tuck sign over the bed. Gerry lay still for a while, his eyes closed. By and bye he spoke.

"Chick?" Gerry waited. "Chick? A long sigh. "Snap out of it, Chick!" Gerry rolled his body against his friend's.

Willard murmured something. Gerry couldn't catch the sense of it.

"I say, Chick!" Gerry waited what he judged to be ten minutes. "Hey, Chick!"

"Who? . . . Who is it?"—definite and sharp.

"Gerry. Roll over on your tummy while I have a try at the ropes with my teeth. Understand me?"

"Yes. . . . They got me . . . pretty good."

Gerry's teeth, strong as a young hound's, found no easy job in gnawing, pulling, twisting; but in half an hour he had Willard's hands and arms free.

"My turn."

"Half a mo', Gerry. I feel a bit sick. They must have given me a bit of dope with the punches. There, I feel better."

Elsie pressed her ear to the wall.

"All right, Gerry. I've got hold of the ends, but it'll take time. The window goes back and forth like the pendulum. . . . What made you groan then?"

"When they knocked me down, I fell upon a thumb," lied Gerry.

Their arms free, the rest of the job was comparatively easy. And in silence they pawed about for bruises, massaging them gently and putting circulation into their legs.

"Gerry, I ran into a full-grown man to-night."

"Uh-huh."

"It was a whale of a fight. All the time he could have knocked me cuckoo with the butt of a gun, but he played it fifty-fifty. Shot at him and missed. And what do you suppose the beggar did? He was half way down the stairs. Jumped headlong down the stairs— a football tackle. . . . Got me on the button. A whale of a fight!"

It certainly had been! thought his companion ruefully. His ribs and thumb hurt worse than his head. That bullet, an inch lower!

"Elsie! Dear God, Gerry, they got her! Elsie, manhandled by rats!"

"She's all right, Chick. In the next room, and she can hear you if you talk loudly enough."

"Which wall?"

"Right."

Willard stood up, but his knees buckled; so he crawled to the wall.

"Elsie, Elsie?"

"Oh, John! You're all right?"

"Yes, but groggy. How did they treat you?"

The woman on the other side of the wall did not purpose to put murder into the heart of her man, not even the thought of vengeance.

"Under the circumstances, they treated me carefully and respectfully. Henry is in the room next to me. Forgive me!"

"For what?"

"For running away for the day—to punish you. I was very angry." She wanted to cry out: "I love you!" But she did not want Gerry to think she was silly.

Gerry stared at the fading night. Jenny. Had she got to his house safely? A hostess in a gunman's club. Damn funny world, when you came to think of it.

"Honey," Gerry heard Willard say, "don't worry about the gems. They're gone by this time. You were right and I was wrong."

Elsie smiled. She could never say to him now: "I told you so."

"The Rajah is bad medicine."

Gerry emitted a sardonic laugh.

"What's there to laugh about?" asked Willard, peevishly.

"More than you'll ever know, old scout. Did you ever learn to hate anyone?"

"You mean war stuff? No; I never hated the poor beggars I sent down. And you didn't hate the chaps you helped to the wall."

"No. But there are some men and women on this dizzy old top, Chick, who are festered with a queer pride; and if you scratch it! Well, you've scratched a man's pride. You made him ridiculous; and he's as full of venom as a cobra."

"I don't get you, Chick. I never made any man ridiculous."

"How about that dear Roger Berks? Remember, when you gave him fifteen thousand heart balm? Did he thank you for it? He did not. You can take it from me, you'll never see the Blue Rajah again."

"Berks? So you thought that, too!"

"Uh-huh. That's the humorist."

"Damn him!"

"Now, now! Don't go into convulsions."

"But what's he kidnapping us for?"

"Every one of us who had anything to do with that mess up at Hood's camp. Wanted me first because he was afraid of me. Well, here we all are, except the sergeant of the state troopers. We made him ridiculous. Are we ridiculous in turn? I'll tell the cockeyed world! And in this queer game of his, Chick, he's had all the luck, all the breaks. Roger will be a vain man. He'll write. And while we're reading the scenario, he and your gems will be upon the billowy sea. He's got us, Chick. He won't have to sell those jewels to a fence. He'll sell 'em, first-chop price, to European collectors. Kiss 'em good-bye, old-timer; kiss 'em good-bye. Now, let's turn in."

Elsie pressed her ear to the wall; but Willard did not reply to his friend's prophecy. He saw the futility of it.

19

THE SUN CAME INTO THE WINDOW OBLIQUELY. Slowly it moved across the floor to the spot where Willard lay in a dreamless huddle. The sharp brightness awoke him; and he blinked, not sure of anything. He moved to get up, and then facts returned to him, mental as well as muscular. His neck and his jaws ached; he could barely see out of one eye; his lips were cut and his torso was sore all over.

Little by little he got up to a sitting position. It was very painful. Then he saw Gerry's face. A black and blue cheekbone, puffed lips, a black eye and a bloody ear, and a thumb that ought to have immediate attention.

Both of them had been somewhere.

There was a table without chairs, but upon this table was a pitcher of water. Willard managed to get to his feet and stagger to the table. He drank slowly and frugally. It was his mouth and throat that needed the soothing touch, not his tummy: though his tummy was in what might be called a balancing condition—the after-effect of the drug, probably.

He touched Gerry carefully with the toe of his shoe.

"Snap out of it!"

Gerry sat up—but as they raise a steel beam to a perpendicular position, a few inches at a time. When sleep was fully gone from his available eye, he stared at his comrade.

"Do I look as rocky as you?" he inquired, with a grimace which was intended to be a smile.

"I should say that you'd been in a fight."

"You don't know the half of it. Talk low. No need of waking up Elsie till we are summoned before our judge. That water? Pass it down." Gerry took a gulp. "What time is it?"

"Half after eight. Bread and water—suppose we go to it?" said Willard. "Tonic."

So he squatted before Gerry, the water and the bread between them. They ate and drank silently.

When the meal was over, Willard said: "So you believe it was Berks?"

"I'm sure."

"Well, Gerry, he wants to buy a long, long ticket. I'm going after him."

"Uh-huh."

"I'm not a man who sits still while someone robs him."

"You proved that once, old scout, and nearly got hanged for it."

"Electrocuted," Willard corrected. "Half a million. That's pretty stiff."

"You never looked upon those gems in terms of cash, did you?"—astonishedly.

"No."

"Well, then, say that Berks has run away with your toys. Toys, because they were playthings which never cost you a nickel."

"They cost my father a neat bit"—drily. "Gerry, do you believe that if things had gone wrong and I had gone to the death house, Berks would have come forward with the truth about Hood's death?"

"Absolutely. You see, it's like this. Berks doesn't handle second-hand stuff. Wanting vengeance, he would not thank the state for stepping in. He may be a great rogue, but he's got sporting blood."

"I always said that."

"Take a peek at it from my side. You'll never catch him. It's a hunch. You know what I mean. Suddenly, without warning, you know somebody's waiting around the corner for you. It's inexplicable, but there it is. Every human being has it—all animals. It isn't fear; it's just knowing something is going to happen. It's this queer thing that makes me tell you that you'll never again see either Berks or the Blue Rajah."

Willard drew up his knees and bent his head. He had mocked Elsie, jeered at her fears. Well, here he was, his gems gone, his body almost beaten to pulp. And they had manhandled Elsie, perhaps roughly. He raised his head.

"It isn't the stones so much—his rats have laid their dirty hands on Elsie. Berks has got to pay for that."

"All right; but bite on this. If you go chasing Berks, Elsie will have to pay for that. Don't you know when you're licked? Haven't you ever had the feeling of being up against a better man?"

"Physically, yes. Particularly last night. But to let a crook like Berks—"

"Curl up in that shady corner and sleep it off. And don't forget that Berks is paying me off, too, and Elsie and poor old Henry—all of us who were vitally concerned in his ignominy. What's going to happen to us will be ultra-modern, as you dub those long-haired ginks who write the musical histories of fireworks and steam engines and Hank Ford's noisy beetles."

But they were not permitted to compose themselves for sleep. They heard light footfalls outside. Soon a key rattled in the door, which opened slowly; and Gerry saw two faces the like of which only Peer Gynt had ever seen. In a second he understood—flesh-tinted rubber masks, which covered up even the ears, with gauze over the eyeholes. One of these creatures held a gun.

"They've got loose! Hey, you! Stand up and march!"

They marched, the unarmed man guiding, the armed man in the rear. Presently they were ushered into a large hall without a gallery. Perhaps three hundred chairs stretched across the hall. There was a small stage upon which stood a table—a speaker's table, there being a gavel and a white pitcher among the objects on the table. Dust everywhere. Willard and Gerry were deposited in two chairs in the front row. They were now bound to these chairs. The two marked men departed.

"Well, Chick, it looks as if we were going to be Elks or Rotaries, or something."

"You're good company, Gerry"—moodily. "When you get a woman all your own, you'll know how I feel."

"Uh-huh," agreed Gerry—moodily.

"Kiss me!" he heard a voice say. Robert Owen, the last of seven generations of born New Yorkers, aristocrat, if you cared to write it that way. And Jenny Lavina, hostess in a sordid booze den—gunmen, dopesters, bootleggers. Gerry's chin sagged to his chest. Couldn't keep the girl out of his head. Straight. That was it. She could play the game in a dump like that and get away with it—straight. Jenny. It wasn't acting; he couldn't tell why he knew. The old hunch again. He had met bad women who could act superbly and were unafraid of anything that walked on two feet or four. Jenny—homespun, as against the Cleos and Gabrielles and Dianas—silk. The lovely spy-bait he had met from time to time. But Louie Lavina, carving the turkey on Thanksgiving! . . . Hell!

Footsteps in the corridor. Elsie and Henry were pushed into the assembly hall, seated and bound. Willard stirred his bonds desperately. Elsie sat at her husband's right. The men who looked like denizens from the Hall of the Mountain King departed. The door was shut and locked. Willard leaned down and kissed Elsie's ruddy head.

"Both of you, beaten and bloody, and I can't help you!" cried Elsie, with a sob.

"Sit loose in the chair—relaxed," was Gerry's advice. "Don't try to get free. Leave the Houdini stuff to me."

"You've been tied like this before?" asked Elsie, fighting to get her voice under control.

"Nothing in my young life," said Gerry. "When they tie you, you strain all your muscles. When they're through you suddenly relax. I've always found a hole somewhere. Once they had me with my back to the wall. But an air bomb spoiled the picture."

"The wall?"

"Why not? They caught me with the goods. I'd done a good deal of damage, and they knew it. All in the game. But what gets me is an empty building with a lift running. For we're up twelve stories. See the envelope, propped against the gavel on the table? There's the whole yarn—if we can get to it."

"All bloody and hurt!" whispered Elsie.

"Keep your hair on, sister. Soap and water will take care of that. But it will take a tub of liniment—"

"They tell me you're something of a detective?" interrupted Willard, ironically.

"Where'd you hear that?"—surprisedly.

"Some rumor floating around. Why didn't you warn me about Berks?"

"I'm human. When I tumbled I straightway called you up. No answer."

"I know. But how did they rope you in?"

"Caught off my guard. One thing, they haven't a first-rate blackjacker in the gang. The only break on our side is that both of us are alive."

Berks, thought Elsie.

20

THEY WERE ALL EXHAUSTED; and it was to be expected that Henry the butler, being weakest, should be the first to succumb to sleep. Soon Elsie took the same road. For a while Willard stared ominously at the stage in an attempt to fight the increasing drowsiness, and fell by the wayside.

Gerry worked at the ropes. It was cruel business since his beaten body was not equal to sustained physical endeavor, particularly such as twisting and writhing. He had known Willard to be an unusually strong person, but he had not expected such punches from those artistic hands. Like his piano, he ran to wire and hardwood. And how Berks must have enjoyed it, even if he could not see it—the sardonic devil!

A perfect crime. Gerry solemnly believed that this had been accomplished and that Willard would never see any of his collection again. Gerry comprehended what had happened: he had walked bang into the finale of this unique adventure—straight into the thunderbolt. Berks must, with the patience of Job, have planned months ahead for these few hours. His several lines of retreat would be perfect. All the breaks in luck, too.

From time to time Gerry was forced to desist in his labors; and it was then that he too nodded—only to bring up his head with a jerk which spangled the hall with stars. Indeed, fighting the ropes helped him to fight sleep. He was determined to miss nothing of the show.

He knew that they would not be held here long; and that all five of them—that would be including Berks—would dine comfortably that night.

One by one the gems would vanish and Berks for them would receive certain sums. The police of America and of Europe would never learn what had become of the collection. Gerry could visualize the rogue. He would probably die in bed somewhere near Dijon, of apoplexy, induced by an overdose of Romanée Conti. A noble death, at that. Gerry chuckled softly. There was something like stage scenery in it all.

There would be a strenuous job, too. There was hot blood in Chick Willard. Could he be made to see that he would spoil Elsie's life if he started out to hunt Berks down? Perhaps his fury would die out after he got home. After all, Berks had only evened up the score elaborately and profitably. The rogue would, in all probability, never commit another theft. If he avoided the tripper routes, he would live grandly and safely till he took to his bed for good.

Jenny. Gerry knew that he wanted her more than any other thing on earth. Damn funny, wasn't it? Seen her three times, and the first didn't count. Kissed her, scared half-way out of his boots, when it had been stage kissing to allay the suspicion of Uncle Louie! Hooey!—and here he was, up to his neck! All these years, making adroit detours—to go bang into Sentimental Ditch this way! He hadn't been hooked, palavered; it was just one of those things. Oh, well. . . . His chin touched his crumpled, bloody shirt and stayed there.

The four of them slept, as soldiers after battle sleep, for hours. It was after two o'clock in the afternoon when a *helloing* awoke Gerry, and he stiffened in his chair.

"Hello!" he called out raucously. "Hello, hello there!"

Hurried tramping of feet.

"Hey, Gerry?"

"Smash in the door with the glass. That you, Art?"

The door crashed, with a splitting and a jingling noise; and Detective Heller, with Dodge and five plainclothes men, entered. They did not ask questions till the ropes lay on the floor.

There followed a rubbing of numb arms and stamping of half-paralyzed feet—actions which were reminiscent of something out of a cinema comedy.

"*Va bene?*" asked Willard, with a grave smile.

"*Va bene,*" answered Elsie, trying to adjust her hair. "I'm all right."

Her smile was grave, too. The show wasn't over; there was yet the anticlimax. She had something to say to him, and she did not know how or when to say it, nor could she imagine what his attitude would be when he heard the amazing confession. The ashes of anger—and the wind the wrong way!—they were bitter in the mouth. Oh, there was a way out, but she knew that she would never take that way—the way of silence. She had, as it were, committed a dishonest act, but she would be honest about it.

She regretted the presence of others. John did not care to have witnesses to his moments of tenderness. With his arms around her, she would have felt a bit of earth under her feet.

Va bene. Italian for "It goes well." But did it? Would it go well when she threw the thunderbolt at his feet?

"How'd you find us?" asked Gerry.

"Dodge, here," answered Heller. "Tailed you here, then went home, drank some beer, and woke up about half an hour ago. He's your product. Later, give him a kick in the pants for me."

"Boss—" began Dodge.

"Never mind, Dodge; we all overslept," said Gerry, tenderly working his broken thumb. "Did you go to my house?"—to Heller.

"Ye-ah. You're a helluva detective, Gerry; but you're always right on your first size-up. You never make any mistakes there. She's straight; a gal with a lot of bad breaks."

"Why didn't you put a guard around Willard's house?"

"No sugar on that pill, but I'll swallow it. I thought it was a ransom case till I saw the wall safe on the floor. They bunged you up considerable. Was our friend Louie in the scrap?"

"No. But what about this place?" asked Gerry.

Heller laughed. "It was hired for theatrical rehearsals, for one week, including the use of the elevator. Janitor ran it daytimes and one of Berks' men at night."

"They might have thrown in a little heat."

"Banked fires, enough to neutralize the cold, but not enough for cheer. But Mr. Berks won't go far."

"No?" Gerry eyed his friend ironically.

"We've got him fenced in—airfield, trains, ships."

"Uh-huh."

"You don't believe we'll get him?"

"No, Art, I don't. There's a letter on that table. Get it, will you please? I know we are expected to read it."

Heller jumped upon the platform, returned with the letter and gravely handed it to Willard, to whom it was addressed.

"Read it aloud, Chick. We're all concerned. Even poor old Henry, who looks pretty ragged."

"Oh, they were not too rough with me, sir."

With more curiosity than he was willing to admit,

Willard tore off the envelope and began to read. "Out loud, Chick, out loud!"

"I beg pardon!" Willard began to read aloud:

"'Willard. When I read in the newspapers, during the Hood muddle, about your exploits in the air, about your shooting elephants in mid-Africa, and stalking snow-leopards in the Himalayas, the picture of my own drab life struck me like a blow. I, too, must have an adventure. So I scribbled one on paper, and then enacted it. Like a play. But I believe I'm a humorist rather than a dramatist.

"'When you gave me that fifteen thousand heartbalm—the commission I didn't get!—I did not thank you, did I? I didn't offer you my hand, to let bygones be bygones, did I? I left you that day, when we were acquitted, wishing you the worst of luck. Sue you in court for abduction and all that, and let the court have all the fun? No, thank you. Not my style. The publicity which I got out of the Hood case really ruined my business. To *say* that a man is crooked in his commercial dealings is nothing; but to have it suggested in type, that is *something!*

"'For all my reputation, I'm a proud man; and for anyone to manhandle me and to get away with it burns me up.

"'To pay my debt to you and to pay it grandly. Cheeky of me, wasn't it, that morning when I came and offered to buy the Rajah? And the joke of it is, I have a customer for it!

"'I wanted your friend Owen out of the way, temporarily. Rather shrewd. He slipped the net because I didn't know that he was a Dempsey in dinner clothes. But the point is this: he thought that attack was the beginning of things, whereas it was the finale. You see, I knew all about the little safe in the wall. So I struck.

"'You have imagination, and I built on that. Your agony as to what was happening to your beautiful wife—the thought of that agony—will comfort me in my old age. *Presto!*—now you see it, and now you don't. Your butler, your wife, your friend, yourself, your gems! As they used to chant at the county fairs: "The hand is quicker than the eye." You know the sleight-of-hand stuff yourself pretty well.

"'They tell me that dramatists write the last act first. So, months ago, I planned my retreat. It is perfect.

"'I'll admit that you had me in a corner last night. You came into the house after we were already in. As you did not turn on any lights, as you went directly to the study, I understood. You were armed and murder bent. I and my companion were in the music room, not knowing just how the devil to handle you in the short time I had. But the amateur detective took care of that *contretemps*. He would guard his friend's treasure. The unexpected pleasure! Damon and Pythias, at each other's throat! Offered to me on a platter, as it were. Oh, Lord, but it was funny! When you fired at Owen, though, I thought the jig was up. For the last thing I wanted in this little comedy was violent death. What I wanted was to leave you a legacy of eternal chagrin. But when it turned out to be a matter of fisticuffs! I couldn't see anything, but I could hear the blows and grunts. When Owen, by the aid of his light, discovered what he had done beaten to pulp his best friend—why, I wouldn't have swapped that moment for ten Blue Rajahs.

"Oh, you will hunt for me! I know you. But will you find me? I believe not. Within six months' time your gems will be scattered in as many private safes. After all, you asked for it—keeping a collection like that in your home. The gem I wanted was, of course, the Blue Rajah, because it meant more to you than all the other gems in the world lumped together.

"To-night I shall dine alone, and the Blue Rajah shall lay on the table beside me.'

"I am, sir, your most obedient servant. (How quaint those old liars were!)

"Roger Berks."

Slowly Willard folded the letter. "You were never going to say anything about it, Gerry?"

"No, Chick."

"And I might have killed you!" Willard held his palm against his aching eyes. "I didn't know you could scrap like that," he added dropping his hand. "I always had the edge on you when we were kids."

Something inspired Heller to send his men out into the corridor. There were no criminals to guard; and there might be some intimate scenes.

Gerry threw his arm across his friend's shoulder. "What's a bullet and a few punches among friends? Here we are, all alive and

kicking. Only, I'm sorry Berks nicked you so badly. I was in a blind
alley till Jenny mentioned Bleak-eye. And Berks' eyes were gray
and bleak. Then I tumbled. Ye-ah. All the way down the stairs."

"Jenny? Who is Jenny?" asked Elsie. When would the moment
come for her to speak? Any temporary diversion!

Gerry heard himself speaking, suddenly and inexplicably, before them all, as if some Cagliostro, standing behind him, *had*
willed him to utter the surprising torrent of words.

"Jenny is the girl I'm going to marry, Elsie. She's the niece of a
dope thug. She's been earning her living as hostess in a bootlegger's
night club called 'The Pink Oven.' The underworld—the most sordid side of it. And she has kept herself clean and straight. The girl
who rang my bell the other night. And ancestors and society and
all that can go to hell for all I care!" Gerry glowered, ready to fight
all and sundry.

Tableau.

Willard's eyes opened widely. Heller grinned. Dodge the chauffeur let down his lower jaw. And Elsie laughed—hysterically. Gerry
drew back, his jaws hard.

"You don't understand, Gerry," she said. "I love you for what
you have just said. That's love. Or it used to be. It made me laugh
because you sounded as if you were ready to bite us."

"Hey, Jenny!" bawled Heller, considering himself master of
ceremonies.

Jenny? Gerry silently damned the detective and then damned
himself. It was horribly embarrassing all around. What, in God's
name, had impelled him to shout like that? With those booming
acoustics!

Jenny, who couldn't help hearing Gerry's explosion, came in,
pale. She turned at once to Elsie. "I can't marry him!"

"And why not?" Elsie asked, gently. The child was lovely!

"I hate men. I like to hunt them. He was different, that's all;
and I couldn't stand by and see him beaten up."

"And you don't love him?"

"No"—stoutly. "Why should I? What the big game was I didn't
know. But I couldn't stand by and see a brave man beaten by a lot

of rats. And then, I'm not his kind—your kind." Jenny spoke brusquely.

But Elsie, through her own agony, saw the agony in Jenny's eyes.

"Owen's a good guy, Jenny," said Heller. "Your protector will go up for a long stretch. You'll be all alone. What'll you do?"

"Oh, I'll find something." Jenny looked at Gerry. "A convict's niece. How would your lady friends like that?"

"I haven't any lady friends," said Gerry, gloomily.

Dodge the chauffeur quietly made his exit. This hall was too crowded for him. This smart little crook, giving the boss the gate!

Queer thing. Gerry suddenly remembered Haig's appeal to his men with their backs to the wall in '18. Been nice of Haig, wouldn't it, to have packed his grip and gone home? Gerry realized that he had spoken bold words. He walked over to Jenny; and the look in his eyes as he approached paralyzed her. He put his arm around her and kissed her.

"And that's that," he said, confidently.

It must have been, because Jenny began to cry against the lapel of his dusty coat.

"Well," said Heller, "suppose we clear out of here?"

"Done!" cried Willard.

"Wait a moment!" It was Elsie who spoke. The words were sharply accented. She stood straight before her husband. "Mr. Berks believes the joke is all his. We have our side of it; but he will only recognize this fact when he puts the micro on the Blue Rajah."

"Elsie, what do you mean?"—from the startled Willard.

"That he has the spurious stone."

"But how?"

"Last spring, before we went fishing, you had a bit of flu. You gave me power of attorney to go to the bank for some bonds that had been called. One of the first things I saw was one of your visiting cards. It looked so odd there that I picked it up. On the other side was the wall-safe combination. It was all accidental. In a flash it was registered in my mind, John. Anything in an envelope, or anything other than you had sent me for—no. It was without thinking that I turned over the card. All my life I've played with models of safes. Always you went to the safe in the dark. I did not know where it was, and didn't care. But the other night you were surprised into revealing the place. You all believed that the copy of the Rajah had been lost at the camp. On the contrary, it has lain in one of my bureau drawers."

Willard began to frown.

"I never knew why I kept the paste; but keep it I did. It's kind of hard to go on. Old-wives' tales. Banshee curses. Witches and broomsticks. You laughed, John, or rather you grew angry."

"And you transposed the stones? When?" There was neither warmth nor eagerness in Willard's voice.

"The night Gerry came in, his head all bloody. Instantly I *knew*. But it was inarticulate knowledge; I couldn't get it out in words. And then, you would have laughed." She pressed her palms against her heart. "It was in here; my heart knew. Gerry had been hurt because of that stone. To all who have owned it—evil!"

"But Gerry did not own it"—mildly, which Elsie knew to be a bad sign.

Thousands and thousands of words, and somehow she could not seize upon the right ones: like a little schoolgirl who had forgotten her piece!

"You were friends," she went on. "Men and women, down the ages, have gone mad over that stone. And that night perhaps I, too, went a little mad—for the hate and fear of it!"

Gerry shook himself out of the hypnosis this queer confession had set upon him, beckoned to Jenny and Detective Heller; and the three of them silently departed. Those two would be saying things no other humans ought to hear.

"Hate?" said Willard, with a shrug.

"Yes," said the resolute Elsie.

"Where is the Blue Rajah?" he demanded.

"Where it belongs. No more murder, battle, and sudden death."

"Where is it?"—in a sharper tone.

"In the mud of the Hudson River, where I threw it the day you gave Berks the order to buy my uncle's emeralds."

Come ill, come good; there it was, in the clear.

Willard sat down, his head in his hands.

21

ELSIE STARED DOWN at his head.

"Filthy hands have touched me, jostled me; I have been man-handled." She paused, but Willard did not stir. "Have I lost you?" she asked. "Was it so dreadful? Because I feared for you? For that was back of it all. Have I torn something out of you that I can never restore? What is baser than to rob and betray a friend—as my poor uncle robbed and betrayed your father? And you could fondle that diamond without recollecting that?"

"I wasn't going to rob or betray anyone"—wearily, without looking up. "The stone brought us together. Besides, it was mine, Elsie."

His! That was it. Inexorably the stone was his!

"I cannot graft my point of view on yours. My brain to think with is mine, individual. What has happened since those gems caught you? Your music. You broke down the other night. You neglected the gift of God for the playthings of the devil. For I am one of those who still believe in both. You can say *bosh* all you want to; those gems were coming in between us. If I had said to you *Choose!* it would have sounded silly, ridiculous. I was too proud. But it should have been enough for you that I hated them. You might have killed your best friend."

"Did I know it was Gerry?" To him, too, there were many elusive words. "I was not to defend my home, then?"

"Which is better—that the stone should lie at the bottom of the Hudson or in the palm of Berks, for him to gloat over?"

"To destroy a thing of beauty! You had no right. I can't quite forgive this. I had rather Berks had it, with the chance of getting, or hoping to get, it back some day."

"Even from the river mud, then, the Rajah mocks me!"—bitterly. "Come, Man-child. I'm tired, and my arm, where they thrust the needle, is painful. What we both need is a bathtub and Dr. Keen. This isn't the hour for Big Talk; rather when we are rested. Come along."

He could argue with her! Instead of taking her weary body into his arms, he could criticise the ethics of her acts! So be it. All of him, or none of him.

Elsie disappeared from the house in Park Avenue that night. Willard made no effort to find her. Eventually she would soften and return to him; or she wouldn't. He knew Elsie. Woman she might be, but the fibre in her was as tough as his own. He offered no rewards for the recovery of the gems. Nor did he make inquiries at headquarters for information as to what was being done in regard to the pursuit of Roger Berks. He did not even go to Gerry for help. Elsie would return on her own; or she would not.

Henry, hiding his distress, went about his household duties as usual. Shortly he began to move on tiptoe. For the master had gone back to his piano. Often, now, when Willard went out to take the air, Henry would find the lunch by the piano untouched.

Willard seldom talked, and Henry never spoke unless given an opening; and then it in no wise resembled conversation.

But Willard thought deeply and constantly. Argue with himself as he would, he could not argue himself into the belief that he was wrong. He was right, a thousand times right. But, dear God, how lonely the house was! He had come to one decision: if she ever came back, never would he mention the Rajah. If she came back. For in one way she had him on the hip: she was, in her own right, as rich as he was.

Not a word, not a note; in her hat and clothes she had gone forth. Sometimes, while prowling through her room, he suffered the tortures of the damned. But she must come back because she wanted to, he would never seek her.

"Henry, do you believe in the devil as well as in God?"

"Well, sir, I believe in God; but the devil was something they used to frighten me with when I was a child."

"Then you don't believe in the devil?"

"I don't know, sir."

Dialogue of this character; scarcely conversational.

Henry waited but waited in vain for Willard to ask him if he knew where his mistress was.

Henry always answered the telephone joyously and departed from it most dejectedly. He missed, too, the cheerfulness, the bubbling energies of the red-headed young man; but Gerry Owen was away on his honeymoon. Henry did not approve of this marriage. But then, since the war, was there anything left to approve of?

The piano could be heard at all hours of the day and the night. The passionate fury began to die away, and a singular sweetness and majesty took its place. Daily Henry waited for the Fantasie Impromptu; but Willard never played it.

In front of one of the great concert halls in New York City a woman paused one afternoon. It was in January; it was snowing; the street scenes were lively and moving. But this woman observed only the printed sheets of paper, framed each side of the entrance. There was no portrait:

JOHN MURRAY WILLARD

FIVE PIANO RECITALS

FOR THE BENEFIT OF DISABLED WAR VETERANS

FIRST RECITAL

THURSDAY NIGHT

The woman approached the box office. "One chair, please. Downstairs."

"The only chair downstairs, madam, is behind a post."

"No matter. Give it to me. Two dollars? Very well. The house is sold out?"

"It is for charity; and many people are curious."

"About the pianist?"

"Yes, madam. It's a good way to try out. If he has the stuff, he'll get professional booking. Mr. Willard is known by his thrilling adventures. Airman, hunter, explorer; that draws. But as a pianist, to-morrow will tell the tale. Thank you, madam."

The purchaser of the ticket went out into the snowstorm.

"Mine!" she said aloud. "He wants me!"

She beckoned to a taxi. She laughed as she got in. She was a very beautiful young woman, imperial. She was dressed in black. The helmet was rimmed by a fringe of ruddy brown hair, and her eyes were brilliant.

"Where to, miss?" asked the cabby.

"Oh, anywhere—to the Park! And put down the windows so that the snow can blow in."

"Yes, miss."

The final number on Willard's program was Fauré's Tarantelle. The applause was generous. A few started to leave; but as the pianist remained in his chair, the few reseated themselves.

Willard began Chopin's Fantasie Impromptu. The critics and the audience remained motionless till the last note vanished on the ear. The critics, if not the audience, knew that they had never heard it played quite so tenderly, so yearningly, so technically perfect, as yonder handsome man played it this night. Silence. Then a burst of applause which would have gratified the greatest of pianists.

Willard swiftly left the stage. In the wings he bumped into a woman.

"I beg your pardon!"—for he was half blind, emotionally.

"It was wonderful, John!"

"Elsie?"

"Yes. You wanted me back. So here I am!"

"It was the one thing you wanted me to do. It was the only way I could call to you."

"And didn't you rather expect me?"

"Dear God, how I hoped! . . . But wait till I get my hat and coat!"

She waited.

Epilogue.

March. The terrace at Ciro's, Monte Carlo. Sunshine, blue sky, and blue sea.

A waiter stood observantly near one of his tables. Four days running he had served this man at noon. The man's face was rubicund and jolly, but his eyes were always as gray and bleak as the rock far above. This stranger liked good things—food, wine, and tobacco; and his tips were generous. The Romanée St. Vivant, 1915, and the fat Corona-Corona wedged between his teeth were unimpeachable evidence. But the stranger had a queer pastime. After his demitasse he produced from a vest pocket what appeared to be a magnificent diamond the shape of a large pecan nut. For all the brilliancy of the object, the waiter was not fooled. No man in his right senses would produce such a diamond in such a place. But it was interesting to watch the stranger play with it, rolling it about with the tip of a finger, smiling at times, frowning at others.

To-day the man abandoned the stone for a little while, leaving it on the table. He opened his Paris edition of the New York *Herald* and turned to the editorial page, that is to say, to the social and artistic events. With the aid of a penknife he cut out half a column, folded it and stowed away. Then he lighted his cigar.

"Gustave!" he called.

"Yes, sir."

"Observe this pebble "—indicating the brilliant.

"Yes, sir."

"Well, once it was worth ten million francs, and now it isn't worth ten centimes."

"What happened to it, sir?" asked the astonished waiter.

"A very beautiful woman's hand touched it. Presto!—now you see ten millions and now you don't!"

"She stole it, sir?"

"Well, you have me there. I don't know; I only suspect."

"Can't you have her arrested, sir?"

"She is rich and beautiful."

"I see, sir. There is sentiment."

"That's it. Sentiment."

With a laugh the stranger pushed back his chair, scooped up the bit of paste, and strode off toward Mentone. Once on the way he paused and took the newspaper clipping from his pocket. For the fourth time he read it.

> John Murray Willard, the noted American pianist, will give his first Continental recital in Brussels next Monday. His success in London was phenomenal. A great musician who is not a professional is a curiosity. He donates the proceeds of his concerts to disabled war veterans. Monday week he will play in Paris. His beautiful wife is with him always. As Miss Elsie Hetherstone she was well known in Paris, having lived for some years in St. Cloud.

Roger Berks tore the clipping into minute pieces and let the wind carry them away. He laughed.

"Well, if he sticks to her," he said aloud to the blue of the Mediterranean, "maybe some day he'll amount to something!"

COACHWHIP PUBLICATIONS

COACHWHIPBOOKS.COM

Murder Ends the Song, by Alfred Meyers
Introduction by Curtis Evans
ISBN 978-1-61646-298-7

COACHWHIP PUBLICATIONS

COACHWHIPBOOKS.COM

Murder in Style, by Emma Lou Fetta

Introduction by Curtis Evans

ISBN 978-1-61646-232-1

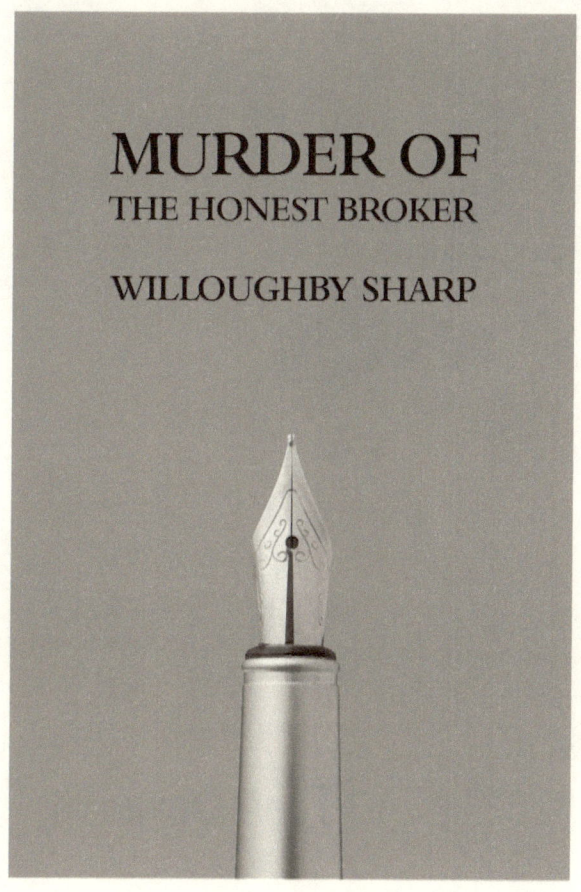

COACHWHIP PUBLICATIONS

COACHWHIPBOOKS.COM

VULTURES
IN THE SKY
A HUGH RENNERT MYSTERY

TODD DOWNING

Vultures in the Sky, by Todd Downing
Introduction by Curtis Evans
ISBN 978-1-61646-149-2

COACHWHIP PUBLICATIONS

NOW AVAILABLE

There is No Return, by Anita Blackmon
Introduction by Curtis Evans
ISBN 978-1-61646-223-9

COACHWHIP PUBLICATIONS

COACHWHIPBOOKS.COM

MARIAN
GALLAGHER
SCOTT

DEAD HANDS REACHING

DEATH'S LONG SHADOW

Dead Hands Reaching & Death's Long Shadow,
by Marian Gallagher Scott
Introduction by Curtis Evans
ISBN 978-1-61646-302-1